THE CHRISTMAS WASSAIL

THE CHRISTMAS WASSAIL

Kate Sedley

This first world edition published 2013
in Great Britain and in the USA by
SEVERN HOUSE PUBLISHERS LTD of
19 Cedar Road, Sutton, Surrey, England, SM2 5DA.
Trade paperback edition first published
in Great Britain and the USA 2013 by
SEVERN HOUSE PUBLISHERS LTD

British Library Cataloguing in Publication Data

Sedley, Kate.
  The Christmas wassail. – (Roger the Chapman mysteries;
  22)
  1. Roger the Chapman (Fictitious character)–Fiction.
  2. Murder–Investigation–England–Bristol–Fiction.
  3. Great Britain–History–Edward IV, 1461-1483–
  Fiction. 4. Detective and mystery stories.
  I. Title II. Series
  823.9'14-dc23

ISBN-13: 978-0-7278-8275-2 (cased)
ISBN-13: 978-1-84751-479-0 (trade paper)

All Severn House titles are printed on acid-free paper.

Severn House Publishers support The Forest Stewardship Council [FSC],
the leading international forest certification organisation. All our titles that
are printed on Greenpeace-approved FSC-certified paper carry the FSC logo.

Typeset by Palimpsest Book Production Ltd.,
Falkirk, Stirlingshire, Scotland.
Printed and bound in Great Britain by
MPG Books Ltd., Bodmin, Cornwall.

ONE

'It's all very well him being called Marvell,' Burl Hodge grumbled, 'so long as the silly old sod doesn't think he is one.'

We were sitting in a favourite corner of our favourite ale-house – the Green Lattis close by All Saints' Church – about to start on a second beaker apiece of our favourite ale. These tasted all the sweeter because both our wives had strictly forbidden us to stay for more than one. Christmas was nearly upon us and our services were required at home.

The Feast of St Nicholas had already come and gone. All over the country the boy bishops had been chosen from among the youths of the choir and were now installed for the next week or two in Episcopal state, making up for all the cuffs, scoldings and general abuse they had suffered throughout the past year. In our household, it had, as usual, fallen to my lot to tell the saint's stories to our children.

Needless to say, Adam and Nicholas, my son and stepson, clamoured for the tale of the two young boys on their way to Athens who stopped in Myra for the night and were murdered by the wicked innkeeper. They particularly relished the part where this evil man chopped the two bodies into bits and pickled them in a barrel of brine, intending to sell them as salted pork and so gain even further from his crime. But, the next day – much, I believe to Adam's and his half-brother's disappointment – Bishop Nicholas arrived at the inn, having had a vision of the two boys during the night, and restored them to life. The murderer then fell on his knees in floods of tears, confessed his sin and expressed his repentance, promising to lead an unblemished life in future. The saint immediately forgave him.

'Pooh,' had said Adam, my five-year-old cynic, 'I don't suppose the innkeeper meant it.' And he had pulled his little knife from his belt, making slashing movements in the air. I didn't feel that he had quite grasped the moral of the story.

My daughter, Elizabeth, naturally preferred the tale of the three young girls whose father had fallen on hard times and who was unable to provide the necessary dowries for them when they wished to be married. St Nicholas, learning of their plight, had tossed three solid gold balls – or three purses full of gold, whichever you preferred – through their bedchamber windows, thus enabling them to wed the men of their choice.

'Do you think Saint Nicholas might do that for me?' Bess had asked wistfully.

'I hardly think so, sweetheart,' was my reply. 'He's been dead for centuries.'

'I'll have to depend on you, then,' she had sighed, grimacing as though her expectations were not very high.

She was probably quite right to be pessimistic, but as she was only just nine, I was none too worried as yet.

Within the city itself, the mayor and aldermen had already carried out their inspection of the wharves and warehouses to ensure that sufficient stocks of wood had been imported to keep both rich and poor, young and old warm for the Christmas season; also that extra supplies of food had been laid in so that not only the citizens could be certain of enough to eat, but any strangers who happened to be visiting Bristol as well. The city fathers had received their annual allowance of furs and wine and fine red local cloth, while the rest of us had worked ourselves up to such a pitch of goodwill that we no longer resented these self-awarded gifts.

Well, most of us didn't. Burl Hodge, an inveterate grumbler, had already had his say on the subject. Now he had found another source of grievance.

I took a deep, satisfying mouthful of ale and swirled it around my tongue before swallowing. Blissful! I smiled at him. 'Our newest citizen been annoying you, Burl?'

The snort he gave would have done credit to pigs at a trough.

'If you call it an annoyance for the stupid old fart to nearly ride over me on that showy bay mare of his and force me into the central drain in Redcliffe Street, then yes! He has annoyed me, as you put it. Who does he think he is? That's what I'd like to know!'

I took another swig of ale and replied peaceably, 'He's Sir

George Marvell, knighted for his bravery on some French battlefield long years ago. He's also extremely wealthy. Inherited wealth from his father, or so I've been told.'

My companion gave another snort and swallowed half his beaker of ale, without pausing to savour it, in a way that made me wince.

'You've been told bloody right,' he snarled. 'And what was his father? A damn brewer who made his fortune by watering his ale.'

'Do you know that for a fact?'

'Well . . . no, not for certain. But I'll wager any money he did.'

'You'd best lower your voice, then. Or, better still, don't repeat it. You never know who might overhear you in a place like this.'

'Even if someone did, he wouldn't tell on me. In here, we're amongst friends. Besides, nobody likes the man. Sir George Marvell' – he uttered the name as though it were an imprecation – 'has made himself more enemies in the ten or so weeks he's been in the city than anyone else I know.'

I had to admit that this was true. The knight was rude, truculent, set up in his own conceit, disliked even by his own family. The list of his failings was endless. At the same time he was a person of some importance whose company, while not exactly courted, was certainly not repulsed by the great and the good of Bristol, and whose father, the brewer, was remembered as a man who had spent his money doing many charitable works in the town.

All this had happened long before I married my first wife, Lillis Walker, and settled in the city, but I knew that the only surviving son of Brewer Marvell had been sent to London back in the late twenties under the patronage of some high-ranking official at the court of King Henry VI, fought in France with the renowned Talbot of Shrewsbury, and eventually been knighted after an act of bravery in one of the many engagements which marked the long, and eventually unsuccessful, campaign to retain our French territories. So much was common gossip. And if you had Margaret Walker as your former mother-in-law, as I did, then you knew every scrap of Bristol history from the Creation to the present day, in this year of Our Lord, 1483 . . .

Burl was still talking, thumping the table with his by now empty beaker. 'What I want to know is why did the old bastard have to move down into the town, eh? Tell me that! He's been quite happy – not that he'd be happy anywhere, the miserable sod, but you know what I mean – up in Clifton Manor in that great house of his, with all his family under the same roof, making their bloody lives a misery, just as he does ours now. So why move down here, acting unpleasant and annoying – your word, not mine – the rest of us? What does Mistress Walker and her two cronies reckon to that? Those three usually have an answer to everything. Especially that toothless old crone, Maria Watkins.'

I couldn't help laughing, but begged him to moderate his language. 'Oh, her theory,' I said, 'and I think it's probably the correct one, is that Sir George has grown worried about his sister, old Drusilla Marvell.'

'Why?' Burl demanded aggressively, as though it were somehow my fault. 'She's lived by herself in that house in Redcliffe Back for as long as anyone can remember. He's never worried about her before.'

I finished my ale and peered sadly into the depths of the beaker, hoping to find a few dregs that I had missed. Discovering none, I wondered if I might order myself a third pot, and if I could persuade Burl to join me. Reluctantly, I decided against the notion, but I wasn't ready to move just yet. Outside, the short December day was drawing towards dusk and it was cold. Earlier, I thought there had been a hint of snow in the air. Inside the Green Lattis all was warm and snug with the warmth of bodies pressed close to one another, a log fire burning on the hearth and a general atmosphere of goodwill in anticipation of the coming season and holiday. The twelve days of Christmas stretched before us like a golden path of peace and plenty and I, for one, was looking forward to it with the greatest of pleasure.

The last two years had been busy ones for me. 'Busy' was not perhaps the right word to describe twenty-four months of action and almost constant danger. If you, whoever you are – and God bless you for it – have read these chronicles of mine this far, you will know that the previous year I had travelled with the army to Scotland, when the Duke of Gloucester, as he then was, had won back Berwick for the English. I had barely returned to London and was looking forward to going home to my wife and children when the duke despatched me on a secret mission to France and another life-threatening situation.

This year had been just as bad, if not worse. In April, King Edward had died suddenly, leaving his twelve-year-old son to inherit the throne. The sudden and unexpected – although not altogether by me – claim of Richard of Gloucester to the crown, on account of the illegitimacy of the late king's marriage to Elizabeth Woodville had, yet again, and through no fault of my own, embroiled me in the duke's affairs. Once more, I had found myself in danger. And as recently as the past month, Fate had shown her contempt for me by jeopardizing not just my life but also that of a member of my family.

So, sitting there in the comfort of the ale-house, the noise of happy, anticipatory voices all around me, old friends raising a beaker to me as they caught my eye across the room, I felt that I had earned a quiet, peaceful holiday in celebration of Our Lord's birth. Perhaps, after all, I would treat myself to another drink. I grabbed a passing pot boy.

Burl's voice continued to rumble on, still demanding answers to his insistent questions. 'Why would he worry about her now, after all these years? Like I say, old Drusilla Marvell's been in that house with no one but her household servants to look after her for as long as I can remember. Became a sort of recluse, she did, after some fellow jilted her almost at the altar steps donkey's years ago. She was quite a young woman at the time, or so I've heard.'

'Well, Bess Simnel and Maria Watkins reckon she's all of eighty-five by now. They say she's at least twelve years older than her brother.'

'Eighty-five?' breathed Burl incredulously. 'Oh, well! Perhaps that's different. That's some age! They must be measuring her up for her coffin. Her brains, if she has any left, must be addled.'

'She's probably growing feeble,' I conceded as my third beaker of ale arrived at the table. I took a sip and sighed contentedly. 'Which is why Sir George thought it wise to move into the neighbouring house when it suddenly became empty back in the autumn. And luckily it's big enough to accommodate all the members of his family as well, plus his servants.'

'How many are there?' Burl asked, eyeing my beaker jealously. 'Family, I mean, not servants.'

I took pity on him, suspecting that it was lack of means rather than fear of Jenny that had made him refuse a third cup of ale, and ordered him another.

'My treat,' I said, continuing before he could demur. 'According to Margaret Walker and her friends, besides the knight himself there's Lady Marvell, his second wife and a good few years younger than he is; Cyprian Marvell, his son from his first marriage; Cyprian's wife and son; and finally Sir George's lad by the present Lady Marvell. His younger son and his grandson are almost of an age. I think there's only something like a year between them.'

'Oh, is that who they are!' Burl sneered. 'I've seen 'em, swaggering about the town. Couple of conceited young coxcombs! I thought they were brothers. There's a likeness that marks them out as kinfolk. What happened to the first Lady Marvell, then? Sir George do away with her, did he, in order to marry a younger woman?'

'For sweet Jesu's sake, man,' I protested, 'keep a watch on your tongue! Unfounded slanders and calumnies such as that will land you in the stocks.'

Just then a pot boy arrived with my companion's third beaker of ale and, from the resentful glance he gave me, I thought for a moment that Burl was going to refuse it. Either that or throw it in my face. We had once been excellent friends, but when, five years earlier, Cicely Ford had died and left me her house in Small Street, Burl had been unable to conceal his resentment at my great good fortune. He had not been the only one by any means. Quite a number of worthy citizens had considered it an imposition to have a pedlar and his family living in the same street as Alderman Foster, former mayor and high sheriff of Bristol, but Burl Hodge's opinion had been the only loss that I had truly grieved over. Jenny and his two sons, Jack and Dick, had continued as friendly as ever, but it was only recently that he had shown signs of wanting to get back on the old footing. Yet even now, all was not as it had been in the past. He was still all too ready to take offence if he considered he was being patronized, and remained reluctant to invite me to his cottage close by Temple Church, in Redcliffe. Moreover, he steadfastly refused to set foot in the Small Street house and, on occasions, was not above making snide remarks about my past relationship with Cicely Ford; remarks he must have known were without foundation if only because of the character of the lady concerned. For Mistress Ford had been renowned throughout the city for her general saintliness of character.

Now, my admonition about his language and the fact that I had paid for his ale made me once again the enemy; the man who – undeservedly in his opinion – had more than his fair share of worldly goods, and certainly more than his fair share of luck. He was still a tenter, working out of doors in the tenting fields in every sort of weather, sweltering in the summer, freezing – to which his rough and reddened hands bore testimony – in the winter, stretching ells of soaking wet cloth, fresh from the fullers, on the tenting frames.

He caught my eye and gave a sort of shame-faced grin, showing that he knew what was going through my mind, then raised the beaker to his lips.

'Waes Hael!' he said, giving the ancient Saxon salutation.

'Drink Hael!' I replied in the same tongue, raising my own cup.

He nodded as though we had reached some fresh understanding, and I gratefully seized the opportunity to give the conversation a new direction.

'How are Jack and Dick doing?' I asked. 'Jack must nearly have finished his apprenticeship with Master Adelard.'

Burl nodded, beaming with pride. 'Master Adelard says he'll be as fine a weaver as any in Redcliffe. He's been a journeyman for more than a twelvemonth now, and he's just completed his Master Piece. If the Weavers' Guild pass it as sound – of good width and texture – he can set up for himself whenever he's able. Provided, of course, he joins the guild and attends its meetings regular. Can you imagine that, eh? Our Jack, with his own workshop and perhaps employing other people to work for him?'

'He was always a bright lad.' I smiled warmly. 'I remember how Dick used to echo everything he said. And how is Dick? I was afraid he might have been put off the baking trade after all that trouble five years back.'

'Not him! It takes more than a bit of murder and mayhem to upset that boy. He's working for Baker Cleghorn in Saint Leonard's Lane. Your Adela would know that. Dick says she buys sweet dough there now and again.'

'I believe she has mentioned seeing him,' I admitted. 'But you know how it is, Burl. You don't always listen to everything women say.'

Burl grunted in agreement, but couldn't resist adding, 'Well, I don't suppose you do. You're not at home often enough.'

'True.' I nodded equably. 'Peddling's a job that takes you far and wide.'

My companion laughed. 'Oh, I wasn't thinking of peddling. I'm not deaf. I hear the rumours and the talk about you, like any other citizen of this fair town.'

I took a deep breath. 'And what exactly do you hear, Burl?'

'That these days you're working mainly for . . . I was going to say the duke, but I'm forgetting. He's the king now, ain't he?'

I ignored – with some difficulty – the provocation in my companion's tone, and leant forward with my elbows on the table. 'I don't know where you and others get your information from,' I said as evenly as I could, 'but it's wrong. I have done several . . . shall we say favours? . . . for King Richard in the past, but that is all. I do not work for him. I am not his spy. I am my own man, as I have always been. I earn my own living. And I rely on you, as my friend, to refute these stories whenever you can.'

Burl shrugged. 'All right, if that's what you wish. But nobody'll believe me. Folk regard you as someone to be reckoned with nowadays, you know. I've even heard it said that the duke – I mean, the king – had summat to do with you getting that house in Small Street. Though no one thought so at the time, mind.'

Words of denial sprang hotly to my lips, but then I gave up. I wasn't going to convince anyone of the truth, let alone my erstwhile friend, whose envy still coloured his perception of me, however hard he tried to do me justice. I propped my chin in my hands and surveyed the ale-room.

It was packed, and I had no doubt that every other inn in the city was likewise full. On this day before the Eve of Christmas, everyone was relaxed and happy, anxious to share that goodwill with friends and strangers alike. Although no one had as yet reached the shouting or singing stage of drunkenness, the noise was none the less deafening, with people calling to one another from table to table, roaring with laughter at friends' jokes and slapping each other on the back as they yelled for more ale. The fire on the central hearth, lit to keep at bay the December cold, had started to smoke badly, one of the logs with which it had just been fed being green and oozing damp. It was becoming difficult to distinguish faces on the opposite side of the room and people were beginning to cough and splutter into their ale. But even their annoyance was good-natured, and there was much ribbing of the landlord for such carelessness in choosing poor fuel.

The door of the Green Lattis opened and closed briefly to allow another thirsty customer to squeeze his way inside and, for a moment, the sudden draught cleared away the smoke on the far side of the room. I happened to be looking that way and, for a few seconds, a face swam in and out of my vision.

'Who's that?' I demanded sharply of Burl.

'Who? Where?' He strained his eyes in the direction of my pointing finger, but the smoke from the fire was again providing an effective screen. 'Who are you talking about?'

'It doesn't matter,' I said. 'You can't see him now. It was just a man I thought I recognized for a moment, but I can't put a name to the face. Probably my imagination, anyway, and I'm certainly not fighting my way through this press to find out.' I stood up. 'I should be going. I promised to be home an hour ago. Adela will be furious with me, and not without cause. Are you coming?'

Burl nodded and also got a little unsteadily to his feet. We shouted our goodnights to the landlord and other friends before supporting each other out into the street. The bells of nearby All Saints' Church were tolling for Vespers. It was later than I thought.

As we rounded a corner of the ale-house, Burl almost bumped into somebody coming from the opposite direction.

He gave a loud belch and mumbled his apologies. The woman, cloaked and hooded, with the hood drawn well forward to cover her face, shrank back in alarm, but whether from a desire not to be recognized or from the stink of Burl's ale-laden breath I shouldn't have liked to hazard a guess. But a lantern, hanging high in the porch of the church, showed her clothes to be of an excellent quality. She was plainly a woman of fashion and some wealth; not the sort to be walking abroad after dusk – although the hour was still early – without a maid in attendance.

I thought at first that she must be going into the church for the service, but she hurried past. Turning to say my farewells to Burl, I was astounded to see her push open the door of the Green Lattis and make her hesitant way inside. There were quite a few women in there, among the rowdy crowd of men, but not of her sort. They were the hucksters, who sold bread around the Bristol streets, washerwomen, who swabbed the floors of the local breweries, spinners and several who belonged to an even older profession, but not one who had any pretensions to being a lady. I was mystified and more than a little intrigued.

'See who that was?' Burl breathed excitedly.

I shook my head. 'Her hood was covering her face.'

'Well, I caught a glimpse of it just as she turned her head away' – he squeezed my arm, his strong fingers biting painfully into my flesh – 'and I'd swear it was Lady Marvell, Sir George's wife. Talk of the Devil!'

'I thought you knew nothing about the family. At least, you were talking as though you didn't just now.'

'Didn't think I did, but I'd forgotten. A few weeks back, Jenny pointed out a woman to me that she said was the knight's wife. And I'd swear that woman we've just seen was her.'

'And what would Lady Marvell be doing going into a place like the Lattis?' I asked scornfully. 'Alone, after dark!'

'You can scoff all you like,' Burl retorted sulkily, aggrieved that his revelation had fallen flat. 'But I'm telling you, it was her.' He hunched his shoulders as a cold wind suddenly blew up from the Backs, and pulled his thin cloak more firmly around him. 'I must be off. You're right! The women ain't going to be pleased.'

We separated, he to walk down High Street and across the bridge into Redcliffe, and I to make my way across the road to Small Street, my steps lagging a little as I steeled myself for Adela's wrath.

I thought I felt a hint of snow in the air. It had certainly grown colder since earlier in the afternoon when I had entered the Green Lattis on my way home from a satisfactory day's peddling of my wares around the town and its immediate environs. The approach of Christmas was always a good time for selling, a time when most folk were prepared to spend an extra few groats for things they really didn't want, and my purse was full. That, at least, should please Adela and soften her very righteous anger. I knew that she and Elizabeth had planned to spend the afternoon making the kissing bush from the branches of holly and mistletoe, bay and alder that my stepson and I had been out into the countryside to pick the day before, and they would be waiting for me to tie it to the hook in the parlour ceiling.

Candlelight gleamed from the windows of houses, stars shone overhead and I suddenly felt happier than I had done for a long time, at peace with all the world. It was the time of Our Saviour's birth, I was at home with my family, King Richard was safely on his throne, the rebellions of the past few months were over and done with at the expense of very few lives, and tomorrow was the Eve of Christmas.

What could possibly go wrong?

TWO

Anything and everything, of course!

Adela and Elizabeth had, between them, made a magnificent kissing bush. The bay and alder branches, the holly and mistletoe had been most skilfully woven in and out of the basket-shaped willow frame which was carefully preserved from year to year, to be brought out every Christmas. In amongst the greenery, red ribbons had been knotted – I had noticed only that morning that my supply of red ribbon was inexplicably low – together with some small bags of nuts and sugared rose petals. Little apples from Adela's winter hoard were spiked on the end of twigs, and tiny figures, cut from stiffened cloth and rag paper, had been threaded on strings and looped around the whole. Some of the latter were even recognizable; a star, what was possibly a manger and certainly a sheep. The only trouble was that the kissing bush had already been hoisted into place, not in the parlour as I had planned, but dangling from a hook driven into the central beam of our small entrance hall.

'Oh, here you are at last, Roger,' my wife remarked on seeing me. 'Supper's ready, and has been this half hour and more. As you see, you're too late to hang the kissing bush. Richard has done it for me.'

I swung round, almost fell over, and steadied myself by grasping at the nearest support. This turned out to be the stocky, red-haired bulk of Richard Manifold, Sheriff's Officer, sometime suitor of Adela before she wed her first husband, Owen Juett, and a permanent thorn in my side. He was still unmarried and consequently always in need of company, particularly, it seemed, my wife's. I won't go so far as to say that he haunted the Small Street house, but he was far too frequent a visitor for my peace of mind. The three older children regarded him with long-suffering tolerance born of familiarity, while I was never quite sure what Adela's feelings for him were. Only my half-nephew, eleven-month-old Luke, but recently fostered by us after the death of his mother, was as yet unconscious of Richard Manifold's (to my mind) disruptive presence in our lives.

Richard smirked at me, and I could have sworn that I caught the glimpse of a halo round his head.

'You knew that I was going to do it. That I enjoy doing it,' I said aggressively, and not altogether truthfully, turning back to my wife. That third beaker of ale was beginning to talk. 'Why did you ask him to do it?'

'You weren't here,' Adela pointed out, keeping her tone reasonable, 'and you know it should be hung up before nightfall on the eve of Christmas Eve. Don't you think it's pretty? Bess and I worked practically all day on it. You have a very talented daughter, my love. She cut out those paper figures using only my working scissors.'

'Yes, I did,' Elizabeth confirmed, 'and you haven't even said anything about them.' Her lower lip trembled. 'I think you're horrid.'

I took a menacing step towards her and she retreated in alarm. 'Don't you dare speak to me like that, my girl,' I threatened, then totally undermined my own authority by adding, 'at least, not in front of strangers.'

Nicholas, flying as always to his stepsister's defence, said truculently, 'Richard's not a stranger.'

'Sergeant Manifold to you, my lad!' I shouted furiously. 'And that goes for the rest of you!'

Hercules, who had just made his way in from the kitchen, hearing my angry tones and considering it his duty, as my four-legged protector, to come to my assistance, began barking ferociously on a high, insistent note. I yelled at him to be quiet; the baby, sat on the floor among the rushes and, unused to such a cacophony, started to scream, while Elizabeth burst into tears and fled upstairs.

So much for a peaceful Christmas! I had been home for less than ten minutes and the place was in uproar. And it was all my fault.

Or the fault of the ale I had consumed. I took a deep breath and apologized all round. My daughter was persuaded to come downstairs again and, between sniffs, reluctantly forgave me;

Luke was picked up and pacified, bestowing on me a beaming smile when I ruffled his copper-coloured curls; Nicholas frowned at me reprovingly, while Adam gave me three or four sharp kicks on the ankles and considered honour satisfied. Richard and Adela continued as if nothing had happened, such behaviour being, they implied, beneath their notice and thus putting me, very properly, in my place. (It did cross my mind to wonder why I was never master in my own house, as other men were, but the answer eluded me.)

Adela held out her hand. 'A kiss under the mistletoe,' she said. I knew what was in her mind.

After the death of our four-day-old daughter, three years before, she had not conceived again, and it seemed possible that Adam would remain our only child. She was a natural mother, a woman who enjoyed motherhood in spite of all its attendant restraints and vexations, which was the chief reason, I felt sure, why she had agreed with such ease to foster Luke, who had no claim on her affection whatsoever. Adam was now five years old, growing up and away from her and leaving a void in her life that cried out to be filled.

'I'm a man,' was our son's frequently voiced assertion, and indeed his sturdy independence had come, I think, as something of a surprise to both of us. It shouldn't have done. His birth had been greeted with resentment by his older half-brother and half-sister who, with a mere fortnight in age between them, had been fast friends from the moment that Adela and I were married. As a baby, they had tried to give Adam away to the mad wife of Baker Overbeck, so he had been very much his own man since he was small. The arrival of young Luke within the past few weeks had strengthened this sense of independence, making him no longer the youngest member of the household and bolstering his self-reliance. He had ceased to need his mother in the way he had done before.

Adela was therefore pining for another child of her own. Mistletoe was supposed to have aphrodisiac properties and kissing beneath it to aid fertility. I didn't think that I had been showing any lack of enthusiasm for my marital duties lately – in fact, it was too often Adela who pleaded tiredness – but if that was the way the wind was blowing, I was perfectly ready to comply. I embraced her warmly and gave her a lingering kiss. She reached up, broke a sprig of the plant from the kissing bush and stuck it in my hair just behind my left ear.

Harmony now being fully restored and Christmas, as it were, back on course, we all repaired to the kitchen to have supper, Richard Manifold included. I suppose it was foolish of me to have expected otherwise.

Tonight it was simply the same stew, reheated, that had provided dinner for Adela and the children, but all around me I could see that preparations were underway for the festive meals of the next few days. Assembled on a side table were the dried plums that would make the plum porridge; the eggs, spices and milk, together with a bowl of boiled wheat, which would turn into frumenty; the butcher's leftovers from the bigger joints of meat sold to the gentry which, with apples and dried raisins, would be encased in pastry to make the minced pies; and a rather small, somewhat withered-looking capon, carefully budgeted for over the past month, which would grace our board on the day of Christ's birth itself.

I could see Richard Manifold eyeing these signs of delights to come as he shared our pottage, and I wondered how long it would be before he made some remark. But it was not until the older children had left the table and Adela, with Luke on her lap, was spooning some of the broth into his ever open little mouth, that Richard could no longer refrain from comment.

'You're well advanced in your preparations, I see, Adela. Are you – er – expecting guests?'

'Only my cousin, Margaret Walker,' my wife replied tranquilly. 'She is Elizabeth's grandmother, after all, and naturally wishes to see her only grandchild on Christmas Day. Do you have any plans, dear Richard?'

I could have screamed at her not to be such a fool. The man was obviously angling for an invitation.

I was wrong, however.

'I shall be eating at the mayor's table,' he said gloomily. 'The sheriff and his assistants have been invited. But I shall be surprised if the other sergeant, Tom Merryweather, and I get through the meal without interruption. The mummers arrive in Bristol tomorrow afternoon, ready to start their plays on Saint

Stephen's Day, and that is invariably the signal for all the young idiots in the town to dress up in masks and go rioting through the streets, making a damn nuisance of themselves and frightening the old biddies half to death. Even Our Lord's birthday's not sacred to them. I don't know what the youth of today is coming to.'

Adela laughed. 'Richard, you make yourself sound like some old greybeard. The young will be young – it's only to be expected. But I didn't know we were to have mummers this year, did you, Roger?'

I shook my head. 'Where are they performing?'

'In the outer ward of Bristol Castle, I believe.' The sergeant rubbed his nose. 'I heard they're to be given accommodation there, as well. It's only a small troupe. Not more than five or six of them, I've been told.'

'The children will be pleased,' Adela said, wiping Luke's mouth on a corner of her apron. She regarded it with dismay. 'Oh dear! Look at that! Now I'll have to wash it again. He really is a messy eater.' She dropped a kiss on the top of the child's curly head. 'You're looking very pensive, Roger. Is something bothering you?'

'Not really.' I chewed my thumbnail. 'It's just that I thought I saw someone in the Green Lattis whom I know. But I can't place him. Which reminds me. Something else rather odd happened. Burl and I—'

'Oh, Burl Hodge, was it!' exclaimed my wife. 'I might have known!'

I ignored this interruption. 'Burl and I,' I continued, 'saw a woman going into the Lattis just as we were leaving. You'll never guess who it was.'

'Tell us, then,' my wife invited, setting Luke down among the floor rushes, where he sat happily subjecting his toes to close scrutiny.

'I have to admit that I didn't actually see her face,' I confessed reluctantly. 'She was wearing a cloak with the hood pulled well forward. But Burl swears it was Lady Marvell.'

There was a moment's silence before Richard Manifold threw back his head and gave a loud guffaw. 'The fool was drunk,' he said. He didn't add, 'like you', but I knew very well it was what he was thinking. In any case, he didn't need to. Adela said it for him.

'You were both in your cups,' she accused me. 'Patience Marvell wouldn't be out alone after dark, let alone entering a place like the Green Lattis.'

I sighed. 'That's what I told Burl, but he would have it that he was right. Said he caught a glimpse of her face under the hood in the light from the lantern in All Saints' porch.'

Richard laughed again and got up. 'I wouldn't believe anything that guzzler thought he saw when he's had a few beakers of ale. Adela, I must be off. Thank you for supper, and I'm glad I could be of use with the kissing bush. If I don't see you again before Our Blessed Lord's birthday, I wish you all the blessings and joy of the season.' He nodded at me. 'Goodnight, Roger.'

Adela saw him to the door. When she returned, I asked irritably, 'And when did Sergeant Manifold become "dear" Richard?'

'Oh, for heaven's sake, Roger!' Her irritation was as palpable as mine. 'It was simply an expression.'

'Not one that I approve of,' I snapped.

She resumed her place at the table and gave me a wan smile. 'Are we going to go on like this? Quarrelling with one another all Christmas?'

She looked weary and suddenly rather frail. I was immediately contrite.

'No,' I said. 'Of course not.'

But I was too sanguine. While she washed the supper dishes, I went into the parlour where a fire burned low on the hearth, sank into my armchair, with its embroidered seat and cushions (all done by Adela's clever fingers), and stretched my legs towards the warmth, expecting, after my busy day and three beakers of ale, to fall asleep immediately.

Chance would have been a fine thing.

I heard the parlour door creak open and the next moment Adam, ready for bed in his little nightshirt, had climbed on to my lap.

'Story,' he demanded imperatively.

I sighed. 'I don't know any more stories. I've told you all the ones I know.'

'Tell again.' He settled himself into the crook of my arm. 'Tell about Balder and Loki.'

I hesitated. 'Sweetheart, you know your mother doesn't approve of my telling you these pagan legends.'

'She won't know,' he answered simply. 'I shan't tell her.' He wriggled a bit, swinging his legs and watching the shadows they made on the hearthstones. The tallow candle, placed near my chair, guttered and went out. My son and I were left in the dancing firelight. 'Balder and Loki,' he repeated.

'Oh, very well,' I said, giving in. 'Balder, who was called the Beautiful—'

'I'm beautiful,' Adam said. He was never one to hide his light under a bushel.

I gave him a kiss and a hug. 'Yes, you are,' I agreed, 'but don't interrupt. Balder the Beautiful was the second son of the god Odin – or Woden as he's sometimes called – and his wife Frigga, or Freya, the mother of the gods. Balder was the god of the sun, of light and peace, and all the other gods loved him.'

'Except Loki,' Adam said with relish.

It was obvious who, to him, was the hero of this story. Perhaps it should have worried me, but I remembered myself at his age. Heroes had always been boring: villains were so much more entertaining.

'I'm coming to that. I told you, don't interrupt. Well, Balder was so beautiful and so beloved that Odin—'

'Or Woden.'

'All right. Odin, or Woden, decreed that nothing which sprang from air, fire, water or earth should ever be able to harm him. So all the gods thought that Balder was quite safe from Loki, the god of earth and strife and darkness, who hated him.'

'But Loki was too clever for them,' my son said, wriggling again in anticipation.

'Much too clever. He fashioned an arrow made from a branch of mistletoe because mistletoe doesn't grow from the earth. It only grows on other trees.'

'The oak and the apple.'

'Yes. And if it grew on an oak, it was especially sacred to the druids, the priests of the old religion. It could only be cut with a knife of pure gold and had to be caught in an equally pure white cloth because it must never touch the ground.'

Adam wasn't interested in this. 'Go on about Loki,' he commanded.

'Where was I? Oh, I know. Well, Loki made an arrow from mistletoe, but he was much too wily to fire it himself. Instead, he gave it to the blind god of war, Hoder, and whispered to him in which direction to aim it . . .'

'And Hoder shot the arrow and it killed Balder,' my son finished excitedly, bouncing up and down on my knee. 'And that was the end of Balder.'

'We-ell, not quite,' I said. 'You know the ending to this story as well as I do. You've heard it before. The other gods and goddesses all missed Balder so much that they begged Odin to bring him back to life. So he did.'

Adam nodded, then said thoughtfully, 'Like Our Lord, Jesus Christ.'

I don't know how long Adela had been standing in the parlour doorway, left open by Adam, or just how much she had heard, but our son's unconscious blasphemy set the seal on her wrath. He was seized from my lap and, to his utter astonishment, given a resounding slap where it hurt the most before his mother turned on me.

'Don't ever,' she raged, 'let me hear you telling him, or any of the children, stories like that again. I won't have you corrupting their minds with such evil, irreligious nonsense.' She turned back to Adam and shook him hard. 'And don't let me hear you repeating it, either. You're to put such wickedness out of your mind. Do you understand me, Adam? Men only made up those stories when they didn't know any better. But we do! There is only One God and Our Lord Jesus Christ is His Son. I don't ever want to hear those pagan names on your lips again.'

I was by now in as much of a temper as she was. 'That's just plain stupid,' I rasped. 'If he can't mention Tue, Woden, Thor and Frig, how is he going to pronounce the days of the week? You perhaps don't realize it, my dear' – there is nothing like a 'my dear' to emphasize how angry you are when arguing with your wife – 'but we talk about them all the time.'

Adela stared at me for a moment or two, her breast heaving, then she quite suddenly burst into tears. 'I hate you!' she sobbed and rushed from the room.

Adam and I stared at one another in consternation.

Of course, she didn't really hate me.

I put Adam to bed in the little room he shared with Nicholas, then went in search of Adela in our own bedchamber, where she always took refuge when upset. It took all my well-known tact and charm to win her round – plus a solemn promise never again to tell the children 'pagan legends' as she called them – and in the end we decided to go to bed ourselves and make up in the usual way. It was pitch dark outside and a fine snow was still falling. As my wife pointed out, it would save candles and more logs for the parlour fire; but as I couldn't help reflecting, rather sadly, there had been a time, not that far distant, when such a mundane consideration would not even have entered our heads.

I woke after some hours with a raging thirst, the result of three beakers of ale and two bowlfuls of rabbit stew, and went downstairs to the water barrel in the kitchen to slake it. The snow had stopped now, as a peep out of the back door into our little yard confirmed. In the distance, I could hear the rattle of the night-soilers' carts as they went about their filthy, stinking business, cleaning out the public latrines and cesspits as well as the private privies of anyone who was willing to pay for their services. Occasionally, I did so myself and decided that if I continued to earn good money at my peddling, I might do so permanently. It was a happy thought and I smiled. Then I went back inside, shutting and bolting the door after me.

I was still thirsty, so I fetched another cup of water and perched on the edge of the kitchen table, swinging one leg. It had not been the best possible start to Christmas, but that had been largely my own fault. I shouldn't have stayed in the Green Lattis, drinking, and I shouldn't have lost my temper when I discovered that Richard Manifold had usurped my right to tie the kissing bush to the ceiling hook. Or should I? I wasn't quite sure.

Thinking about the Green Lattis brought back the memory of the face I had seen across the ale-room. I was still unable to put a name to it, but I was possessed of the strong conviction that it had been in the wrong place. It hadn't been in its familiar surroundings. Had it been, I felt certain I should have known who the man was.

'You'll recollect, given time,' I told myself. 'Let it alone and it'll come to you. It always does.'

But I couldn't stop worrying at the problem, like probing an aching tooth with one's tongue, so I deliberately diverted my thoughts to a different worry, and one that I could do nothing about. It was a month or so now since rumours began circulating that King Richard – a man I loved and deeply admired and who had, on several occasions, claimed me as a friend – had had his two nephews murdered. These stories had started during the late rebellion, and I thought I knew who was their author: one of the king's most implacable enemies, John Morton, Bishop of Ely. But once the rebellion had been put down, skilfully and with very little loss of life or retribution, I had confidently expected the king to deny the calumny publicly and to produce the two boys, alive and well, for all the world to see. It hadn't happened, and although I kept telling myself that my belief in King Richard's humanity and probity was as strong as ever, now and again I felt that belief to be a little shaken . . .

It was useless to think like that. I stood up abruptly, swallowed the remaining water, replaced the cup on the shelf and went back to bed. In spite of my cluttered mind, within five minutes I was asleep and snoring. Or, at least, so Adela informed me in the morning.

It was at breakfast that Adela, looking a little heavy-eyed as though she had slept badly, informed Nicholas and myself that our first task on this Eve of Christmas would be to go down to Redcliffe Wharf where, so she had been informed, the Yule logs were being distributed.

'Now you know what to look for, Roger,' she instructed me. 'A log that's not too wet, so that it won't burn at all, but not too dry, either. A bit green and damp so that it will burn throughout the whole twelve days until Twelfth Night. If it stops burning, that's bad luck for the coming year.'

'I wanted to go and watch the mummers arrive,' my stepson protested indignantly, but his mother was adamant.

'That's not until this afternoon,' she said. 'There will be plenty of time for that afterwards.'

'How do you know it's this afternoon?' Nick, though normally a quiet and amenable child, could be awkward when he chose.

'Sergeant Manifold said so.'

'I didn't hear him.'

'That'll do, Nicholas!' Adela so rarely called her son by his full name that he looked startled. 'You'll do as I tell you.'

Not another Christmas disagreement, please Lord, I prayed silently. Out loud I said, 'I should appreciate your company, Nick. Then, if I choose the wrong log, I'll have someone to share the blame with.'

That made him grin and restored his good humour. 'Can we take Hercules?'

'Yes, if you like. Although I warn you, he's bound to be more of a hindrance than a help.'

So as soon as breakfast was finished, I set out with the two of them for Redcliffe Wharf. Before leaving, I gave Adela a smacking kiss and the purseful of money I had made the preceding day. Pleasurably surprised by the amount, she not only returned my embrace with interest, but actually conceded that perhaps, after all, I had earned those extra two beakers of ale in the Green Lattis.

Early as it was, the streets were already crowded as people began their last-minute preparations for the holy day on the morrow. As we made our way across the bridge and along Redcliffe Street the crowds grew thicker, and several times Hercules was obliged to growl menacingly at strangers who jostled us too closely. Like ourselves, many of those on foot were making their way towards the quayside where the Yule logs were being handed out. My hopes of getting one exactly suited to my wife's requirements faded.

We had just turned into one of the narrow alleyways which run between Redcliffe Street and the Backs, when a great shout went up from some of the people ahead of us. 'A mill! A mill!'

Every man loves a good fight, and immediately all those behind us began surging forward. I hauled Hercules up into my arms, told Nicholas to hang on to my cloak and on no account to let go, then used my height and bulk and strength to heave aside my neighbours and push us clear of the alley.

A circle of spectators, about eight deep, had already formed about the two contestants, but I edged my stepson to where a pile of Yule logs, a little apart from the rest and so far unnoticed by others, formed a platform from which the fight could easily be viewed in comfort.

To my astonishment, this was no bout of fisticuffs between a couple of crane workers or dock-hands – which was not an unusual sight along the Backs – but a set-to between two young men who, judging by their clothes, were of some wealth and standing. The savagery of the blows which they were inflicting on one another argued an enmity deeply felt and of long duration, but they had, at least, chosen to fight with their fists rather than their daggers or swords which, together with their cloaks and hats, were piled at the feet of an onlooker.

It was not easy to distinguish between them. They were of a similar age – somewhere, I guessed, around nineteen or twenty. Both were of slender build and both had brown curly hair. Indeed, except for the fact that one wore a blue tunic and the other a green it would have been almost impossible to tell them apart.

After a few minutes watching them, it became apparent that 'blue tunic' was getting the worst of it. He had been knocked to the ground twice in the last few seconds and was obviously tiring. His opponent, on the other hand, still seemed fresh and ready to continue handing out punishment indefinitely. And perhaps he would have done had there not, at that moment, been an interruption.

Some of the spectators were suddenly and violently scattered by a horse and rider plunging between them. A whip flashed, catching 'green tunic' across the shoulders, and a stentorian voice shouted, 'Stop this! Stop it at once!'

It was Sir George Marvell.

THREE

S ir George threw himself from his horse and seized 'green tunic' by the scruff of his neck, at the same time bellowing, 'You great oaf! You young bully! Leave your uncle be!' He then gave the lad a shove which sent the latter sprawling on the ground and turned to the other, who appeared to my eyes as the slightly younger man. But if he had expected sympathy, he was disappointed. 'Get up, for Sweet Christ's sake, Bart! What are you, a man or a jellyfish? If you can't stand up to a lout like James, God help you! You should be ashamed of yourself!'

The man in the green tunic, referred to as James, got to his feet and gave a snort of laughter. 'There's one thing to be said about you, Grandfather: you don't have favourites. We all get to feel the rough edge of your tongue.' He stooped and proffered a hand to his opponent, still struggling to rise. 'No hard feelings, Bartholomew. But you shouldn't be insolent to your elders and betters, you know, even if I am your nephew.'

'You're not better than me. Father!' The other youth, now on his feet, laid a hand on Sir George's arm. 'Tell him to stop teasing me. He's always on at me and I don't like it,' he whined.

The onlookers had fallen silent, delighted by the spectacle of an aristocratic family, oblivious of dignity and pride, tearing itself apart. But the charade was not yet played out. A female voice, shrill and full of venom, demanded, 'What have you been doing to my son, you hulking brute?'

The knight spun round, his face as black as thunder. 'Leave this to me, Patience! This has nothing to do with you. Just a lads' quarrel, that's all. Bart's not hurt. Go home!'

Patience! This, then, was the present Lady Marvell, mother of 'blue tunic' and the woman Burl swore was last night's visitor to the Green Lattis. I craned my neck in order to obtain a better view of her and was rewarded by seeing her clearly in profile as she turned her head to look at another woman who was pushing her way angrily through the crowd. I saw a thin face with a sharp, prominent nose and very black eyebrows, the latter finding an echo in her son's slightly coarser features. Her slender frame was expensively dressed in a brown fur-trimmed velvet cloak and hood, which was definitely not the garment she had been wearing the previous evening – had it indeed been her whom Burl and I had seen.

The second woman who had joined the group was equally, if not quite as richly dressed in a cloak and hood of red wool with a trimming of marten fur framing her face. This I was unable to see because she was turned away from me, addressing Sir George, but her voice was as high-pitched as Lady Marvell's and every bit as vituperative.

'What is going on here?' She stabbed a forefinger at Bartholomew Marvell. 'What has that little bastard been doing to my son?'

The youth called James stepped forward hastily and, putting an arm about her shoulders, said something in a low voice, plainly remonstrating with her, but gently.

She put up a hand to caress his cheek, her response to his words carrying easily to where Nicholas and I were standing.

'No, I will not be silent! If your own mother can't be your champion, who can? You have been pushed to one side all your life for that idiot there, who she says' – the woman rounded fiercely on Patience Marvell – 'is your grandfather's son but who might be anyone's by-blow for anything we can tell. After all, he was an old man when he married her and quite probably impotent by then.'

You could have heard a pin drop. This was entertainment of a very high order; better than the mummers, who were arriving that afternoon, could offer. This would provide gossip in every home and tavern in the city for months ahead. But there was still more to come. With an ear-splitting shriek, Lady Marvell threw herself on her tormentor, clawing at her face and neck and giving voice to imprecations which no lady of breeding should even know, let alone utter.

Sir George seized his wife by the shoulders, spun her round and slapped her face with the full force of his arm behind it. At the same time he addressed a thickset, middle-aged man whom I had noticed standing quietly at the front of the crowd watching the unfolding of the little drama with, I thought, a certain cynical detachment. 'Get your wife home this instant, Cyprian! I shall have something to say to you all once we're there.'

With that, the knight, his face contorted with fury, mounted his horse and moved her about preparatory to riding off along Redcliffe Back to one of the tall, three-storied houses that lined the southern bank of the River Avon and which had so lately become the Marvell family home.

But he found his path blocked by the arrival of authority in the shape of Richard Manifold, followed by his two henchmen, Jack Gload and Peter Littleman.

'What's going on here?' demanded Richard. 'I've information that there's a breach of the peace. A couple of ruffians brawling, I was told. Where are they? Let's be having them.'

'Get out of my way, you dolt!' Sir George exclaimed furiously. 'There's no breach of the peace. Just my son and grandson having a disagreement, that's all. I suppose honest citizens can have a bit of a turn-up without bringing the law down around their heads.'

Richard Manifold looked startled. He had not immediately perceived that the man on horseback was Sir George and for a moment or two was unsure how to proceed. But he was not easily intimidated and, although he had a natural deference for anyone with a title, he was not prepared to overlook any misdemeanour which contravened the laws laid down in Bristol's Great Red Book.

'I'm sorry, Sir George,' he said respectfully, yet firmly, 'but fighting in the city streets is not allowed. You can see for yourself what crowds it attracts. All these fools blocking the king's highway.' He indicated the rest of us with a dramatic sweep of his arm. 'I'm afraid I'll have to take the culprits into custody, although I'm sure they'll be released on the payment of a fine. Are these the two lads here?'

James Marvell grinned at the other man. 'Looks like we're due for a spell in the Bridewell cells, Uncle,' he remarked good-naturedly.

'I won't! I won't!' The younger man seemed appalled at the thought of such an indignity. 'Mother!' He turned imploringly towards Lady Marvell. 'Don't let them arrest me.'

Patience Marvell caught at her husband's bridle. 'George, do something! You can't allow your son to be taken into custody like a common criminal!'

The knight wheeled his horse about with such violence that she was almost thrown to the ground.

'I wash my hands of the pack of you,' he snarled. 'If my son and grandson behave like common louts, then they must take the consequences.' He addressed Richard Manifold. 'Tell the sheriff that I'll be along to bail them out later. Much later!' And with that, he rode off along the wharf without a backward glance.

Richard Manifold, plainly relieved that Sir George had seen reason and bowed to the authority of the law, and with the assistance of Jack Gload and Peter Littleman, marched his two prisoners away, having first permitted them to gather up their hats and cloaks, swords and daggers from where they had left them. Lady Marvell, her stepson and the second woman, who was presumably the stepson's wife, were left staring uncomfortably at one another, suddenly aware of the interested crowd around them. Cyprian Marvell cleared his throat awkwardly.

'Come, Joanna! We'd better go home and – er – face the storm.' He offered her the support of his right arm, then held out his left to his stepmother. 'Patience?'

But she was staring after her departed husband, her face contorted with anger.

'I'll never forgive George for this,' she said. 'Letting Bart be carted off like a criminal by that officious sergeant and those two horrid, common little men.'

Whilst treasuring up this description of Jack and Pete for use at some future date, I couldn't help feeling a certain admiration for Cyprian Marvell. I knew nothing about the man, or his family if it came to that, apart from what I had seen during the recent unsavoury spectacle, but of them all he seemed the most reasonable. The two women had started hurling invectives at one another again concerning their respective sons – each blamed the other's for the recent brawl – and with the greatest good humour he placed himself between them, admonishing them gently, and urged them in the direction the knight had taken.

As they disappeared from view around a slight bend in the river bank, the crowd began slowly to disperse, suddenly remembering what we were all really there for; the distribution and collection of Yule logs.

'Well, I did enjoy that,' said a voice in my ear as Nicholas and I descended from our perch.

It was Burl Hodge, grinning all over his round, freckled face.

'Did you get a good look at Lady Marvell?' I asked. 'Do you still think she's the same woman we saw last night?'

'Stake my life on it,' Burl responded cheerfully. 'Oh, yes! It was the same woman all right.'

'I don't see how you can be so certain. The light was too dim.'

'I wasn't three parts drunk like you,' Burl said outrageously, depriving me temporarily of speech. 'I use my eyes.' He nudged me. 'Here! If you're on the same errand as me, we'd better line up for our logs before all the best ones get taken. I don't know about your Adela, but my Jenny's given me strict instructions what to look for. And if she don't get what she wants she can be a right Tartar.'

'Oh, my Adela's reasonable enough,' I answered smugly, but conscious of a sharp look of surprise from Nicholas. 'All the same, perhaps you're right – we need to be able to pick and choose.'

I set Hercules down on the ground, handed his rope to my stepson with instructions to hang on to it tightly – there were always a number of stray cats along the wharves looking for rats – and pushed my way to the front of the crowd now forming about the dispensing official. A short time later, we were on our way home.

I congratulated myself that I had managed to grab just the right log, not too dry but not too damp either; one which, when lit the day after tomorrow, St Stephen's Day, would slowly burn and smoulder throughout the twelve days of Christmas. Adela should be pleased, I told Nicholas. I had taken a length of rope to tie around the log so that it could be dragged behind us to Small Street, but in the event was forced to carry it, Hercules taking instant exception to my having anything on a lead apart from himself. The weight of it nearly broke my arms and I staggered indoors, letting the log drop on to the hearth in the hall with a thud that shook the painted overmantel.

My wife, daughter and son came running to investigate the

crash, while the dog, anticipating trouble, escaped to the kitchen as soon as Nicholas released him. Adela, however, was so delighted with the size and condition of our Yule log that she forbore to mention the flakes of red and green paint that had been shaken loose and lay scattered on the hearthstones. And later, during dinner, when I recounted the scene at Redcliffe Wharf, she was even more forgiving, filling my plate, unasked, with a second large helping of pottage.

'Sir George must have been mortified,' she murmured. 'And the two women quarrelling, as well! It'll be the talk of Bristol for weeks.'

I nodded. 'The only one who came out of the affair with any credit was Cyprian Marvell.'

'Cyprian! That's a stupid name,' Elizabeth opined scornfully.

'It's a saint's name,' Adela reproved her.

'Saint Cyprian,' I added, never one to hide the light of my knowledge under a bushel, 'was Bishop of Carthage during the third century. A scholar and an orator. As a Christian, he was beheaded on the orders of the Emperor Valerian, which makes him one of the Church's martyrs.'

My daughter was unimpressed. It worried me sometimes – whenever I had the time to think about it – that she had inherited a little of my ambiguous attitude towards religion. Moreover, her maternal grandparents, Margaret Walker and her dead husband, Adam, had dabbled in Lollardism. My former mother-in-law had, at one time, even possessed a Lollard Bible.

Elizabeth said now, in a flat little voice, 'Being a martyr's silly. You might just as well pretend to agree with people and then go your own way afterwards.'

I could see by the horrified expression on Adela's face that a storm of protest was about to burst around my daughter's head – not to mention my own for being too lax a father in these matters – so I said quickly, 'Who wants to see the mummers' arrival at the castle this afternoon?'

Immediately four hands shot into the air, including that of the baby, who simply copied his foster siblings' actions. As the other three clamoured and shouted their acquiescence, he gave us all a beaming smile, which made Elizabeth swoop to pick him up and give him a stifling cuddle, which only seemed to make him smile the more.

'You'll come, too?' I asked my wife.

'If Luke is to go, I shall have to. I wouldn't trust him with any of you.'

She gave me a little half-smile, indicating that she knew she had, for the present, been outmanoeuvred, but also letting me understand that the subject of my daughter's irreligious attitude had merely been postponed, not forgotten.

'At what hour are they expected?' she asked.

I shrugged. 'No one knows. But if we want a good view we'd best be at the castle as soon as we can. There's bound to be a crowd waiting to see them.'

I was right. News of the mummers' arrival for the Christmas season had attracted not only hundreds from within the city itself, but also many from beyond its walls, from the surrounding villages and hamlets. With four children and a dog, and even arriving well before midday, I had my work cut out to force a passage across the barbican bridge and, once in the castle's outer ward, to find a place where we could all see comfortably and without being too badly jostled by the smellier and more scrofulous riff-raff of the city streets. Adela and I shared the burden of Luke's weight between us and Elizabeth, Nicholas and Adam took it in turns to be responsible for Hercules.

While waiting, I took the opportunity to look about me, not having been inside the castle for some little time and, although I knew from general report that it had fallen into a bad state of disrepair, I was nevertheless surprised by how swiftly it had deteriorated since my previous visit. One building, a guardhouse, was practically roofless, while the chimney of yet another – the castle bakery – had tumbled to the ground, leaving merely a hole in the tiles. Loose bricks and stones lay scattered everywhere to trip up the unwary, while huge cracks were opening in the walls of various other outhouses and even in the great keep itself.

I had learned something of its history from Alderman Foster who also lived in Small Street and who, unlike many of the other residents, had never resented my family's presence there. I knew, for instance, that the castle's construction had been started only a year or so after the Conquest under the auspices of Geoffrey de Mowbray, the warlike Bishop of Coutances (and later, for services rendered, of Exeter). The keep, however, with its six-foot-thick walls, had been built at the instigation of Earl Robert of Gloucester, bastard half-brother of the Empress Matilda, with stone brought from his birthplace of Caen, in Normandy. Every tenth stone had been set aside for the glory of God and the building of St James's Priory.

Two kings had lain within its walls. Stephen, fighting his cousin Matilda for the English throne, had been its prisoner for some little time after his capture at the Battle of Lincoln. And, later, the future Henry II, Matilda's son and half-nephew of Robert of Gloucester, had spent much of his boyhood, from the ages of about nine to thirteen, there; carefree, happy years which he acknowledged in later life by the granting of Bristol's first Great Charter, exempting its citizens from certain taxes and tolls. He had married the wealthy heiress and former Queen of France, Eleanor of Aquitaine, who had given him what she had been unable to give Louis VII: four healthy sons. But Henry quarrelled with them all, just as he quarrelled with Thomas Becket, his Archbishop of Canterbury. He was, nevertheless, one of England's greatest kings, the Law Giver, and I liked to think that, as he lay dying at Chinon, surrounded by his enemies, he perhaps took comfort from memories of happy, childhood days in Bristol, fishing in the Rivers Frome and Avon and riding his pony through its cobbled streets or out into the surrounding countryside as far as Clifton and the gorge . . .

Adela nudged me painfully in the ribs. (She has a very sharp elbow when she likes.) 'Wake up, Roger! You're daydreaming again. What's more, if I hadn't managed to catch him in time, you would have dropped Luke. And I think the mummers must be coming. I can hear people cheering out in the streets.'

'Sorry,' I muttered, uncomfortably aware of my failings as a father and husband. I ruffled Luke's curls by way of an apology and was rewarded with a beaming smile and the flash of a new tooth. I did not deserve it.

The shouting and cheering was growing louder as the mummers approached the castle, but I thought the tone of their reception was rather muted. And when, finally, they rattled across the barbican bridge and into the outer ward, I realized why.

This was no King's Troupe which had been hired for our Christmas entertainment. Typically – and indeed what one should have expected knowing the city fathers' obsession with saving money and doing everything on the cheap – it was a company of only five, two of them more than a little advanced in years. But they had made as brave a showing as they could with what they had, coloured ribbons and evergreens decking the first cart, which obviously also served as their stage. The second, smaller cart which rumbled behind was piled with chests of clothes, from which the occasional stray sleeve or leg of hose had escaped, and with rolls of painted canvas – the backdrops to their plays.

In spite of our general disappointment, we all raised a cheer as the carts came to a standstill in our midst. The young man driving the first one clambered from the box seat on to the 'stage' and raised his arms for silence. He was a tall, slim youth of about nineteen, with a ruddy face, ready smile and a generally pleasing appearance. I guessed that the young woman seated beside him, obviously pregnant, was his wife.

'Friends!' he shouted. 'We are not a big company, as you can see.' We all laughed and there were some disparaging remarks from the back of the crowd, but he took no notice and continued, 'But what we lack in numbers we make up for in quality. We are, in short, the best.' There were more cries of derision, but all good-natured and accompanied by laughter. 'We shall give our first performance the day after tomorrow, on Saint Stephen's Day, and it will be the enactment of Saint George and his epic struggle with the dragon. No character will be omitted. As well as the saint and his terrible opponent, you will also see depicted the Turkish Knight, the Saracen, Old Man Winter, the Doctor' – there were roars of approval at this mention of the Doctor – 'and Beelzebub Himself! Friends, you are all cordially invited to as many performances as you care to attend.' He grinned broadly, adding, 'There will, of course, be a collection for the players at each one.'

'I thought the city fathers were paying you!' yelled a voice, which I recognized as Jack Nym's, from somewhere to my left.

The young man answered drily, 'This is Bristol, master.' There was a delighted roar from the crowd. He went on: 'The mayor and aldermen are giving us free lodgings in the castle.' He cast a disparaging glance around him and nodded in the direction of the roofless guardhouse. 'The very best, as you can see' – another roar – 'but we have to keep body and soul together, so all donations will be gratefully received.'

He got down from the 'stage' and resumed his place beside the girl preparatory to driving forward into the inner ward, where one of the castle stewards was waiting patiently for him by the gate. Before the two carts disappeared from sight, however, I took quick stock of his companions. Apart from the young woman, there was another man of perhaps some thirty summers sharing the box seat with them, and whose features bore a sufficient resemblance to the girl's to convince me that he was probably her brother.

The second cart was driven by a much older pair; a man and woman both well over sixty, and maybe nudging seventy if I were any judge of the matter. In spite of it being December, with a cold, nipping bite to the wind, the woman's arms were bare to the elbow and, like her face, her skin was the colour of hazelnuts. Her clothes were nondescript and shapeless, while the hands which held the horse's reins were remarkably large for her sex and appeared extremely strong. Around her head she had tied a broad strip of faded cloth from beneath which a few strands of grey hair were escaping, and between her teeth she clenched a long piece of straw which she chewed with slow, deliberate movements of her jaws. At first glance and until I noticed her skirts, I had mistaken her for a man.

Her companion on the box seat was undoubtedly male, bald but for a fringe of almost white hair which grew nearly to his shoulders. These were rounded and suggested a once tall man who was now permanently stooped with age. His skin was as brown as the woman's, indicating, as did hers, the wandering, outdoor life. But his most distinctive feature, which I noticed as he turned his head in my direction, was the puckered skin around his right eye, drawing the corner upwards as though, at some time, it had been seared with a red-hot brand. At least, I thought that this was his most distinctive feature until he put up his right hand to flick a strand of hair from his cheek and I saw that the first two fingers were missing.

The leading cart had by now disappeared through the gate into the castle's inner ward and the second was preparing to follow suit when a disturbance beyond the archway and voices raised in anger caused the woman to pull on the reins and bring the horse to a standstill. People, including Adela and myself, who had begun to disperse, came to a halt, craning over our shoulders to discover the cause of the commotion.

'Oh, no!' groaned a voice in my ear. 'Not him again!'

But it was indeed Sir George Marvell riding out from the inner ward, together with another man, and loudly cursing the mummers' carts which were impeding his progress.

'Get out of my way, you idle layabouts!' he shouted. Then, turning to his companion, he demanded in ringing tones, 'What's this riff-raff doing here, Robert?'

I knew Robert Trefusis by sight, although I knew very little about him. He was a tall, very upright, grey-haired man of roughly Sir George's own age, and I understood him to be, again like Sir George, a man of inherited wealth. He was, I believed, an alderman who, on occasions, acted as one of the sheriff's deputies, a role I suspected he had been playing that afternoon. It was my guess that Sir George had been to the castle to pay his son's and grandson's fines for breaking the King's Peace that morning.

Alderman Trefusis shrugged. 'It's the Christmas mummers. None of my doing, George,' he replied with equal clarity. He glanced contemptuously at the second cart and the old pair seated on the box. 'We were too late to hire a decent troupe and this rubbish was all we could find.' He laughed loudly. 'As you can see for yourself – the old, the halt and the blind. Well, semi-blind, at least. Not worth their board and food for my money.'

There was an uncomfortable murmuring amongst the crowd but, to their credit, the old couple showed no reaction of any sort. They merely stared at the two men as if they weren't there, as if they were looking right through them. Then the woman removed the straw from her mouth in order to spit over the side of the cart and the man picked his teeth with a grubby fingernail before the horse, responding to a flick of the reins, moved forward and entered the inner ward.

The gate closed behind them and the crowd once more began to move.

'What've we done to deserve that he should come and live amongst us, eh?' demanded the same voice as before, and I turned to find Jack Nym beside me. He continued without waiting for an answer, 'That Sir George got a lovely gert house up in Clifton what he's abandoned. All empty it is now. Weeds growing everywhere. Wood beginning to rot. Why he don't make it over to his son and daughter-in-law and their boy is more'n anyone can tell. But he's one o'them controlling sort. He holds the purse strings and doles out the money.'

I grinned. 'You've been talking to Burl Hodge.'

Jack frowned. 'No, I ain't. What d'you mean?'

'Burl doesn't like Sir George, either.'

'Does anyone?' was the explosive answer. 'Do you?'

'Not much,' I admitted. 'Although I believe he's a brave man. Fought in the French wars with great credit.'

'Huh!' Jack dismissed this with a wave of his hand. 'I'll tell you one who hates his very guts, and that's his sister.'

'Why?' asked Adela as we struggled across the bridge, hemmed in on all sides.

Jack shook his head. 'Too long a story an' I've got a load of sea coal to deliver before today's out. You ask Mistress Walker or one of her cronies. They'll know.' He began ruthlessly elbowing his way through the people ahead of us. 'God grant you a merry Christmas,' he called back over his shoulder.

The next moment he was lost to view.

FOUR

We did not see Margaret Walker until the following day, when she came to take her Christmas dinner with us.

We were all tired after the excitement of the mummers' arrival, and Adela decreed we must go to bed as soon as supper was finished, especially the children, if we were to be up at midnight for the first of the day's three Masses. This, the Angel's Mass, we always celebrated at St Giles's Church, in Bell Lane, as it was the shortest distance from our house and entailed the minimum of walking at an hour when none of us was at our best. Strangely, the children always seemed fresher than either Adela or myself, and enjoyed the novelty of being abroad at an hour when they were normally tucked up securely in their beds. This year, the newest addition to our family, eleven-month-old Luke, he of the curly hair and ready smile, protested a little at being roused from his first deep sleep, but, as I have already indicated, he was of too sunny a disposition to be disturbed by anything for long, and the sight of all the other people and the flickering candlelight in the church soon restored him to his normal good humour.

St Giles, as I have explained elsewhere in these chronicles, is built on the foundations of the Jewish Synagogue which stood upon the site for a hundred years and more until the first Edward expelled the Jews two centuries ago, and for me, that knowledge has always added something extra to the sanctity of the place – although that was not a sentiment I dared communicate even to Adela, Or, perhaps, especially not to Adela. We managed to push our way to the front of the crowd thronging the nave, so that even Adam could see everything without being picked up, while my wife and I shared the burden of our foster son between us. The figures of the saint – the mentor, so it is claimed, of Charlemagne – and the deer he rescued from King Flavius's huntsmen had both been newly painted and glowed in the light from the altar candles and wall cressets. Luke was enchanted, clapping his little hands and dribbling with enthusiasm as he tried to express his joy. Walking the short distance back to our house, he bounced up and down in my arms with sheer exuberance.

Adela groaned. 'He's never going to settle, and we must be up again at dawn for the Shepherds' Mass.' She added, 'I thought we'd walk up to All Saints.'

The three older children jibbed a bit at that but, like myself, they knew better than to take issue with the decision. There were times, and this was one of them, when once Adela had made up her mind on some matter, it was useless to argue with her. She could be as stubborn as a mule and invariably carried her point. Consequently, after a few hours sleep, we were all to be found trudging wearily up Small Street and crossing Corn Street to All Saints' Church.

Yet again, the building was full and we were not so lucky this time in our attempts to reach the front of the nave. This, after all, was not our church and the regular worshippers quite rightly resented our efforts to take precedence over them. As a result, we were some way back, not far from the door, so that my attention was distracted by the arrival of every latecomer (and also of every early departure, if it came to that). To my astonishment, among the former was Lady Marvell, who hurried in about ten minutes after the Mass had started, alone except for a young girl who I guessed to be her maid.

The Marvell family naturally attended the great church of St Mary in Redcliffe – or St Mary Redcliffe as it was commonly referred to, as though the saint had a second name – and I was amazed to see Patience appear on this side of the river, at All Saints. That she was by herself was obvious when, after ten minutes or so had gone by, no other member of the family had joined her. Watching her closely, I thought she seemed anxious not to draw attention to herself, lingering at the back of the congregation and keeping her eyes cast down in an attempt to avoid people's gaze. She was wearing the same fur-trimmed brown velvet cloak as the day before, and kept the hood drawn close about her face. Her whole demeanour seemed to me to be slightly furtive, and I was not entirely surprised to see her slip unobtrusively out of the church before the Mass was finished. The maid had plainly been told to stay where she was and made no move to follow.

Fortunately, Adela had only recently relieved me of Luke, so I was able go in pursuit without my absence being noticed, for a while at least. I was just in time to catch a glimpse of Patience Marvell's cloak as she turned into Corn Street and caught her up with very little trouble, keeping a dozen or so paces behind her. She appeared to be heading for the Frome quayside, but then suddenly stopped short a few yards before reaching the entrance to Marsh Street. Here, she cast a quick, furtive glance around, withdrawing into the shadow of an adjacent doorway, huddling even further inside the protection of her cloak and looking extremely ill-at-ease. Almost immediately, a man joined her; a man who must have been loitering in the vicinity awaiting her arrival.

I sucked in my breath. Marsh Street! Otherwise known as 'Little Ireland'! And even though the light was still poor, the winter sun not yet having climbed above the rooftops, I recognized Patience Marvell's companion and knew whose face it was that I had seen two nights before in the Green Lattis. It belonged to someone with whom I had had dealings once or twice in the past. His name was Briant of Dungarvon and he was an Irish slave trader.

For a moment I felt thoroughly bewildered, then suddenly everything began to fall into place and make sense. There could only be one reason why Lady Marvell was making secret assignations with an Irish slave trader and that was because she wished to have someone illegally transported to Ireland and sold into slavery. My first thought was of Cyprian Marvell, but I quickly rejected him. He was too old to be of any use as a servant and, I guessed, too astute and too resourceful to allow himself to be caught. But his son, James, the next heir to the Marvell fortune after his father, was, from what I had seen of him the previous morning, the sort of arrogant, self-confident young bravo who might easily be flattered into doing something stupid and lured into a trap. And with James removed, Bartholomew, Patience's son, would be assured of his inheritance when Cyprian died, for I doubted if Joanna Marvell, from my glimpse of her, was young enough to bear more children.

I stood irresolute, not quite believing what I was seeing and unsure what to do. If I brought myself to the conspirators' attention – and if they had turned their heads and glanced up the street they could have seen me plainly – then that must surely nip in the bud any transaction they were about to make. On the other hand, Briant of Dungarvon knew me, and although in the past our relationship had been one of mutual, if guarded, respect, he was unlikely to thank me for spoiling a lucrative deal. An attempt at retribution would undoubtedly follow. I decided, therefore, that my best course of action was to make myself scarce before I was spotted and tell my tale as soon as possible to Richard Manifold. And if he were unwilling to accept my interpretation of what I had witnessed, I should have to go to Cyprian Marvell himself. I suspected I should have no difficulty in convincing him.

I was just about to withdraw in the direction of All Saints' Church, desperately hoping to remain unobserved, when the little drama unfolding before me took a totally unexpected turn. Patience Marvell had just handed her companion a purse which she had withdrawn from beneath her cloak – a very weighty purse by the look of it – and was saying something more to him, probably in the way of information which he might find useful. But then, suddenly, he was violently shaking his head and trying to thrust the purse back into her hands. Patience, plainly as astonished as I was, refused to accept it, and from where I was standing, rooted to the spot, I could hear her voice raised on a high, shrill note of enquiry. Her protestations did no good, however, and the Irishman, having flung the purse at her feet, vanished around the corner into Marsh Street without a backward glance.

I waited no longer, and made my way back to the church as quickly as I could, but not quickly enough for my absence to have gone unnoticed by Adela. In answer to her whispered demand to know where I had been, I pleaded an urgent call of nature.

'Rather a long one,' she accused me suspiciously, at the same time thrusting Luke into my arms.

I offered no defence. I was too preoccupied trying to interpret what I had just seen. It was apparent – at least it seemed apparent to me – that Briant of Dungarvon had agreed to some transaction with Patience Marvell, the preliminaries of which had probably been argued out two nights ago in the Green Lattis, only to renege inexplicably on the deal at the last moment. But why, I could not begin to guess and, judging by the lady's expression when she re-entered the church a few minutes later, neither could she. She was looking angry, confused and more than a little frightened and, touching her maid on the arm, left the church again almost at once, as the Shepherds' Mass was drawing to its close.

I was still pondering the riddle when we arrived home just as the early morning sun burst forth in all its Christmas splendour over Small Street. There was now no hint of snow, the air being crisp and cold and the roofs of the houses sparkling with frost. By this time, Luke was asleep in Adela's arms and Adam in mine, while the two older children could barely put one foot in front of the other. Indeed, all four were far too tired to eat any breakfast and my wife immediately took them all off to bed so that they could get some much-needed rest before the third and final Mass of the day – the Mass of the Divine Word – for which we had arranged to walk over to Redcliffe and join Margaret Walker at her parish church of St Thomas.

But when, two hours later, we met my former mother-in-law (and Adela's cousin) outside her cottage door, it was my suggestion that, instead of St Thomas's, we go only a little further on, to the church of St Mary Redcliffe.

'Why?' Margaret demanded bluntly. 'The children look exhausted, and anyway I've arranged to see Bess Simnel and Maria Watkins at Saint Thomas.'

I raised my eyebrows. 'You mean you haven't already seen them twice this morning? I know you, Mother-in-law. You're not one to shirk your Christmas worship.' She looked pleased and flattered, so I pressed home my advantage. 'I was hoping to catch a glimpse of the Marvell family to make sure that they were all present, because Lady Marvell and her maid favoured us at All Saints for the Shepherds' Mass earlier this morning.'

This was as much news to Adela as it was to her cousin as, in her usual devout way, she had been concentrating too hard on the service to notice what had been going on around her. I mentioned no more of what had happened and what I had witnessed in Corn Street, but I had said enough to intrigue both women and to win their approval of my suggestion. So, in spite of some grumbling from the three older children, we arrived at St Mary's in good time for the impressive entrance of the entire Marvell family.

Sir George, resplendent in a fur-lined russet velvet cloak over a knee-length tunic of yellow brocade and boots of the very finest Cordovan leather, embroidered gloves clasped in one hand, led the way to places reserved for them at the front of the congregation. The two women were also dressed in their best attire. As befitted their estate, jewels glowed on their fingers, flashed on their wrists and winked among the gauze of their headdresses. Furs and silks gleamed in the candlelight and, from where I was standing, I was able to get a good look at Joanna, Cyprian's wife. My first impression of a thin-faced woman of about forty, with dark eyes and eyebrows was confirmed, and I could see now the thin-lipped mouth set in a discontented, almost straight line.

Cyprian Marvell was plainly dressed with no ostentation of any kind, but the two younger men more than made up for this lack on his part. Both wore tight, particoloured hose, shoes with pikes so long that they had to be chained around the knees, and tunics so indecently short that the elaborately decorated codpieces were well displayed. I saw a number of elderly ladies hurriedly and modestly avert their eyes as James and Bartholomew passed them by, their velvet cloaks flung well back over their shoulders.

'Disgusting,' Margaret Walker hissed to Adela as she forcibly turned Elizabeth's head away from the interesting spectacle.

But there was still more to come. The Marvell family had scarcely taken their places when there was a fresh disturbance at the main door. It was again thrown open, this time to admit the astonishing figure of Sir George's older sister, the eighty-five-year-old Drusilla Marvell.

She wore the high, double-horned headdress fashionable many years earlier but no longer, or very rarely, seen. Her cloak, which was held up by a diminutive page boy, was made of rich purple velvet – probably prohibited by the sumptuary laws to all but royalty – and lavishly trimmed with sable. Her face was thin and deeply lined with a sharp beak of a nose and dark, glittering eyes that darted from side to side as her steward, wearing the same red and gold livery as the page boy, forced a passage for her through the interested crowd of worshippers. She leant heavily on an ebony stick.

But it was the quantity of jewels adorning her skinny person that commanded attention. Rubies, sapphires and emeralds sparkled in the candlelight and turned her into a veritable rainbow of colour. Every arthritic finger and both thumbs displayed a magnificent ring of heavily chased gold supporting a gemstone the size of a walnut. Diamonds hung in clusters from her earlobes and encircled her neck and wrists, while the front of her silk gauze gown – most unsuitable for both her age and the winter weather – shimmered with silver medallions. If she had had a herald walking before her crying, 'This is a woman of very great wealth and importance,' her message could not have been more plainly delivered.

Her steward having conducted her to the head of the congregation, she ostentatiously ignored her brother and his family, taking up a position immediately opposite where she could look right through them as though they didn't exist. Whispered details of this highly entertaining comedy were passed from front to back of the assembly and resulted in so much inattention that the priest was forced to reprimand us in no uncertain terms and to remind us that it was Our Lord's Nativity, one of the holiest days of the Christian calendar.

Sir George, it was reported later, had turned scarlet with mortification and rage, and even, after the service, attempted to remonstrate with his sister. This had been a mistake, giving the lady a chance to show yet more disdain by informing him, through her steward, that she had no wish to bandy words with him.

'Well, I did enjoy that,' I remarked as we walked home to Small Street, taking Margaret Walker with us for her Christmas dinner. 'I wouldn't have missed it for the world.'

'I wish I could believe you meant the service,' Adela reproached me, shifting Luke from one arm to the other.

But Margaret only laughed and agreed with me that it had been worth walking the extra distance to St Mary's for such a piece of unlooked-for entertainment.

'Of course, Drusilla Marvell will never forgive her brother,' she added with a chuckle. 'If she disliked him before – and I may say that they never got on – she hates him now.'

'Why?' I asked.

My former mother-in-law laughed. 'I'll tell you later,' she promised.

She was as good as her word, but the excellence of the meal, and doing it justice, delayed the story for some while.

We started with plum porridge followed by the capon, roasted on a spit over the fire earlier that morning, between the Shepherds' Mass and the Mass of the Divine Word, and kept hot in a box of warm hay. It was, admittedly, a very small bird, but Adela made it stretch amongst seven of us without making it too apparent that her portion was smaller than that of anyone else except Adam. Our son, who has always had an extremely sweet tooth, was far more interested in what was to follow, namely frumenty – he loved the spices and honey mixed with the wheat – and a plate of 'Yule dolls'. He picked out all the currant 'eyes', 'noses' and 'buttons' before eating the little gingerbread figures themselves. A minced pie apiece rounded off the meal, the sweet and savoury combination of fruit and meat making the perfect ending to a repast which otherwise might have left a cloying taste in the mouth.

By this time the three older children were almost asleep, suffering from the effects of an exhausting morning and more food than they were used to, so Adela drove them all upstairs to take another much-needed rest. Even Adam went without a backward glance. She then put Luke, stuffed with plum porridge, down in the large rocking cradle which I had made for our younger son, and she and Margaret carried it into the parlour while I made the three of us a large jug of 'lamb's wool'. This, together with the necessary beakers, I took into the parlour after them, and we settled around a fire of logs and branches gathered by myself some days before from the many trees to be found on the downs above the city.

'Now, Mother-in-law,' I said, pouring out the 'lamb's wool', 'tell us about this quarrel between Dame Drusilla and Sir George.'

'How do you know all these things, Cousin?' Adela asked admiringly. She was sitting on the window seat, rocking the cradle with one foot and, when not drinking, keeping her hands busy mending a rent in one of Elizabeth's gowns. (It has always intrigued me how women manage to do several different things at the same time.)

'My dear child,' Margaret laughed, 'I've lived in Redcliffe all my life, as you very well know. You lived there yourself until you married that first husband of yours and went off to Hereford with him – something I never approved of, but we'll say no more about that. You must know what a hotbed of gossip it is! You can't sneeze without someone calling round to find out if you're suffering from a rheum. And Drusilla Marvell has lived there longer than I have. In fact, she's lived in that old house on the waterfront all her life. She was born there, as was her brother. And after he went away to London and then to fight in the French wars, and her parents died, she just stayed on. She's a very rich woman, you know. Not only did she inherit money from her father, but an uncle – a brother of her mother's, I believe – who had no children of his own and was very fond of Drusilla when she was young, left her all his fortune. She's wealthier than Sir George. Who will get her money when she dies – and that can't be far off, she's eighty-five now – is a matter of great conjecture in Redcliffe. The rumour is that she favours Cyprian Marvell's son, James. Certainly, he seems to be the only member of the family she has any time for.'

I immediately found myself thinking of Lady Marvell's meeting with Briant of Dungarvon. Had she indeed been making arrangements to have her step-grandson abducted and sold into slavery, as I had conjectured, in the hope that with his disappearance her sister-in-law would be forced to leave her fortune elsewhere? But whatever had been her intention, it had gone awry.

I took a gulp of my 'lamb's wool', Adela's excellent pear and apple cider warming my throat and belly, and wiped away the froth from the roasted apple with the back of my hand.

I addressed Margaret again. 'You said that Dame Drusilla and her brother never got on.'

She nodded. 'That's true. He's a great deal younger than she is. She was twelve or thereabouts when George was born and had been the only child until then. But naturally the arrival of the much longed-for son very quickly relegated Drusilla to second place in her parents' affections. Her resentment of him descended rapidly into dislike and, later, into something more akin to hatred.'

'Natural enough,' I said, a remark that earned Adela's instant disapproval. She believed that you should never give in to the baser instincts of your nature.

Margaret, however, merely nodded. 'Understandable, I agree. But then, of course, relations improved somewhat between them. When he was grown, George went away and was away for some years. When he eventually came back to Bristol, he was married to his first wife, Lydia Carey, and Cyprian had been born. They didn't return to the family home on Redcliffe Wharf but settled outside the city in that big house in Clifton Manor, close to the great gorge.

'Now if my memory serves me aright, old Brewer Marvell died the following year and his wife a few months later, leaving Drusilla the sole occupant of what, for some obscure reason, has always been known as Standard House. When I say "sole occupant",' she added, 'I'm not including the army of servants who attend upon Drusilla. She likes to be pampered and to tyrannize over people.'

'Why did she never marry?' I asked. 'I can't imagine it was for lack of suitors. Not with a fortune the size of hers.'

'You're a cynic,' Adela told me, pausing in her stitching. 'Or you pretend to be.'

I laughed but said nothing, merely looking at Margaret, waiting for her reply.

She drank some more of her 'lamb's wool', emptying the beaker and holding it out for me to refill. 'You're right, Roger. There were suitors in plenty when she was young, and I understand from Maria Watkins that she was betrothed at least twice. But, mysteriously, these affairs never came to fruition and Drusilla remained a spinster. She seemed content enough.'

'And her relationship with Sir George?'

'It was always distant, and she took very little interest either when he was widowed or when he married again. My guess is that she never really forgave him for being born. But there was no open animosity until three years ago when a handsome young cockerel of about your own age came on the scene and laid siege to her.'

'My age?' I demanded incredulously. I was thirty-one.

'Your age,' Margaret confirmed. 'Drusilla was by then, even by her own calculations, at least eighty-two and should have known better, but madness set in. Whether or not her brain had softened because of her great age is a matter for speculation, but suddenly she announced she was getting married.'

Adela frowned. 'I heard nothing of this.'

Margaret chuckled. 'Hardly surprising, my love. It was all over before the gossip had time to spread to this side of the river. Once Sir George got wind of what was happening, he descended in Jehovian wrath from Clifton and the young man was gone in a cloud of dust. No one knows if he was bought off or simply succumbed to good, old-fashioned threats, but either way he disappeared and has never been seen again. What he had managed to wheedle out of the old lady before he was so summarily dismissed is anybody's guess, but those few who had contact with him described him as a knowing one, so no doubt he didn't depart empty-handed.'

'And Dame Drusilla blames her brother for this destruction of her plans?'

'Blames him!' Margaret almost choked over her beaker. 'Blames him? Word is that she threatened to kill him with her own two hands when she discovered what he had done. She hasn't spoken to him since, but if necessary addresses him through a third party. And when she found out, after her neighbour, an elderly, childless bachelor, died, that Sir George had bought the house and was moving in next door to her, it was reported that she actually foamed at the mouth and fell down in a fit. It's probably an exaggeration – but not much of one.'

'Why did he do it?' Adela asked, laying aside the mended gown and removing her foot from the cradle's rocker as Luke was now fast asleep. 'He must have known that his sister wouldn't thank him for it.'

Margaret shrugged. 'Of course he knew. But she is eighty-five now and bound to be getting senile. His conscience may have pricked him. Perhaps he felt she needed caring for. And after the affair of three years ago, maybe he thought he should keep a closer eye on her in case madness seized her again. After all, Sir George has young Bartholomew to provide for as well as Cyprian.

He won't want Drusilla's fortune falling into anyone's hands but his own.' She leant back in her chair – the one usually occupied by Adela, opposite my own – and regarded me shrewdly through half-closed eyes. 'You've suddenly gone broody, Roger. Something's bothering you. What is it? What do you know?'

'Know? Why, nothing,' I denied hastily.

But she wasn't fooled. 'There's something going on in that head of yours,' she accused me. After a few moments' silence, she added with a sigh, 'But you're not going to tell me, are you?'

'I was just mulling over what you've been telling us,' I protested feebly. 'An interesting story.'

She glanced at Adela, looking for support, but my wife was almost asleep, her head fallen forward on her breast, worn out by the exigencies of the morning and lulled by the warmth and the intoxicating effects of the 'lamb's wool'.

I leant back in my own chair and smiled sleepily at Margaret. 'I know nothing,' I lied, closing my eyes.

She didn't believe me.

She knew me too well.

FIVE

After supper – another rich meal, but one which the children
especially had been almost too tired to enjoy – I escorted
Margaret home to Redcliffe.
Although it was growing dark and the curfew bell had sounded,
there were plenty of revellers still abroad in the streets, quite a
few wearing the animal and bird masks brought out of cupboards
and attics at this season of the year, and not necessarily for festive
purposes. Some of the more stupid or malicious youths thought
it great fun to lurk in the shadows of overhanging houses and
street corners in order to jump out on unsuspecting passers-by,
giving them the fright of their lives. The previous Christmas, at
least two little old ladies, returning home unattended from supping
with their families, had been reduced to hysterics by such antics.
This year, on the orders of the sheriff, the numbers of the Watch
had been increased, but I was taking no chances. My former
mother-in-law was a strong-minded woman and not easily frightened, but she accepted my company without demur and even
seemed glad of it.

We encountered no trouble, in spite of seeing a number of
masked figures, but then at thirty-one I was an even more impressive figure than I had been at eighteen. Then, it was true, I had
had youth on my side, but if I was somewhat slower on my feet
than I used to be, I now had weight as well as height – as my
womenfolk were never tired of pointing out to me, my girth had
increased – and I still swung a pretty cudgel. This was an impressive weapon, half as tall as I was and weighted with lead at one
end.

I saw Margaret safely into her cottage by St Thomas's Church,
kissed her a dutiful goodnight and issued strict instructions that
she must open the door to no one during the hours of darkness.
Then I waited outside until I heard her shoot the top and bottom
bolts into their wards. Satisfied that I had done my duty, I turned
to retrace my steps before deciding on a sudden impulse to walk

down St Thomas's Street to Redcliffe Street and so, by way of one of the little alleys, out on to Redcliffe Wharf.

It was a cold night, frosty, and the stars rode clear and high in a cloudless sky. There was a three-quarter moon and the shadows from the houses were deep and black, lying like ink stains across the cobbles. I grasped my cudgel a little more tightly, aware of a sudden silence as the walls of the buildings of the alley cut off all sound . . .

But not quite all. A frenzied cry of 'Help! Murder!' sent me running on to the wharf as fast as my legs would carry me. I paused to look around.

Then I saw it, a dark shape huddled at the foot of one of the cranes. I reached it just as the door of a neighbouring house opened cautiously and lantern light spilled out across the cobbles. A voice quavered, 'What is it? What's happening? Is someone hurt?'

I knelt down and turned the dark shape over. 'It's a man,' I said. 'I think he's been stabbed.' I felt for his pulse. 'He's still alive, but only just. Quick! Come and help me. We must get him under cover, out of the cold. Is this your house?' And I indicated the tall, three-storey building behind the man who was now proceeding with even more caution towards me.

'No,' was the reply. 'It belongs to Sir George Marvell. I'm his steward.'

'Then go quickly and tell Sir George what's happened.' The light from the lantern fell across the victim's face as the steward stooped to take a closer look. 'God's toenails!' I exclaimed, startled. 'Hurry, man! Go! This is a friend of your master's, Alderman Trefusis.'

By the time I had staggered into the house with my burden, laying him down in front of the fire in the great hall and then gone back for my cudgel – which I had, out of necessity, been forced to drop – not only the knight himself but also his wife and daughter-in-law, both sons and grandson had also come running from other parts of the house and were gathered about the dying man. For there was no doubt in my mind that he would not last many minutes. Indeed, the only surprise was that he had survived the attack at all, for a bloody gash marked his throat almost from ear to ear.

'Robert!' Sir George was kneeling with his friend's head in his lap. 'Who did this to you? Did you recognize whoever it was?' He turned furiously on his wife, who was having a fit of hysterics. 'Hold your noise, woman,' he bawled, 'or I'll thrash you to within an inch of your life. Bart, see to your mother! Knock her unconscious if need be.' He bent once more over his friend. 'Robert!' His tone was urgent. 'Do you know who did this?'

His voice seemed momentarily to penetrate the other's failing senses. The dying man struggled violently against the encroaching darkness.

'Dee . . .' he began. But that was as far as he got. The death rattle sounded in his throat, his eyes rolled up under his lids and the grizzled head fell back against the other's chest. The alderman and occasional deputy sheriff was dead.

Sir George looked up at me. 'Did you see anyone?' His voice was harsh.

I shook my head. 'No one. The wharf was deserted but for myself.'

The knight's lips pinched together in a thin, straight line. His expression became even grimmer. 'Well, there's no help for it. I suppose we'll have to send for that idiot, Richard Manifold.'

But it was not Richard who arrived some short time later; his fellow sergeant, Thomas Merryweather, came instead, attended by his two corporals. Merryweather I knew only by sight, having had almost nothing to do with him in the past, but he had always struck me as a plodder, thorough but slow. I had heard people refer to him as dim-witted, but I doubted this, or he would not have remained in his post. Nevertheless, he was not quick on the uptake.

'Footpads, no doubt of it,' he said ponderously, looking down at the dead man. 'Christmas,' he added, as though that explained everything.

Sir George made a choking sound deep in his throat. 'Footpads!' he snarled. 'You cross-eyed, ale-swilling numbskull! Can't you see he's still wearing all his rings and a sapphire pin in his hat? And that his purse is still attached to his belt? What manner of footpads would leave such pickings, you dolt?'

Sergeant Merryweather appeared unperturbed by this mode of
address. Indeed, if anything, he seemed used to it.

'This gentleman' – he indicated me – 'disturbed the robbers
before they had time to finish their work. They were baulked,
that's what they were. Baulked.'

'Nonsense!' Had there not been ladies present, I felt certain
the knight would have used a much stronger word. He turned on
me. 'How long was it, Chapman' – I was going to get no title
from him – 'before you reached the alderman after hearing his
cry?'

'Not long,' I answered. 'I was halfway along Bear Alley when
I heard him shout. As you know, Bear Alley is one of the shorter
turnings between Redcliffe Street and the wharf. Moreover, I ran.
I would estimate thirty seconds or so, no more. But the quayside
was deserted. There was no sign of any attacker.'

The sergeant nodded his sandy head. 'That's what I said. They
were baulked.'

The knight let out a roar that sent Lady Marvell off into another
bout of hysterics. Bartholomew patted her ineffectually on the
shoulder.

Sir George ignored his wife and vented his spleen on Tom
Merryweather. 'You dunderhead! Footpads wouldn't have run off
like that, before they had cause to. They would still have been
kneeling over the body, trying to rob it. But they weren't. In the
very short time it had taken the chapman here to run from Bear
Alley on to the wharf, whoever did this heinous deed had disappeared. Now that would suggest to anybody but a fool like you
that the murder was his – or their – main object, not robbery.
This must be reported immediately to the sheriff. Christmas Day
or no Christmas Day, I demand that he be brought here at once!'

I thought his argument a sound one. I had almost reached the
same conclusion myself. Lady Marvell's sobs had abated again,
so I ventured to raise my voice.

'There is also the fact, Sergeant, that when Sir George asked
Alderman Trefusis if he had recognized his assailant, or assail-
ants, he uttered what sounded like the name Dee.'

Sergeant Merryweather frowned heavily. 'This is the first time
such a circumstance has been mentioned. How am I to do my
job if vital information is being withheld from me? Dee, you

say? And known to the alderman? That puts an entirely different complexion on the matter. Not,' he added slowly, 'that I know of that name in the city, and I pride myself on being acquainted with most families within these walls.'

To my astonishment, Sir George, instead of corroborating my story, hastened to refute it.

'The alderman mentioned no name,' he snapped, glaring at me. 'It was simply a noise he made as he lay dying. I doubt if he was even aware of my question. He was too far gone. A moment later, he was dead.'

I was about to appeal for support to the others who had been present, when I realized that the knight knew perfectly well what his friend had said, but that for some reason or another he did not want it repeated. Moreover, he was frightened. There was something in the rigidity of his stance, the way in which his hands were clenched by his sides, the fixed look on his face that spoke to me of fear. Why the name Dee should provoke this reaction, I had no idea, but I was positive it was so.

'Maybe I was mistaken,' I muttered.

The sergeant was pardonably incensed. 'Well, which is it?' he demanded irritably. 'Did the deceased mention a name or no?'

'No,' Sir George said, and with an emphasis that brooked no argument. 'He died without saying anything. But that doesn't alter the fact that he was deliberately murdered in cold blood. I want no more talk of footpads. I want the sheriff fetched before another hour has passed. That's an order. See that it's obeyed.'

Suddenly it was easy to see that he had once been a soldier, in charge of other men. He had an indisputable air of authority and command. But if I was impressed, Sergeant Merryweather stolidly refused to be so.

He removed his hat and scratched his head vigorously before replacing it again. 'What was the alderman doing, I wonder, out alone on the wharf, in the dark with no attendant?'

I thought for a moment that Sir George would explode with frustration. Instead, he spoke very slowly and carefully, as if dealing with a more than usually stupid child.

'He had been taking his Christmas victuals with us, Sergeant. We have known one another for years. As for being out alone in the dark, apart from the fact that it is not late – the church bells have not yet rung for Vespers – he soldiered with me in France. Robert Trefusis was not afraid of danger or of darkness.'

The sergeant drew down the corners of his mouth. 'Well, it seems he had cause to be this time. Whoever set upon him for whatever reason was intent on taking his life. I still think it was footpads, but I daresay you're right, Sir George. He's a man of some standing in the community. We'd best send for the sheriff. Not that he'll be pleased at being disturbed on Christmas Day, but there you are. It can't be helped. Did the alderman have any family that you know of? Can't say I've ever heard tell of anyone. But you seem to know him better than I do.'

'He had a wife once,' the knight said shortly. Then added, 'She left him many years ago.'

It was an hour or more before the sheriff arrived and I was able to make my deposition and go. I arrived back in Small Street to be met by a wrathful Adela.

'The children were too tired to stay up any longer,' she said accusingly, 'and you promised to play Snapdragon with them before they went to bed. Where have you been? You can't have been talking to Margaret all this time. If you've been drinking, Roger . . .'

But when I had made my explanation, her anger gave place to curiosity, intrigue and a certain amount of exasperation. When she had finished exclaiming over the murder and speculating aloud as to who could have done such a thing, and why, and trying to recall anyone she knew by the name of Dee, she demanded, 'What were you doing on Redcliffe Wharf, anyway? It's not on your way home from Margaret's.'

'Not directly, no. I just thought I'd walk that way round to the bridge and get a breath of river air.'

'And ran straight into a murder.' She sighed. 'What is it about you, Roger? You just seem to attract trouble and mayhem as a magnet attracts pins.' An alarming thought occurred to her. 'They don't suspect you, do they?'

I was able to reassure her on that score, then suggested we retired to bed ourselves.

'It's Saint Stephen's Day tomorrow,' I pointed out. 'We must be up early to light the Yule log, and then it's the mummers' first performance in the afternoon. The children will be excited about that. So let's get some rest while we can.'

'Oh, well, if it's rest you're talking about . . .' Adela answered and let the sentence go.

'Not altogether,' I admitted as we started up the stairs.

I have to admit that of all the twelve days of Christmas, I like St Stephen's Day the least. Even as a boy – and I was as callous as most children are – I never liked the custom of going out and stoning wrens to death, then tying the poor, broken little bodies to poles and parading them around the streets. People were supposed to give you money in return for one of their feathers, a talisman that apparently averted shipwreck; but as there were very few, if any, sailors in inland Wells, the custom seemed pointless. In Bristol, of course, where sailors abounded, it was a different matter; but even so, I had always forbidden our children from joining the early morning forays into the surrounding countryside to kill the birds.

Similarly, I always hated the bleeding of horses that took place on that day. I know it was said to be good for the poor beasts in order to ensure their health and vitality throughout the coming year, but some owners rode their mounts almost to death before bleeding them, so that they would be too weak to resist. Burl Hodge, I knew, had always scorned this sensitivity in me and had once taunted me about being too 'womanish' for my own good. Indeed, I deplored my own squeamishness, but could do nothing about it.

There were, however, some enjoyable customs on the Feast of Stephen. As I have said, the lighting of the Yule log, making sure it burned steadily until Twelfth Night, was one, and sword dancing in the streets as well as the start of the mummers' plays were others. All three older children were up and downstairs early to assist at the former ritual, and although none of them was allowed to put flame to the bed of straw and twigs, they nevertheless crowded close enough about the pair of us to make both Adela and myself apprehensive. But no one did anything foolish and eventually the Yule log itself caught alight, ready to be tended and cosseted for the next twelve days.

We heard Mass at St Stephen's Church so that the children

could gaze upon the statue of the martyred saint in all his glory, but I was very much afraid that their minds were more upon the coming afternoon's entertainment than the service. As for the adult members of the congregation, there was little doubt where their interest lay. If I heard the whispered words 'Alderman Trefusis' and 'Robert Trefusis' once, I heard them a hundred times. At that point no word seemed to have got about concerning my connection to the crime, but by the afternoon, when we entered the outer ward of the castle for the mummers' opening performance, everyone appeared to know.

Jack Nym, who had obviously been lying in wait for me at the end of the drawbridge, seized my arm the moment I was fairly under the portcullis.

'What's this story I hear about you finding Robert Trefusis's body last night?' he demanded. 'Is it true?'

'Yes,' I answered wearily. 'But it was purely accidental, I do assure you. I know no more about his death than you do.'

'This man Dee they're all talking about,' he whispered confidentially, while gripping my arm in a painful squeeze. 'There's no one of that name in Redcliffe or anywhere else in the city that I know of. Mind you,' he added on a dissatisfied note, 'at this season of the year there are always a lot of strangers around visiting friends and kinfolk.'

We were joined by Burl Hodge, his cherubic countenance alight with a mixture of eagerness and envy. 'Roger, I've just been told it was you who found the alderman's body last night. Why is it,' he demanded, echoing Adela's words, 'that this sort of thing always happens to you? You must be perpetually snooping.' I ignored the jibe, so, having failed to draw blood, he continued, 'This rumour that the dying man mentioned a name – Dee, was it? – is apparently false. I have it on good authority that Sir George utterly denies it.'

Jack looked disappointed but unsurprised. 'Pity,' he said gloomily. 'But as I was just saying to Roger, there ain't no one called that what I know of in the city.'

As the word had spread coupling my name with that of the dead man, a little crowd had gathered around me and my friends and I was now being pelted with questions from every butcher, baker and candlestick-maker demanding his curiosity be satisfied.

After all, it was not every day that a city alderman was done to death in circumstances of such gruesome barbarity. And my involvement was enough to convince some people that another treasonable plot against our new king had been uncovered. I was quick to disabuse their minds of this notion, but whether or not I managed to convince them was another matter.

Fortunately, at this moment there was a fanfare of trumpets – well, one trumpet blown slightly off-key – the gates to the inner ward of the castle were thrown open and the mummers' carts appeared. And a brave show they made, decked with coloured ribbons, holly and other evergreens, the banner of St George fluttering in the cold, wintry breeze.

There was a ragged cheer.

The first cart, the one which served as a stage, came to a halt in the middle of the crowd and there was a pause while the elderly couple, assisted by the man who I had guessed to be the brother of the pregnant woman, unfurled a canvas backdrop of badly painted meadows, trees and a distant castle. This they fixed between two poles at the back of the 'stage', and then the youngest man, dressed as the saint, came forward to introduce the cast of characters.

'Friends! Good people of Bristol!' Loud and prolonged cheering. 'My name is Tobias Warrener and I take the part of Saint George. My wife, Dorcas' – the young girl was helped up on to the cart – 'is the Fair Maiden I must rescue from the terrible, fierce Dragon, played by my wife's brother, Master Arthur Monkton.' The man who had helped with the scenery came forward and bowed to a chorus of good-natured booing. 'My grandmother, Mistress Tabitha Warrener, will take the part of the Turkish Knight' – he indicated the elderly woman who wore a turban and flowing eastern robes – 'while the Doctor' – screams of delighted laughter from the crowd – 'is brought to life by our very good friend, Ned Chorley.'

The man with the missing fingers and scarred eye made his bow with a flourish, then stepped back into the semicircle formed by his fellow players and the performance finally started. I wondered if I was the only person who had noted how the old man's eyes had raked the crowd as though searching for someone in particular. Or had that just been my fancy?

The play proceeded. St George killed the Dragon, who died writhing in agony to ecstatic cheering, but was then challenged by the Turkish Knight, who killed him in his turn and ran off with the Fair Maiden. This, of course, was the cue for the entrance of the Doctor, whose appearance was greeted with gales of laughter in anticipation of his comic monologue and antics. Adam found the character so funny that, at one point, he was in danger of choking, but after a hearty backslapping from every member of his family – so hearty on the part of Nicholas and Elizabeth that he became belligerent and threatened to retaliate in kind – he recovered sufficiently to enjoy the rest of the performance. The Doctor produced his miracle cure, St George sprang back to life and rescued the Fair Maiden, slaying the wicked Turkish Knight in the process, and then everyone, 'dead' and living alike, went into the final dance. This, despite its lack of musical accompaniment, was so successful, and so rapturously received, that a second and third reel was called for, while the undoubted comic talents of the maimed old man playing the Doctor were applauded to the echo. The crowd was loth to let them go even then, and it was not until the two younger men had performed a sword dance and a jig that people began looking anxiously at the sky, muttering reluctantly that it was time to be moving.

The performance, with all its encores, had taken longer than anyone had bargained for and, while we had been watching, the sky had darkened towards evening and there was a sudden hint of sleet in the air. It had been Margaret Walker's intention to return with us to Small Street for supper, but in view of the advanced hour, the deteriorating weather and the events of the previous evening – events which had taken place almost on her own doorstep – she announced her intention to return home at once. We couldn't blame her and so, when I had seen Adela and the children safely indoors, she and I set off, as we had done the night before, for Redcliffe.

Yet again I saw her into her cottage, repeated my instructions of yesterday and left to the sound of bolts being driven into their sockets. There was to be no detour tonight: I was determined to go straight back to Small Street and the comfort and safety of my own four walls. I took a firm grip on my cudgel and made for the bridge which gave the city its name. Bricgstowe, our Saxon forebears had called it, the Bridge Place, and so it had more or less remained. Some people still call it Bristowe today.

As I stepped between the houses, towering five stories high on either side of me, I was aware of a man leaving the chapel of the Virgin, which bisected the bridge, mounting his horse, which had been tethered outside, and riding towards me. It was the by now familiar figure of Sir George Marvell who had, presumably, been offering up prayers for the soul of his dead friend. I felt a sudden and unexpected stab of sympathy for him and, drawing to one side, was about to accord him the courtesy of a respectful bow when someone rushed past me, pushing me out of his way with such force that I lost my balance and fell heavily on my left side. By the time that, swearing and cursing, I had picked myself up, my assailant had reached his real target and was dragging George Marvell from his horse with obvious murderous intent. The knight had plainly been taken completely by surprise and, apart from the whinnying of his frightened animal, there was no sound except a great grunt as he fell awkwardly on to the cobbles.

I saw the flash of a knife blade as an arm was raised. Yelling at the top of my voice, I ran forward, swinging the weighted end of my cudgel in a lethal arc, and the would-be assassin turned a startled face in my direction just as a wall cresset flared into brightness above his head. It was apparent that he had been unaware of my presence, or of having barged into me until he heard me shout, so intent had he been on his fell purpose. As our eyes met his face was clearly visible in the light from the cresset, then, with a snarl of desperation, he turned to finish what he had started before I could reach and prevent him.

Unfortunately for him, the brief pause had enabled Sir George to recover his wits and strength and, with an enormous effort, he heaved himself free of his attacker just as I hit the man's right hand with the knob of my cudgel. The latter gave a screech of pain and dropped his knife, but his sense of self-preservation was sufficiently strong to get him up and running before I could make any attempt to lay him by the heels. He had flashed past me and reached the end of the bridge, turning right along the Backs, before I had time to realize what was happening.

'Where is the bastard? Did you get him?' Sir George panted, struggling to his feet.

I held out a hand to assist him, but this was impatiently spurned. 'I'm afraid not . . .' I was beginning, but a roar of frustration was let loose about my ears.

'You stupid dolt! You dunderhead! Don't tell me you've let him escape!'

In spite of my anger, I had to admire the man. He was old, well past his three score years and ten, and he must be badly shaken. But there he was, as aggressive as ever, taking me to task for sins of omission instead of gratefully thanking me for saving his life.

I said coldly, 'There is no need for me to run after him, Sir George. I not only know who your assailant is, but I also know where he can be found when he's in Bristol.'

The knight glowered at me. 'You do, do you? So who is the murdering rogue? Out with it! We don't want to be standing here all night. Master sheriff and his sergeants have work to do. Who was it, eh?'

I waited for him to finish ranting, then answered quietly, 'I don't know what you've done to incur his enmity, Sir George, but the man who just tried to kill you is an Irish slave trader by the name of Briant of Dungarvon.'

SIX

There was a long silence; long enough at least for me to be conscious of rats scrabbling in the central drain, scavenging for food. Somewhere in the distance a dog barked, and nearer at hand an owl hooted.

After my revelation, I had expected Sir George to demand immediate action; to send me at once for the sheriff or command that I lead him without delay to Marsh Street and indicate the ale-houses where the Irish slave trader lodged. Instead, he said nothing for several seconds, but stood staring at me while he soothed his frightened horse, which was still trembling in every limb.

Finally, he spoke. 'A slave trader, eh? Probably mistook me for someone else. One of his "marks". Must have realized his mistake when the torchlight showed him how old I am.' He gave an uncertain laugh, not at all like his customary confident bellow. (Not that I had heard him laugh much, I had to admit.) 'Nothing to be done about it, then. The lord sheriff won't thank me for turning his men out to raid "Little Ireland", especially not after dark. Somebody's sure to get hurt. Those rogues will resist any form of authority. So it will be just as well for you to keep your mouth shut about this, Master Chapman.' His new-found politeness slipped a little as he added menacingly, 'I don't want to hear this story being bandied around the town. If I do, I shall deny it completely and imply that you are only wishful of drawing attention to yourself. There are no witnesses.'

He was right. Even my yells had provoked no response. No one had opened a door or a casement or called out to know what the matter was. Such incidents were all too frequent in the Bristol streets after dark, and last night's murder had made everyone doubly wary of getting involved. A killer was abroad; and if an alderman, with his short sword and dagger at his belt, was not safe, then why should a common man with nothing more than his meat knife and stick to protect him, fare any better? It was wiser to stay indoors and shut one's ears.

I answered coldly, 'If you wish me to say nothing about this affair, Sir George, then naturally I shall keep quiet. But I must point out to you that no slave trader worth his salt tries to kill his "mark", as you call it, only to kidnap him. Or her. I have heard it said that the slavers' code of honour' – the knight snorted derisively – 'forbids murder for money and that anyone of them breaking this unwritten law is summarily dealt with in the same fashion.'

The knight's explosion of fury was so sudden and so violent that I took a hurried step backwards and almost fell again. In the light of the overhead cresset I could see that his face had turned purple and was contorted with an almost animal-like rage. He was fairly slobbering with anger and the spittle ran out of his mouth and down his chin as he gibbered, 'Th-Those s-scum have no honour. They d-don't know the meaning of the word.' He took a deep breath to steady himself, but even so, he found it difficult to speak coherently. I caught the words 'mad', 'arrant rubbish' and 'dangerous theories' before he jerked his horse's reins and pushed past me, mounting at the Redcliffe end of the bridge and vanishing in the direction of Redcliffe Wharf.

I stared after his retreating form, leaning against the wall of one of the houses, waiting for the beating of my heart to steady and trying to make sense of what had happened. My overriding impression was that George Marvell had been badly frightened, not simply by the murderous attack on his person, but also by my remark concerning the slavers' code of honour and the retribution exacted for its flouting. The name Briant of Dungarvon had meant something to him – that was obvious. He was acquainted with the man, but their association was to remain a secret and so he had threatened to make me look a fool if I should make the incident public.

But something else occurred to me as I stood there in the darkness of the bridge; an explanation of the little drama which I had witnessed between Lady Marvell and the Irishman played out the previous morning. She had solicited his services for some purpose of her own and he had been perfectly willing to comply until . . . Until what? Until he learned her name, of course. Until he realized that she was the wife of a man he had marked down as his enemy and whom he intended to kill. Perhaps he had not previously known that Sir George moved from Clifton Manor and was now living in the heart of the city, so close to 'Little Ireland'.

I heaved myself away from the wall and continued my journey home, suddenly confident that my reading of the situation was the right one. All that remained now was to try to discover, if I could, what the connection between the knight and the slave trader might have been.

'I don't believe it!' my wife exclaimed in exasperation when I had offered my explanation of why I had again been delayed returning home. 'Why are you always present at the exact moment when these things happen? Why do they never occur when other people are nearby?'

I gave a sheepish grin. 'Luck?' I suggested.

Or God's will? It had always been my contention, although not one I shared very often with other people, that the Almighty nudged me into these affairs where my natural powers of deduction were used by Him to bring evil to justice. Perhaps it was arrogance on my part to believe so, but all too frequently I seemed to be involved through no volition of my own. As had happened last night and again this afternoon, I was on the spot when events unfolded more often than seemed warranted by simple coincidence.

Adela snorted. 'Ill fortune, more like,' she retorted. 'Now come and eat your supper. And remember! The children are expecting that game of Snapdragon with you that you failed to give them yesterday.'

The game of Snapdragon in our house, with three excitable children and a cautious mother, was played not as it was by the gentry, with pieces of exotic fruit floating around in a pool of flaming brandy, but with slices of apple and a handful of raisins swimming in ice-cold water and having to be bobbed for with the teeth. There were screams of merriment as Nicholas, Elizabeth and Adam bent over Adela's largest bowl and attempted to catch the fruit in their mouths. The trophies were not immediately eaten, but lined up in front of each child, to be counted when the bowl was empty to see who had managed to catch the most.

It was almost a foregone conclusion that the winner would be

Adam. It was an equally foregone conclusion, of course, that he would cheat, butting with his head and jogging with his elbows to ensure that he had an unfair advantage. But as he shared his 'snapdragons' with Luke, who had been frantic to join in, but been forcibly restrained by Adela, his older siblings and I let him get away with it for once. The three older children and I now being extremely wet and cold, we towelled one another dry, then played a vigorous game of Hoodman Blind to warm ourselves up. This was followed by Oranges and Lemons, although with only five of us able to participate (Luke was carried round with Adela and screamed with delight whenever they were captured) there was no prospect of the tug of war which should always succeed the game.

We were, in any case, starting to flag and even I was beginning to look forward to my bed.

'It's your age,' my wife said unkindly as she began herding the three older children upstairs, leaving me with Luke to entertain until such time as she could attend to him.

I quite properly ignored this remark and carried my foster son into the parlour, where I was able to rest my ancient bones in an armchair and rock him on my knee. Tomorrow, I reflected with relief, would be St John's Day, and he being the patron saint of booksellers and writers – and now, presumably, of those who practised this new-fangled art of printing – it was likely to prove a quiet, uneventful day. At least, so I hoped.

But the next day, pushing my way through the Saturday morning crowds milling around the Tolzey marketplace, I felt a tap on the shoulder. Turning with a smile, expecting to see someone I knew, I was confronted by the lugubrious, bearded features of Humility Dyson, landlord of the Wayfarers' Return in 'Little Ireland'. He was not himself Irish – a native of Bristol born and bred, so I had been given to understand – but he was trusted by all the slavers as one of them and treated as though he were in fact an Irishman. Indeed, I believe he thought of himself as one of them and would have no more considered betraying them to the authorities than he would of cutting his own throat.

'You're wanted,' he said tersely, jerking his head vaguely in the direction of Marsh Street.

'Who wants me?' I stalled, though I could guess.

'Him.'

'Who's him?'

'You know who.'

I sighed. This conversation could continue all day. 'If you mean Briant of Dungarvon, why don't you say so?' I snapped.

The landlord gave a start and glanced nervously around him. 'Lower your voice,' he growled. 'Yes, him.'

'And what does he want me for? To stick a knife in me like he tried to do to Sir George Marvell yesterday evening?'

He shoved me – and I am not an easy man to shove – behind one of the booths with surprising ease. His hirsute face was pushed within an inch of mine. 'He won't harm you. I'll vouch for that. And if you doubt my word,' he added belligerently, 'I'll twist your head round so that it's facing the other way.'

'Very well,' I said, considering it politic to submit. 'Where is he?'

'The Turk's Head.'

This I knew to be the other ale-house in Marsh Street, also nowadays owned and run by Humility Dyson. I nodded. 'But I'll walk two or three paces behind you. I don't wish to be seen in your company.'

He accepted this readily, knowing it to be a sensible measure and one which he would have suggested himself had I not done so.

'Except,' he amended, 'you'll walk two or three paces ahead of me so that you don't decide to disappear.'

As it happened, I was too anxious to hear what Briant had to say for himself to do anything of the kind.

The Turk's Head was twenty or so yards nearer the gate which opened on to the path bordering the great marsh itself than the Wayfarers' Return, and strange to me. On the two previous occasions when I had visited Marsh Street, the Irishman had been lodging at the last named ale-house, but this time he appeared to have altered his habits. It was difficult to see why as the interior of one was very similar to the interior of the other; if anything, slightly more cramped and fetid with the stink of unwashed bodies.

There was the usual sudden silence as I walked in, followed

by a resumption of conversation as it was seen that I was accompanied by the landlord. Briant had chosen his customary dark corner and motioned me to take a seat on the opposite side of the table to himself. I swung my long legs over the bench, cursing, as always, as I scraped my knees against the board, and requested Humility Dyson to bring me some ale.

'And he can pay,' I added shortly, indicating my companion.

The Irishman laughed. 'Getting bold, aren't you, Chapman?' he asked. Nevertheless, he nodded at the bar keep, who prowled away in the direction of some kegs lined up along the further wall. Briant leant towards me, lowering his voice.

'Our friend hasn't called out the forces of law and order against me, then?' There was no point in pretending not to know who he meant, so I shook my head. Briant grinned. 'I knew he wouldn't. He'd be too afraid of what I'd say.'

A pot boy came with my ale. I took a generous swallow. It was very good. I looked at my companion over the rim of the beaker. 'You intended to kill him,' I said, following his example and not mentioning Sir George by name.

'I did. And would have but for you interfering.'

His face was suddenly grim and my heart missed a beat. Had Briant got me here to take his revenge? I shifted uncomfortably on the bench. 'You'd be facing the noose if I hadn't. The sheriff wouldn't let you get away with killing a knight of the realm. His men would have braved Marsh Street for that. And if all I hear is true, your fellow countrymen wouldn't have lifted a finger to save you. They don't hold with murder.'

'For some things they do.' His voice and face were even grimmer than before. 'Moreover, they might have come after you for informing against me. You were the only witness.' He stared me down for a moment or two, then drew a deep breath and seemed to relax. 'However, you did prevent me and unless you change your mind and go to the authorities, we'll hear no more of the matter. But I'll wager the old bastard has instructed you not to.'

I drank some more ale. 'You'd win your wager. Sir George told me that if I did, he'd deny the whole incident and make me appear a fool.' There was a pause while the hubbub of the tap room went on around us. 'So why am I here?'

Briant shrugged and glared at another man who would have joined us at the table. The newcomer hurriedly slunk away.

'I like you,' the Irishman said unexpectedly, finishing his own drink and calling for another. 'I want you to know why I tried to kill that piece of shit. I want you to know what sort of man he really is.' I raised my eyebrows and, after his ale had been brought, he continued, 'The first time we ever spoke, I was with my friend, Padraic Kinsale. Do you remember?'

'Yes. But when I commented on his absence at our second meeting, you refused to say what had become of him.' My companion's lips tightened into a narrow, ugly line and he fell silent. 'So what happened?' I prompted.

After a moment or two, Briant said abruptly, 'He was taken and hanged.'

For some unaccountable reason, I was shocked. 'When was this? I don't remember anything of it.' But then, I probably wouldn't. I was absent from the city so long and so often, and no one would think the incident important enough to tell me of it on my return. A thought struck me. 'Was Sir George Marvell concerned in the affair?'

The Irishman drank his ale, emptying the pot in almost one go before slamming it down hard on the table. 'He was,' he said. 'But he didn't live in the town in those days. He had a house on the heights above Bristol.'

'In Clifton Manor,' I agreed. 'He still owns the place, but today it stands empty.' There was another pause. 'Go on.'

Briant chewed a thumbnail that was already bitten down almost to the quick. 'Know the family, do you?'

'I've only made their acquaintance very recently, but yes, I think I've managed to work out who each one is.'

Another couple of drinkers, anxious to secure a seat at our table, were glared away, just like the first man. I reflected that Briant seemed to be of some importance. No one argued with him or even uttered a word of protest.

'There's a son from the first marriage –'

I nodded. 'Cyprian Marvell. Stocky. Middle-aged.'

My companion bit his thumbnail some more. 'This happened five, maybe six years ago. He was younger then. He was married and his wife had a much younger sister. Constance Trenchard, she was called. Very pretty by all accounts, but for some reason still unmarried.' He shouted for more ale and then sat waiting, tapping his fingers on the table.

'And?' I said, growing impatient.

'Sir George coveted her. Old enough to be her father. Nearly old enough to be her grandfather, the old ram. Somehow or other, he persuaded her into becoming his paramour. Mind you,' Briant added fair-mindedly, 'I suppose he isn't bad-looking even now and this, as I say, was five, six years back. Some women like 'em old and I daresay it wasn't his face she was interested in.' He gave a sudden loud guffaw. 'Looks like a man who might have plenty tucked away in his codpiece.'

His ale arrived and he downed it without pausing for breath, then wiped his mouth on the back of his hand. I waited resignedly for him to resume.

After a while, he leant forward again, his chin propped between his fists. 'I don't know how long this love affair, or whatever you want to call it, was carried on between this pair, but in the end, as you could guess, the old man's wife began to get suspicious. His second wife, that is, and a great deal younger than he is.'

'I know,' I said. 'I've met her.' I didn't add, 'And so have you.' I was saving that revelation until later.

Briant grunted. 'He seems to like 'em young.' He scratched his cheek. 'Well, as I was saying, Sir George's wife was growing suspicious and he needed to get rid of Constance in a hurry. He had no intention of soiling his whiter than white reputation, so he told the girl it was all over between them. That's when the trouble started. She wouldn't accept that it was finished and threatened to make the affair known to her sister.'

'How do you know all this?'

'Padraic told me. George Marvell had offered him a very large sum of money not just to abduct the girl, but to kill her. I begged him to have nothing to do with it. I warned him over and over that it was too dangerous; that if the English law officers didn't get him, our own people would. I reminded him that you can't trust any Englishman farther than you can see him. That you're a treacherous race. That if anything went wrong, Sir George wouldn't hesitate to throw him to the wolves.'

'Your friend didn't agree with you?'

'Oh, he agreed with me all right. Any Irishman would. But Padraic's trouble was thinking he was cleverer than he really was. And the amount of money he was being offered would have tempted a saint. Furthermore, he said he thought he could screw some more out of the old man. He could retire. Buy that farm near Waterford he'd always wanted. Settle down and get married.'

'But it didn't turn out like that?'

'Of course it didn't turn out like that! I told him it wouldn't, but he refused to listen to me.'

'So? What happened?'

'That old devil wheedled all Padraic's plans out of him. Where, when and how he was going to meet this Constance and kill her. I don't know how he managed it because Padraic wasn't a stupid man. I think more money must have been promised. I don't know the details, but the result was that the law officers arrived just in time to find Padraic with the body, but not in time to save the girl.'

I sucked in my breath. 'But what a blackguard the man is,' I muttered, and Briant knew that I wasn't referring to his friend; although, when I thought about it, the description could just as easily have applied to both men. 'I don't suppose it was any good Master Kinsale telling the truth?'

'What would have been the point? No one would have believed him. Sir George would have utterly denied the accusation, and it would have been his word against that of an Irish slave trader. Who would have been listened to? Not Padraic.'

'He might have sowed the seeds of doubt in one or two minds. Lady Marvell's, for instance. If she'd begun to have doubts about her husband's fidelity, some of them might have taken root.'

'True. But Padraic probably didn't feel he could let himself come between man and wife. At least, that was my guess for I never spoke to, nor saw him again after he was arrested. The fraternity disowned him, and orders went out that we were to keep our heads down until people had forgotten the affair, which wasn't long. Folk have short memories. I went back to Ireland and stayed there for a month or two, and by the time I returned no one even remembered the incident. Padraic was just another felon whose body had been left to rot on some dunghill, but I didn't forget. I know Padraic did wrong, but he was tempted into it by that old devil, and I swore to get Sir George Marvell when I could.'

'You waited a long time,' I commented.

'It wasn't possible while he lived in Clifton. I'd have stuck out like a sore thumb on a woman's white hand if I'd been seen up there. Sir George would have been alerted within an hour and would most likely have guessed my intention. But then, a day or so ago, I learned he had moved down to the city. My chance had come.'

I nodded. 'And you learned that from none other than Lady Marvell herself.'

He had been looking down at the table, but now his eyes flew up to meet mine. 'Now how do you know that, Chapman?' he asked softly.

So I told him about recognizing him in the Green Lattis and seeing Patience Marvell go into the ale-house just as I was leaving. 'And on Christmas morning, I followed her out of All Saints' Church during the Shepherds' Mass and witnessed your second meeting with her. I saw money change hands and then you push it back at her, refusing to accept it. I didn't understand why at the time, but now I do. She'd mentioned her name and you'd realized who she was. You couldn't do business with someone whose husband you intended to kill.'

'One of these days,' Briant said, leaning across the table and bringing his face close to mine, 'that long nose of yours is going to be the death of you, Master Chapman.' He breathed heavily for several moments, his ale-laden breath hot on my cheeks, and I saw an angry glint in the dark brown eyes. My belly felt queasy and I could almost feel the cold steel of a knife gliding between my ribs. But then he withdrew and sat back again on his bench. 'You're right, of course. I hadn't known who she was until that moment. Humility Dyson had simply informed me that a respectable woman – a lady, he said – needed my services.' He laughed. 'That was nothing new. It's only the respectable and those with well-lined pockets that can afford our services. This woman wouldn't come to Marsh Street; was afraid to be seen anywhere near it. Again, that was normal, so I made arrangements to meet her elsewhere. That night in the Green Lattis people were too drunk to take notice of what their neighbours were doing. Except you, of course. We arranged to meet again on Christmas Day, at dawn, during the Shepherds' Mass, when she was to give me details of the man she wanted abducted, and also pay me. As you guessed, that was when I learned who she was. I told her I was no longer willing to go through with it, but I didn't tell her why. I just left her to think what she would.'

'And who did she want removed?' I asked.

Now Briant really was angry. His hand went to the knife in his belt and his eyes seemed to have turned red. 'Do you think I'm going to tell you that?' he snarled.

'No, I don't,' I replied calmly, although my heart had started to thump a little. 'But I'll make a guess. It was her step-grandson, James Marvell. With him out of the way, her own precious boy, Master Bartholomew, stands a better chance of inheriting not only his father's wealth – for I doubt if Cyprian Marvell can father another child – but old Drusilla Marvell's fortune as well.'

The Irishman regarded me thoughtfully, the anger slowly draining out of his face. 'I've heard rumours about you,' he said after a while. 'You've a reputation in this city. And of course, four years back when you persuaded me to take that Scottish nobleman, or duke, or whatever he was, over to Ireland, I knew you were dabbling in treason. I suppose that's why I like you. You're not afraid to step outside the law when it suits you.'

I was indignant and about to refute this accusation, when honesty compelled me to admit that it was true. I grinned in acknowledgement.

'But,' I warned him, 'if I wake up one morning to find that Sir George Marvell has been murdered, I shan't hesitate to tell everything I know.'

He shrugged. 'Well, if someone does eventually kill that swivel-eyed piece of dirt, it won't be me. I've finished with him. If God had meant me to be the instrument of his destruction, he wouldn't have let you thwart me.' He crossed himself. 'I've learned my lesson. I shall be going home to Ireland in a few days' time. The Clontarf's due to drop anchor along the Backs on Tuesday, if the weather holds and she can navigate the Avon safely. Even your fucking rivers lay snares for foreigners.' He held out his hand. 'I'm glad we've had this conversation, Chapman.' He smiled, showing a chipped and blackened tooth. 'I seem to recall that years ago, when we first met, either Padraic or myself gave you some good advice. Watch your back. One of these days you'll make an enemy too many.'

I gripped his proffered hand, for, in spite of what he was, I returned his liking. All the same, 'I meant what I said,' I reminded him. 'I'm law-abiding enough, whatever you may think, not to tolerate murder.'

'I believe you,' was his answer. 'But I also have enough faith in your sense of justice to know that you would want to bring the right man to book. And that man won't be me, I give you my word.'

I grinned. 'And I might even believe you,' I said.

SEVEN

I was just in the act of leaving when a thought struck me and I turned back. 'I don't suppose,' I said, 'you know anything about the death, on Christmas Day, of an alderman of this city by the name of Robert Trefusis?'

Briant's face immediately became suffused with blood and his right hand flew to the evil-looking dagger tucked in his belt. 'Are you accusing me—?' he began.

'No, no!' I exclaimed hastily. 'I just wondered if there had been any talk along the Backs concerning it.'

Mollified, he shook his head. 'Never heard of the man until yesterday when chat of a murder went round. I fancy someone did say that he'd been a deputy sheriff, but why he had been killed, nobody seemed to know. Nor was anyone very interested and there were certainly no rumours as to who might have wanted him dead. But if it matters to you, I can ask around, here and at the Wayfarer's. Someone could have heard a whisper.'

'Nothing was said of a man named Dee? Or of a woman, I suppose, if it comes to that. Although throat-cutting isn't usually a woman's crime.'

Briant snorted. 'I've known women who would cut a throat without a moment's hesitation. I grant you such creatures are rare, but they're to be found, nevertheless. I remember one. Dressed like a man, walked like a man, talked like a man. Swore like one, too. She was a member of the Fraternity. Best slaver on either side of the Irish Sea. So it's not impossible. Unlikely though, I agree. However, as I said, I can make enquiries for you if it's important.'

I hesitated a moment, then shook my head. 'I won't put you to so much trouble. The death is nothing to me. I wasn't acquainted with the man. But if you should hear anything before you return to Ireland . . .'

Briant tapped his nose, 'I'll let you know, of course. Humility will get word to you one way or another.'

We shook hands once again and I left the ale-house amid a positive flurry of goodwill. Rogues I had never seen in my life before saluted me or flashed a smile from the depths of their overgrown beards. From now on I would most probably be known in 'Little Ireland' as 'that friend of Briant's'. I could only trust that such a description did not extend beyond the confines of Marsh Street.

Adela, for some reason, did not appear to have noticed my delay in returning home. She had been too busy keeping an eye on Luke who, at eleven months old, was eagerly exploring everything within the orbit of his peculiarly crablike, sideways crawl. Finally, she had done what she used to do with Adam and tied him to the leg of the kitchen table with a length of old linen.

'He doesn't like it, but he'll have to learn to,' she said firmly as the child raised an indignant, tear-stained face to mine. 'Did you get all the things for the Twelfth Night cake?'

With a flourish I lined up my purchases along the centre of the table, taking a piece of the sugared lemon peel from its wrapping and handing it to Luke. His tears turned instantly to smiles as he started to suck it, and Hercules promptly bit my ankle to remind me that he, too, had a sweet tooth.

That afternoon I took the older children to see the second of the mummers' plays as, in a rash moment, I had promised to do. Adela elected to stay at home in order to make her Twelfth Night cake so that the brandy with which it was laced would have plenty of time to soak into the rest of the ingredients. (This Christmas was costing me a fortune.)

'Don't forget to put in the bean and the pea,' Elizabeth instructed before we left the house, 'or we shan't have any King and Queen of the Feast.'

'How long do you think I've been making . . .' Adela was beginning furiously when I pulled my daughter outside and firmly closed the door behind us. (Even now, as a mature woman, she still has no sense of danger.)

The outer ward of the castle was once more crowded, although not quite as full as it had been the previous day. And the general talk was still of Alderman Trefusis's murder, but

I could sense that interest was beginning, very slightly, to wane. In a day or two other topics would have superseded it in the public mind.

The mummers' arrival, too, was greeted with a little less warmth than on their first appearance, but this may have been simply that the choice of play was less popular than that of St George. In spite of featuring Old Man Winter and Beelzebub – both parts taken by the elderly couple – and a very realistic fight between a Saracen Knight and a Christian Knight for the love of the inevitable Fair Maid, it was not as humorous a play as yesterday's. Adam, for one, whined all the way home because he had not seen the Doctor – 'that funny man', as he called him. In the end my patience ran out.

'Just stop moaning, Adam,' I admonished him. 'It's not my fault the mummers didn't play Saint George and the Dragon again today. You just have to take what you're given in this life. You're five. It's time you accepted that.'

'Tomorrow,' announced my stepson, 'is Childermass. You have to be especially kind to us all day.' Nicholas could be annoyingly sententious when he wanted to be.

'Specially kind,' echoed Adam severely, thrusting out his lower lip.

'You can't scold us or be nasty or anything like that,' said my daughter, adding her mite to the conversation.

It was true that tomorrow, as well as being Sunday, was also Holy Innocents' Day on which the children slaughtered on the orders of King Herod were remembered. And, if one were not careful, it could also be a time of extreme bad luck. It was, I reflected bitterly, just my sort of day.

We went, next morning, to our customary church of St Giles for the Childermass service, and were early enough to find ourselves places near the front of the nave. All four children were dressed in their best clothes and shone with cleanliness, even Luke honouring the occasion by managing to dribble a little less than usual. At Adela's behest, I wore one of the two decent suits of clothes bestowed on me a year earlier by our present king when he was Duke of Gloucester. Consequently, in my brown woollen hose and green tunic with its silver-gilt buttons, I already felt miserably overdressed long before I realized that the five mummers had entered the church and were standing next to me.

I had been conscious of some little commotion, a sudden whispering amongst the congregation, but had not bothered to turn my head to discover its cause. Now, however, a certain smell assailed my nostrils; the smell of very old clothes which have been washed, then put away without being properly dried. Glancing to my left, I saw the puckered skin of the older man's right eye and his right hand with its missing first two fingers raised to scratch his cheek. Next to him stood the old woman and, beyond her, the three younger members of the troupe. All five had obviously taken trouble with their appearance, shabby though it was, and the young woman had tied a knot of red ribbon in her long fair hair which she wore loose under a veil of white lawn (an unconventional headdress for a married woman and one which was causing hushed comment amongst the matrons).

It became apparent why they had pushed their way to the front of the crowd thronging the nave, to stand with the parents and children, when it came time for the latter to be blessed. As each child went forward to receive the priest's benediction, the girl followed them, thrusting out her swollen belly so that her unborn child would also receive a blessing. And although, in general, mummers were regarded as on a par with rogues and vagabonds and outside respectable society, there was a murmur of approval from the gathering.

I thought that the young woman – whose name I suddenly recollected to be Dorcas – looked extremely pale as she returned to stand beside her husband, so it came as no surprise when, a moment or two later, she gave a queer little sigh and fainted. There was immediate consternation, and several of the women standing close by, including Adela, who pushed Luke unceremoniously into my arms, stepped forward to lend their aid. This was not needed, however, as the husband, who must have been a great deal stronger than he looked, stooped and, picking his wife up as if she had been a featherweight, carried her out of the church, closely followed by the other three mummers.

And closely followed, also, by my wife.

I sighed. I might have known it, I thought: at present, anything and everything to do with babies had Adela's undivided attention. With a jerk of my head, I indicated that Elizabeth, Nicholas and Adam should accompany Luke and myself outside to where Adela was already insisting that the five mummers must return home with us to share our dinner and allow the younger woman to rest.

'For you can see that the poor child is quite worn out,' my wife was saying, one arm about the shoulders of the girl, who seemed to be recovering a little, revived by the cold, fresh air. 'You can't be very comfortably housed in the castle. The place is falling to bits.'

The old couple demurred, not wanting to be beholden to anyone not of their own kind, but the two younger men, who were plainly anxious concerning Dorcas's well-being, accepted with alacrity.

'Our lodgings aren't what a woman in Dorcas's condition should have to put up with, and that's a fact,' the man who was her brother admitted. 'Truth is, we'd all be glad of a meal and a rest in a decent home.'

The husband – Tobias Warrener? Was that what he was called? – nodded in agreement. The old woman would have made more difficulties if she could, but the excitement of our children at the prospect of having the mummers actually under their roof put paid to any further argument. We set off without further delay for Small Street.

Fortunately, because it was Christmas we had a greater store of food than usual; in addition to which, Adela was never without a supply of pottage kept in a small iron cauldron and ready to be heated over the fire at any time of the day. Furthermore, the girl, Dorcas, professed herself uninterested in food for the moment and was swept off upstairs by Adela to lie down upon our bed, a proceeding I regarded with the greatest misgiving.

The older woman, who reintroduced herself as Tabitha Warrener, proved to be very handy in the kitchen, skilled at making a little go a long way by adding a bit of this to that, or that to this, ideas over which my wife enthused to me later. ('I suppose she's had to skimp and scrape all her life, but she's certainly a remarkable cook.') The old man, Ned Chorley, was also worth his weight in gold by keeping our three imps and myself amused with tricks and 'magic' in the parlour while the women prepared the food. (I couldn't help reflecting that Adela wouldn't approve of such things on a Sunday, but unless one of the children informed her, she would never know. And what she didn't know couldn't hurt her.) Meanwhile, Tobias Warrener and his brother-in-law, Arthur Monkton, sat with Dorcas until they were called downstairs to dinner.

During the meal, Adela and I tried to draw them out about their life in general, but although they were all perfectly willing to recount amusing anecdotes of their life on the road, and although Tabitha was happy to talk about her girlhood in Hampshire, where her father had been head warrener on one of the manors near Southampton and a young Ned Chorley one of his assistants, I couldn't help feeling that there was a large part of the older couple's lives that remained veiled in mystery.

('You're imagining things, as usual,' Adela said tartly when, later, I suggested this to her.)

But I was satisfied I wasn't. They had both talked perfectly freely about their younger days with her father, but then, suddenly, her parents were dead and she was married with a child. And I remembered distinctly her telling us that she was quite old when her son was born. Indeed, she reckoned she was well past twenty, maybe nearer thirty. So what happened to the years in between?

Tabitha went on to tell us how her ne'er-do-well husband had deserted her shortly after the birth of their only child, never to be seen again; how she had reverted to using the surname of her girlhood; how she had been helped in those dark days by her old friend, Ned Chorley; how her son, who had borne my name, Roger, had married very young 'a sweet, pretty little maid, but with no strength in her', who had died when Tobias was born. 'And poor Roger, he took and died of a broken heart less than a twelvemonth later,' she concluded. 'So I set to and reared Tobias all on me own. Not that it were any hardship,' she added, smiling fondly at her grandson on the other side of our kitchen table. 'I'd done it once. I could do it again.'

'And a very good job you done of it, too, my old sweetheart,' endorsed Ned Chorley. ''E's a credit to you, and that's the truth.'

'When did you decide on the mummers' life?' I asked.

The old man shrugged. 'Some twenty years back, maybe. Times were hard. The nobles were still fighting each other. Sometimes we had one king, sometimes another. A man didn't know where he was. We' – he jerked his head at Tabitha – 'were living near Romsey at the time trying to keep body and soul together, selling a few vegetables, taking in washing. And then this troupe o'mummers arrived and every single one o'them died of the plague. Terrible summer for plague, it were.' Tabitha nodded gravely. 'So there was their stuff all left with no one to claim it, lying rotting in a field. I says to Tabitha, why not? Shall we try our luck? May make a better living at it than what we're doing now. She said yes and we've been on the road ever since. Young Toby then were only two. He ain't ever known any other way o'life.'

'You can read?' I asked.

'Grandmother can,' Tobias answered, spearing a slice of goat's milk cheese on the end of his knife. 'She teaches the rest of us our parts. Tried to learn me my letters once,' he added cheerfully, 'but I ain't got no head for words. Not written down, that is. I'm all right at reciting.'

They went on talking for quite a while after that, answering the children's eager questions as to how certain stunts and tricks were done, while I poured more ale for us all and watched with anxious eyes as the level in the barrel slowly dropped. And it was about that time that I began to reflect that there was a gap, quite a big one, in both Tabitha Warrener's and Ned Chorley's life histories that they hadn't told us about. And neither had mentioned how the latter came to be so maimed, even though he obviously had difficulty using a knife with his right hand. He had seen me looking curiously at him, too, but had offered no explanation.

Not, of course, that it was any of my business. And to be fair, I'd noticed how they all stared curiously around them, obviously wondering how a mere pedlar – for I had told them that much – could afford such a house. So, in the hope of encouraging equal frankness, I briefly recounted how I and my family came to be living in Small Street and the service I had rendered Cicely Ford which had provoked this generous return.

'You'm clever with your brain, then,' Ned Chorley remarked admiringly. 'Can read and write.'

I have no idea what made Adela say what she did next, for she is normally as reticent concerning my achievements as she is about her own.

'Oh, he's clever all right.' She smiled proudly at me. 'He's done favours for a lot of people, including our present king. Indeed, he was given a place at the coronation and at the feast afterwards as a reward for his services.'

I'm not sure that any of them really believed her, but they had the good manners to pretend that they did and exclaimed suitably. But the conversation then naturally drifted to the dramatic events of the past year and to the fact that this same time last December no one would have believed that King Edward would be dead by now.

'And if we had believed it,' Tabitha said, 'no one would've thought to see the old king's brother wearing the crown instead of his little son.'

Ned Chorley then proved himself to be a man after my own heart. 'Well, a good job Richard o'Gloucester did take the crown,' he said positively. 'We didn't want no Woodville brat on the throne and all his family ruling the roost. Like cocks on a dung-hill, they'd have been. And a very good king King Richard's proving to be.'

'I dunno about that,' Arthur Monkton demurred. 'What about this here story that he's had the boy king and his brother killed?'

Before I could say anything, the old man spluttered, 'You don' want t'believe shit like that, lad. That's a lot o'moonshine, that is.'

'Then why don't he produce the boys and say, "Look! Here they are, so stop yer chattering!"?' demanded the other man.

I waited with bated breath to hear what Ned Chorley's answer would be, for the question was still troubling me.

'Strategy!' he exclaimed scathingly. 'Strategy, son! Something what you young fellows knows nothing about. He's a good soldier is our present king. Fighting in the field, he were, long before he were our Toby's age.'

'What strategy?' Monkton scoffed.

Ned stabbed at him across the table with the point of his knife. 'There's been one rising already on behalf o'them boys, and if King Richard produces them and says, "Look, here they are!" like what you want him to do, there'll be another. So, he don't say nothing.'

'But if the king says nothing,' Tobias objected, 'all them lords as don't like him and think he ain't entitled to the throne, they'll just go and join that there Henry Tudor.'

'No, they won't!' Ned thumped the table in his excitement. ''Cos they won't be certain, neither, that the boys are dead.' He glanced triumphantly around him. 'That's the beauty of it. That's what I mean by strategy! King Richard's a soldier to his finger-tips. He knows how to keep the enemy guessing. They'm para-lysed now, not sure which way to jump. That's what your true strategist does. He keeps everyone guessing.'

I had to restrain myself from getting up and hugging him. All the same: 'Where do you think the children are then, Master Chorley?' I asked, refilling his beaker with a generous measure of ale.

'Still in the Tower?' Adela wanted to know.

'Nah!' Ned took a drink, then chewed a split fingernail. 'I reckon as he's had them moved secretly up to Yorkshire, to one of them big strongholds of his. Middleham. Sheriff Hutton, maybe. Travelling under cover of darkness – and at this time o'year there's plenty of that – they could be there before anyone got wind o'the move.'

'And what happens when they grow up?' Tabitha asked in her practical way. 'The elder's twelve already. Nearly a man. They won't be content to remain in the shadows.'

Ned snorted. 'King Richard will've established himself by then. Everyone'll know what a good king he is. They won't want no other.'

Tabitha shook her head. 'I don't believe that. Oh, not that he won't be a good king! He were a good soldier and strategist, as you said. No need to get up in yer high ropes, Ned. But if Saint Peter himself were king, he'd make enemies of someone. There's always some malcontents wanting a change, no matter how sweet you try to keep them. That there Duke o'Buckingham's a case in point. And the boys' whereabouts aren't going to remain a secret for ever.'

Ned looked irritated, but he knew she was right. 'That's for the future,' he said, brushing her objection aside. 'He can't be expected to think of everything right now. He'll take it one step at a time. What d'you think, Master Chapman? If what your dame says is true, you know His Highness a deal better than the rest of us.'

'I think you're probably correct,' I agreed. 'In some ways, the king's a very trusting man. Lets his heart rule his head more than he should. *Loyauté me lie* is his watchword as well as his motto, which is why I suspect that Buckingham's betrayal must have hit him hard.'

'Oh, well, maybe it'll serve as a warning to him,' Tabitha said, pushing back her stool and getting to her feet. 'That were a tasty meal, Mistress Chapman. All the same, we can't impose on your hospitality any longer. Toby, come upstairs with me and see how Dorcas is going on.'

But when they returned a few minutes later, it was to report that Dorcas was sleeping so soundly they hadn't wanted to wake her.

'Quite right,' said Adela. 'You must all stay and have supper with us. I'm sure you'll all be more comfortable here than in that draughty castle.'

I saw the old couple hesitate and glance at one another, refusal in both their faces. But then Tabitha shrugged. 'That's very kind of you, mistress. I won't deny that the accommodation there leaves a lot to be desired. And it's a cold day. A very cold day.' She looked at her grandson. 'Toby ought to take a walk, though, and make sure our gear is safely locked away. We didn't bargain on being absent for longer than the Mass at Saint Giles and we took no extra precautions.'

'I'll go at once,' the young man said, pulling on the thick

frieze coat he had dropped carelessly on the floor on entering the house.

'Good lad.' Tabitha nodded her approval. 'No need to hurry. Dorcas won't wake for a while yet, I reckon. Sleeping like a babe, she is.'

'So you three just be quiet and don't go waking the lady up,' I charged my children when he had gone, while Adela took Luke on her lap and began feeding him some frumenty.

Adam regarded me beneath lowering brows. 'It's Childermass,' he reminded me. 'That means we can do as we please.' Trust him to get the wrong idea!

I was about to remonstrate with him when Ned Chorley seized him by the wrist and, with the other two in tow, bore them all off to the parlour again, promising a whole lot of new tricks they hadn't yet seen. I saw Adela frown, so, indicating that Arthur Monkton should go with us, I followed them out of the kitchen before she could voice any misgivings.

In spite of the mummer's sleight of hand, I must at some point have fallen asleep, for I came to with a start as the parlour door opened and Tobias Warrener slipped into the room. I realized that it must be well past noon by the quality of the light filtering through the unshuttered window. Elizabeth, Nicholas and Adam were still sitting in a spellbound semicircle at Ned Chorley's feet, so I went in search of the women, only to bump – literally – into Tabitha Warrener as I stepped out into the hall. She smiled at me before putting her head around the door.

'Everything all right, Toby?' she asked.

'All's well, Grandmother,' was the answer. 'The truth is I don't think anyone thinks we have anything worth stealing.'

Tabitha laughed. 'More'n likely,' she agreed.

The short afternoon wore away and, after supper, the two women went upstairs again to see how the invalid was faring. Their report was not as encouraging as it might have been.

'Mistress Warrener is feeling well rested,' my wife told Tobias, 'but a little sick and dizzy when she moves her head. I'll take her up some broth and a sup of ale which should revive her, but I think she should remain here tonight. I can lend her a night-shift and she can sleep with me. Roger, you'll either have to bed down with the boys or sleep in the parlour in a chair.'

'Don't make the poor man do that,' Ned Chorley protested. 'He can come back to the castle with us. The bedding's clean and there's enough beds to go round. I think they must've been expecting a bigger troupe than ours.'

There was no way I could gainsay these arrangements without appearing churlish. Nevertheless, I gave Adela a very speaking look as she passed me on her way upstairs to collect my night-shirt, and I promised myself that I should have something to say when I returned home the following morning on the subject of my wishes being consulted in future before plans were made on my behalf. I fancy Tabitha felt much the same, for on the short walk to the castle she was apologetic.

'Not what you're used to, Master Chapman,' she said more than once.

I assured her, truthfully, that I had slept in many worse places in the course of my travels. And, indeed, I was pleas-antly surprised by the room in which I eventually found myself. I had never, so far as I could recall, been in the castle's inner ward before and was surprised to find it in as great a state of disrepair as the outer ward with crumbling walls and the door into the orchard hanging drunkenly on one hinge. I reflected that there was little point in locking the gates at night, as Dick Manifold had once told me they did, when anyone could simply walk in and out at will through the gaping holes in the masonry.

But, as I say, the building in which the mummers were housed was rain- and windproof with a roof of solid lead tiles, and was afforded additional protection by standing in the lee of the orchard wall. The beds, too, had good straw palliasses and clean, if coarse, linen sheets as well as blankets, and I had to admit to myself that I had not expected such consideration from the city fathers for a group of travelling players. There was, of course, no privacy, but as Tabitha and Ned fell into bed more or less fully clothed, and the two younger men did the same, I followed suit, merely removing my outer garments, tunic and boots. I did think longingly for a moment or two of my own goose feather mattress and Adela's comforting presence and wonder if I was going to be kept awake by the others' snores. But within five minutes I was soundlessly and dreamlessly asleep.

EIGHT

For a few moments after waking, I was at a loss to know where I was.

A cock was crowing somewhere in the distance and through a hole in one corner of the roof, where a tile had broken away, I could see a single star shining high and far off in a patch of sky lightening towards dawn. The room stank of bad breath, stale sweat and unwashed bodies, while to my right someone was snoring loud enough to waken the dead. I forced my eyes wide open, staring at the rafters overhead and trying to remember where I was. Slowly, memories of the previous day's events came crowding back to me, and I knew that I was in an outbuilding of the inner ward of Bristol Castle while young Dorcas Warrener slept in my bed at home. As for what day it was, I gradually and painfully worked out that it must be the twenty-ninth of December, the Feast of the Martyrdom of St Thomas Becket, the day on which, all those centuries ago, the 'holy, blissful martyr' was hacked to death in his own cathedral of Canterbury by four knights come from Normandy to carry out what they thought to be the wishes of King Henry II; that same Henry who had spent part of his boyhood in this very castle where I was now lying.

There was the sudden scrape of a flint and, seconds later, a candle flared into brightness. I rolled on to my left side to find Tabitha Warrener, fully clothed and seated on the edge of her bed, regarding me with some amusement.

'You slept well,' she said.

I grunted. 'I don't think I stirred all night.' I pushed back the bedclothes and swung my feet to the floor, thankful that I had removed only my outer garments the night before. (I felt sure that Tabitha would have appreciated my manly charms, but there was a cynical gleam in her eyes that made me uncomfortable.) 'My mouth is so dry I can barely speak. Is there anything in this barn of a place to drink?'

She laughed. 'You don't think they supply us with "all-night", do you? We take our meals in the common refectory with the reeve and other castle officials, and I can tell you, Chapman, that they are meagre and generally undercooked. That's why it was such a pleasure to eat with you and your dame and family yesterday. She keeps a plentiful table.'

'Adela's a good housekeeper,' I agreed, swallowing hard to moisten my mouth. 'Where do you go after Christmas, when you leave here?'

'Back into winter quarters.' Tabitha fished in the pocket of her ancient skirt and produced a small bottle from which she removed the stopper before handing it to me. 'Try this. It's strong but it's wet.'

I sipped cautiously, recognizing the liquid as mead, a drink I generally found too sweet for my taste. But it eased the dryness of my throat. 'Where are these winter quarters of yours?' I asked, handing back the bottle.

''Tween Winchester and S'ampton. Sweetwater Manor. Master Tuffnel gives us all shelter there every year without fail twixt Our Lord's Birth and Resurrection.'

'This Master Tuffnel, you know him well?'

'All my life. My father was warrener to his father. Ned worked on his land.'

'You grew up together, then?'

'In a manner o'speaking. Apart from him being the master's son and me the warrener's daughter – he's a few years older 'n me. But he was always good to me and Ned. Helped us when we needed it most.'

I waited for her to enlarge on this last remark, but she offered no more information, getting abruptly to her feet, lighting a second candle and shuffling over to wake the other three men who were still asleep.

'Wake up, you lazy bastards,' she said affectionately, prodding each one in the back with a bony forefinger. 'You'll be late for breakfast.'

'I'd better be getting home for breakfast, too,' I remarked, pulling on my boots and tunic. 'I'll escort young Mistress Warrener back here as soon as she's ready.'

Tabitha shook her head. 'We won't put you to so much trouble, Master Chapman,' she said. She nodded at her grandson. 'Toby and I'll come and get her when we've eaten. We need to thank Mistress Chapman for all her kindness.'

'As you please.' My foot hit against something and, bending down, I picked up a battered tin plate on which reposed the remains of something black and sticky. A faint, sickly-sweet aroma drifted up to me. 'What's this?'

Tabitha smiled and held out her hand. 'That's my poppy seed and lettuce juice lozenges. Or what's left of 'em. I always carry a supply when we're on the road. Set light to them and they burn slowly all night. The perfume helps us sleep when the accommodation's poor and the beds are hard.'

'I wouldn't have thought you needed them here,' I said. 'I've slept on far worse mattresses than these.'

Tabitha shrugged. 'Force of habit. And Dorcas is finding it difficult to drop off just now. She's getting to be an awkward shape.'

I said my goodbyes and went home to find our unexpected guest much recovered and anxious to be reunited with her husband. I assured her that he and Tabitha would be coming to collect her as soon as they had had breakfast and settled down to my own with a will. I also promised myself a change of clothes and a wash under the pump as soon as I had eaten. Adela, bustling around the kitchen, reminded me that she would need a further supply of apples fetched down from the loft.

'You haven't forgotten it's Wassail Day, have you?'

I had, as a matter of fact, and my spirits lifted. This was the fourth day of Christmas and my neighbours and I would be calling on one another throughout the afternoon and early evening with bowls of hot, spiced 'lamb's wool' in order to drink each other's health; an ancient Saxon custom which the Normans had never quite managed to stamp out.

Waes Hael!

Drink Hael!

By nightfall we should all be as drunk as lords.

We went to church again that morning to celebrate the martyrdom of St Thomas Becket and to beg for his intercession in heaven, then walked home through a sudden, but brief flurry of snow. Adam wanted to know if we were going to see the

mummers again in the afternoon but, much to his disgust, I
said no. It wasn't that I didn't like them or find their plays
amusing, but I felt that I had had a surfeit of their company
for the time being. Besides which, I had a nagging headache.
Adela left us at the street door, saying she had to walk on up
to the market and to set the pottage over the fire to heat. 'I
might be a little while,' she added – which meant that she had
arranged to meet Margaret Walker and possibly other friends
for a gossip. So I was astonished when, only a very short time
later, she reappeared in the kitchen accompanied not only by
her cousin, but by the latter's two cronies, Bess Simnel and
Maria Watkins, as well.

Before I could express my surprise at this intrusion, all four
women began speaking at once, sending the three older children
from the room with hands clapped over their ears. Luke began
to yell in competition.

I picked him up. 'What's happened?' I demanded. 'For the
Virgin's sweet sake, Adela, speak one at a time!'

My wife indicated that the other three should be quiet for a
moment.

'It would seem,' she told me a little breathlessly, 'that Sir
George Marvell has disappeared.'

'What do you mean?' I asked. 'Disappeared?'

'What it usually means,' Maria Watkins said waspishly.
'Vanished! Unable to be found!'

I ignored her and raised my eyebrows at Adela, but it was
Margaret who answered.

'The story is all over Redcliffe this morning,' she said, 'that
he retired as usual last night, but this morning there's no trace
of him in his chamber and the bed has not been slept in.'

I handed Luke to my wife. (He was teething again and dribbling all down my neck.)

'Where's his horse?' I asked. 'Is the mare missing, too?'

The women looked at one another. 'I don't know,' Margaret
admitted at last. 'I didn't think to ask. I know Sir George uses
the stables in Redcliffe Street . . . But I don't think it can be or
the family wouldn't be so anxious.'

'Are they anxious?' Or was this just an incident blown up out
of all proportion by the gossips – especially by the three now

filling our tiny kitchen – just to make life a little less monotonous?

'Word is,' Maria Watkins told me sharply, 'that the three other Marvell men have been out scouring the whole of Redcliffe since dawn.'

'Since dawn,' Bess Simnel confirmed, her beady gaze darting eagerly around the room, taking note of all that was going on. 'Adela, my dear,' she added, grinding her almost toothless gums together, 'is that the remains of a bowl of plum porridge that I see?'

My wife sighed. 'Help yourself, Bess. There's a clean bowl and spoon on the chopping bench.'

While Goody Simnel was eagerly doing just that, Maria Watkins astonished me by asking, 'Well, what are you going to do about it, Roger?'

'Me?' I replied indignantly. 'It has nothing whatsoever to do with me. Moreover, it's my guess that Sir George's horse is also missing and he will come trotting home in an hour or so having been for an early morning canter across the downs. Has Cyprian Marvell enquired of the gatekeeper at the Redcliffe Gate if his father passed through at first light this morning?'

'I've no idea,' my former mother-in-law said thoughtfully. She nodded briskly at her friends. 'I think we'd better go back and find out what's happening. Put that Yule doll down at once, Bess, and come with us. You're eating poor Adela out of house and home! You've finished all that plum porridge.'

The three elderly ladies then departed, leaving Adela and myself to enjoy a quiet laugh at their expense.

'All the same, do you think there's any substance in this story, Roger?' my wife asked, setting Luke down again among the rushes while she stirred the pottage and set the table for dinner. 'What was the gossip in the market?'

She shook her head. 'I didn't have time to find out. I met the three of them at the top of Small Street. They were full of the story and insisted on coming here straight away to tell you.'

I snorted. 'What did they think I would do? Or could do? Nevertheless,' I continued thoughtfully, 'I'll walk up as far as the High Cross when we've eaten, but not before. Going to church always gives me an appetite.'

* * *

We had barely finished our meal, and I was descending from the loft with a basket of apples for the 'lamb's wool', when a knock on the street door heralded the arrival of Richard Manifold, looking harassed.

'Ah, Roger!' he said as soon as he saw me. 'We need men to search the town. Sir George Marvell has disappeared.'

'It's true, then,' Adela said from the kitchen doorway.

He turned towards her, his face lighting at the sight of her. 'You've heard. Who told you?'

'Margaret Walker, Goody Watkins and Bess Simnel.' She smiled. 'Come and have a cup of ale. Sit down a moment. You look tired.'

He shook his head. 'I daren't, my dear. We've been straitly charged by the mayor himself to discover what has happened to the knight as soon as possible. Roger, can you come? We need every able-bodied man we can muster.'

I nearly said, 'And who asked you to call my wife "my dear"?' but thought better of it. He did look exhausted and, besides, my curiosity was aroused. So I enquired instead about the horse.

'Still in its stable,' was the answer. 'So he hasn't left the city.'

'He could have walked.'

Richard again shook his head. 'None of the gatekeepers remember seeing him.'

That made me laugh. 'There are half a dozen ways you can get in and out of this town at any hour of the day or night without being seen. You must know as well as I do that the walls are generally in a bad state of repair.'

Richard shrugged. 'But why would he go anywhere on foot and in the middle of the night? It makes no sense. No, no! He must be somewhere near at hand. The fear is that he might have fallen into the river and drowned. In this weather the waters are freezing.'

I handed the basket of apples to Adela. 'I'll get my hat and cloak.' Two minutes later we were striding up Small Street buffeted by an unpleasantly cold north wind. 'What's the family's story?'

Richard grimaced. 'They all tell the same tale. They wished Sir George goodnight at around his usual time for retiring and didn't see him again. When one of the servants went in to wake him first thing this morning there was no sign of him and his bed hadn't been slept in.'

'Could he have left the house last night without being observed?'

'Easily. At this time of year everyone – family and servants alike – goes to bed early on Sir George's orders to save candles. If he'd waited an hour or so, he could have crept out and no one would have seen him.'

A large gathering of men was assembled by the High Cross, receiving instructions from Sergeant Merryweather. I recognized Burl Hodge and his sons, also Nick Brimble and Jack Nym, but foiled the latter's attempts to attach himself to me by indicating that I was accompanying Richard Manifold. I wasn't, but by giving Richard, in his turn, the impression that I was going with Jack and Nick, I managed to slip away on my own.

I made my way without hesitation to Marsh Street, to the Turk's Head, and enquired for Humility Dyson. So high was my standing now in 'Little Ireland' since my appearance in Briant's company, that someone offered to fetch the landlord for me. He arrived, cross and out of breath, a few minutes later from the Wayfarer's Return.

'What's this all about?' he panted angrily.

'Where's Briant?'

'Gone.'

'Gone where?'

'None of your business.'

I gripped his arm and shook it. 'It might be,' I said. 'Sir George Marvell is missing.' And I told him about the incident on the bridge three nights previously.

The landlord called the Irishman a number of uncomplimentary names, some of which were new even to me. Then he ran a hand through his beard and drew me out of the ale-room into the street.

'Word was brought late last night that the Clontarf was berthed at Rownham, near the ferry. Her captain wouldn't bring her right up into the Backs: the river was too low. Said Briant could join the ship there at daybreak and they'd sail on the late-morning tide. But Briant announced he weren't going to wait for morning and went straight away.'

'On foot?'

'They don't come over here with horses, now do they?' Humility scoffed. 'Of course on foot. There's plenty o'ways to get in and . . .'

'Yes, yes! I know,' I interrupted impatiently. 'You don't think . . .?'

'No, I don't!' was the violent retort. 'He's a man of his word, is Briant. If he promised you he'd let Sir George Marvell be, then he will. The knight'll turn up sometime, safe and sound. Mind you, it wouldn't worry me if he didn't. As nasty a piece of work as God ever made, and that's the truth.'

'Well, don't go spreading that opinion abroad,' I advised him, to which he demanded to know if I supposed he was a fool.

Having reassured him on that point, I took my leave and walked slowly back to the High Cross wrapped in thought. But the crowd had dispersed, each man now, presumably, busy searching every odd alleyway and corner of the city in the hope of running the knight to earth. This disappearance, coming as it did so soon after the murder of Alderman Trefusis, must be giving the sheriff and his men a collective headache that had nothing to do with the Christmas wine and ale.

I hesitated for several seconds, wondering where to start, before deciding on another course altogether and setting off across the bridge to Redcliffe.

I was shown into Drusilla Marvell's presence by a servant almost as venerable as she was herself.

'I'm sorry to disturb you, mistress,' I said, careful to make my bow a deep one. 'I was hoping to have a word with the other members of your family, but they are all out, looking for your brother. I understand he's disappeared.'

The room, on an upper floor of the house, was plainly the old lady's bedchamber, and although, today, she herself was dressed in funereal black, her surroundings fairly blazed with colour. What first drew the eye was a counterpane of scarlet silk covering an enormous bed draped with curtains of emerald velvet embellished with gold and silver thread. Even the woodwork of the bedstead itself was painted in shades of crimson and vermilion. There were no rushes on this floor, but the luxury of a carpet patterned in red and yellow, while the rest of the furniture, including the chair Drusilla sat in next to the window, was of the finest oak.

She regarded me balefully, striking an ivory-handled cane against the leg of her chair. 'What is it you want? Who are you? I didn't catch what my steward said.'

I realized she was deaf and raised my voice. 'I'm sorry to disturb you, mistress . . .'

I was interrupted by another furious hammering. 'You don't need to shout! That's the trouble with people. They think if you're deaf you can't hear anything! I'm able to hear you speaking perfectly well. I just find it hard to distinguish the words. The English are scared to death of moving their lips. For some reason we think it makes us look stupid. Use your mouth, young man! Use your mouth! Then I can see what it is you're trying to say.'

Feeling much as I used to do when chastised by my mother or by my novice master at Glastonbury, I shuffled my feet, unhappily conscious of my dirty boots on the carpet, and repeated my message.

The dame snorted. 'Disappeared, has he, my little brother? They needn't worry. He'll turn up again like a bad surprise. Those sort of people always do. There's no getting away from them. They harass people, that's what they do. Harass people! It wasn't enough for George to stick his nose into what didn't concern him and ruin my chances of happiness. Oh, no! He had to move himself into the house next to mine, instead of staying where he was in Clifton, so that he could spy on me some more. Said it was because he was concerned about me, the lying toad! Concerned about my money more like, and which of his precious sons I'm going to leave it to.' She paused for breath, but before I could say anything in answer, resumed her tirade. 'Mind you, it wouldn't surprise me to know someone had dealt him his comeuppance. He's made enough enemies in his life. And I'll tell you this, young man!' She thrust her stick at me and waved it about in the air. 'It wouldn't upset me if one of them had.' She broke off suddenly and a beringed hand crept up to her mouth. 'I wonder,' she muttered, more to herself than to me. 'Now, I wonder . . .'

She seemed momentarily to have forgotten my presence, plunged into some reverie of her own.

'You wonder?' I prompted after a moment or two, then repeated it more loudly.

Drusilla jumped, then treated me to a second diatribe about shouting at deaf people. Finally, however, she condescended to continue. 'You say he went missing last night?' No one, it seemed, had thought it necessary to inform her.

I nodded. 'Sir George was first missed when his servant went to wake him this morning. His bed had not been slept in.' I was careful to enunciate as clearly as possible.

The dame pursed her thin lips. 'So my brother must have let himself out of the house sometime during the hours of darkness.' She turned her head and stared out of the window. 'He might,' she mused, 'have gone in answer to a summons.'

'That's possible,' I agreed, and waited.

My patience was rewarded. After a few moments, she went on: 'There was a man stood over there, opposite George's house, yesterday afternoon. He stood there quite a long time, just staring.'

My pulse beat quickened. 'What was he like?' I asked eagerly.

Drusilla turned back to look at me and gave a cackle of laughter. 'Can't tell you that. He was wearing one of those masks young idiots adopt at this time of year. A bird mask with a great beak. Going about frightening old ladies like me,' she added viciously.

I thought to myself that it would take more than a bird mask to frighten Drusilla Marvell, but merely said, 'From what you could see of this man, did you get the impression he was young or old?'

Having watched my face intently while I spoke, she answered at once. 'Young. Well, it wasn't an old man's body. More like yours.'

'Did he enter the house?' I asked.

She shrugged. 'Don't know for sure. I watched him for a while, but then I had to use the chamber pot. Your bladder gets weak at my age and if you don't go when you need to, there could be a nasty accident. When I came back to the window he'd gone.'

'What was he wearing? Apart, that is, from the mask.'

She stared. 'What men usually wear. Boots, hose . . .'

'A cloak, perhaps? It was very cold yesterday afternoon.'

The old lady considered this suggestion. 'I don't remember a cloak,' she said at last. 'But then, I don't remember anything much except the mask. Maybe one of those thick coats that workmen wear. Not that I'd be sure about that.'

I could see that I should get little more out of her in the way of a description, so I changed the subject.

'Dame Marvell,' I said, 'do you know about the murder of Alderman Trefusis on Christmas Day?'

'Of course I know about it,' she snapped. 'I'm not that deaf! No one's talked of anything else since it happened.'

'Do you also know that the last word he uttered before he died was the name Dee? Does that mean anything to you?'

If I had not been watching her so intently, to make sure that she was reading my lips, I might not have noticed the slight tell-tale flicker of her eyelids. As it was, it was so brief that I almost missed it.

'No, the name means nothing to me,' she said sharply and with a shake of her head. 'I know of no one called Dee.'

A sudden inspiration came to me, and I wondered that the thought had not occurred to me before. 'It might, of course, have been just the beginning of a longer name; one merely starting with the letters D-E-E,' I suggested.

This time, she shook her head even more vigorously. 'No!' she exclaimed, banging on the carpet with her stick. 'I've told you! Now, go away! You're upsetting me!'

She reached for a little handbell that stood on a table beside her chair, but before she could ring it I heard the bedchamber door behind me open and someone tread heavily across the floor.

'Aunt Drusilla,' said Cyprian Marvell, bending to kiss her cheek. 'I've come to give you some disturbing news.'

'I know it already,' she snapped, 'thanks to this man.' She again stabbed at me with her stick. 'None of my family thought it necessary to inform me that my brother is missing. Oh, no! It takes a stranger to do that.'

Cyprian Marvell turned and, somewhat hesitantly, held out his hand. 'Master Chapman, is it? Yes, I thought so. You've been pointed out to me.'

I explained hastily that I was supposed to be a member of the search party looking for Sir George. 'I called on you first, sir, but everyone being out, it occurred to me that Dame Drusilla might have some information that could be useful.'

He smiled pleasantly. 'I don't suppose she has.'

'You would be wrong.' I returned the smile. 'Dame Drusilla did see something yesterday afternoon. But I'll leave her to tell you all about it. I've trespassed enough on her time already. Now I must go and join in the search. I assume Sir George has not been found yet?'

Cyprian shook his head. 'I'm afraid not.'

He didn't strike me like a man who was very worried by his father's mysterious absence, but then, I reflected, appearances can be deceptive.

The steward was summoned to show me out and, once in the street, I stood for several moments deep in thought. Then, instead of hastening to rejoin the search party, I turned my feet in the direction of Margaret Walker's cottage.

NINE

My knock was answered almost immediately.

'Oh, it's you,' my former mother-in-law grunted, and with this unenthusiastic greeting turned back into the cottage. She added over her shoulder, 'Come in then and close the door. You're letting in all the cold air.'

I did as she bade me. 'You don't sound very pleased to see me. Are you expecting someone?'

'I thought it might be Bess or Maria with some news.' She picked up a sharp knife from the table and went on with her task of splitting the skins of a dozen or so apples which she was preparing for the evening's wassailing. 'I'm taking these round to the baker's in High Street in a moment or two and he'll bake them in his oven for me. You can't get a really good baked apple over an open fire. What does Adela do with hers?'

'I don't know,' I admitted. 'I've never thought about it.' She snorted and muttered something under her breath about 'men never do'. 'Margaret,' I went on, ignoring the provocation, 'can you remember the name of the man you told me came courting Dame Drusilla a few years back?'

Her head jerked up at that and she paused in her work to look hard at me. After a long moment's consideration, she slowly shook her head. 'No, I can't. I don't think I ever heard it. Why? Is it important?'

'I don't rightly know. It might be,' I said cautiously.

'To do with Alderman Trefusis's murder and now with Sir George's disappearance?'

'Perhaps.'

She handed me her knife and indicated the remaining fruit. 'Finish slitting these apple skins for me.' She twitched her cloak from its peg. 'I'll be back in a few minutes.'

'Where are you going?'

'To fetch Bess and Maria, if I can find them.' The door banged to behind her and the latch clicked into place of its own accord.

Margaret was as good as her word and, before I had time to add the last apple to the basket waiting to be taken to the baker's, the latch clicked again as she and her two friends entered the cottage.

'What's this all about?' Goody Watkins asked peevishly, while Bess Simnel's beady eyes darted around the room in search of sustenance. 'Don't tell me you've interrupted my after-dinner nap to talk to him.' She gave a scornful jerk of her head in my direction. 'He doesn't know any more'n we do. Less, I expect.'

'Got 'nything to eat, Margaret?' Bess whined. Her small, bird-like frame seemed to need constant nourishment.

Impatiently, Margaret handed her a stale oatcake, left over from her breakfast, then turned to address Maria. 'Roger wants some information,' she said, 'and I can't give it to him. He says it could be important. I thought one or the other of you might know.'

At these words, both women came to attention, quivering like a couple of dogs scenting a bone. The challenge was a clarion call to arms. Their very honour was at stake.

'What information?' Maria and Bess demanded in chorus. (At least, it would have been in chorus if the latter's mouth had been empty. As it was, she made a kind of champing, gurgling noise, but its meaning was obvious.)

I repeated my previous request to Margaret. 'Did either of you ever know the name of the young man who wanted to marry Drusilla Marvell three years ago?'

'Not so young a man as all that,' Goody Watkins retorted. 'He were about your age as I recall.'

''S'right,' Bess Simnel agreed. She ran her tongue around her almost toothless gums, trying to find the last remnants of oatcake. 'That were stale, Margaret,' she accused her hostess before bending her mind to the problem in hand. A look of deep disappointment contracted her little features. 'I can't say for sure I ever heard it, did you, Maria?'

But Goody Watkins wasn't going to admit defeat so easily. She chewed her lips, paced up and down and breathed heavily through inflated nostrils.

Finally, in desperation – not having wished to give them a lead of any kind – I said, 'Could it have been Dee? Or could it have started with Dee?'

At these words, Bess Simnel choked over a crumb she had just discovered lurking behind one of the few ancient teeth remaining in her mouth. But as soon as it had been dislodged by a good back thumping from both her friends, she gave a hoarse, triumphant cry.

'Deakin! That were his name! Miles Deakin! Fancy me rememberin' that, and at my age, too!'

It was plainly a victory she would not let the others forget, and their sour expressions told me that they knew it. I was hard put to not to burst out laughing.

'You're a wonder, Bess,' I said, leaning over and kissing one withered cheek. She gave a little scream and skip of pleasure.

'Behave yourself!' Maria Watkins admonished her.

'You, also, Roger,' Margaret told me sharply. 'Why did you want to know?'

'About the young man's name?' I laid a heavy emphasis on the word 'young'. 'Because the last thing Alderman Trefusis said before he died was the word Dee. No one I've spoken to seems to know of anyone in the city called that. And then it occurred to me that it might just have been the beginning of a name.'

'So why did you think of old Drusilla's beau?' This was Margaret, hot on the trail of what could prove to be a truly fresh piece of gossip.

I hesitated. The information I had culled that afternoon should first have gone to Richard Manifold or Sergeant Merryweather, but I was grateful to the three women for their help, so I told them of my visit to Dame Drusilla and of the man she had seen staring up at her brother's house. I also explained how my suspicions had been aroused by the dame's reaction to my mention of the name of Dee.

I finished by asking, 'You don't happen to know where this man, Miles Deakin, hailed from, I suppose?'

'He weren't from the city,' Maria Watkins said positively.

'Maybe he was from Clifton,' Margaret suggested. 'That's how he knew about Drusilla and her money.'

'Not necessarily,' I said. 'If he was staying with kinfolk in the town – an aunt, uncle, grandparents – they could as easily have given him the information. Did Alderman Trefusis have any connection to this story? Might this Deakin have had a grudge against him for any reason?'

'I think Trefusis were always a friend of Sir George,' Maria said at last, and the other two nodded.

'Soldiers together they were, in the French wars,' was Bess's contribution. 'Leastways, so I've allus been told. P'raps he were the one who let Sir George know what was going on. Sir George lived up in his big house in Clifton in them days.'

'That's likely enough,' Margaret agreed. 'That would give the young man a grudge against him.'

'And you never heard a word as to where Miles Deakin came from?'

Margaret shook her head regretfully. 'No, never. Not so much as a whisper. What about you, Bess? Maria?'

But neither woman could throw any further light on the subject. All three looked a little shame-faced at this important gap in their knowledge and were inclined to excuse the lapse as if, somehow, they had failed me. Soon, however, they were anxious to be gone, eager to spread their newly acquired information amongst friends and acquaintances. Long before nightfall there would hardly be a soul anywhere in Redcliffe who had not heard of the stranger in a bird mask who had been seen staring up at Sir George's house the afternoon before he disappeared.

I arrived home to find Richard Manifold seated in our kitchen, but no sign of Adela; an absence soon explained by a message left with the sergeant that she had taken her apples to be baked at Master Cleghorn's bakery in St Leonard's Lane.

'Any news of Sir George?' I asked, sinking down on to the second stool and pouring myself a beaker of ale. Overhead, I could hear the three older children playing.

Richard gave me a curious glance. 'Weren't you present when I made my announcement at the High Cross half an hour ago?'

I shook my head. 'As you can see, I've only just got back.'

'Where have you been? Didn't you get my message that I was calling off the search until tomorrow? Jack Gload and Pete Littleman thought they'd spoken to most folk. And everyone was asked to pass the message on to those who might not have heard. I requested people to assemble at the cross so that I could give them instructions for Tuesday.' There was a short pause while he eyed me speculatively. He was naturally suspicious of me. 'Where did you look? I don't recollect having seen you.'

He was at his most irritatingly self-important. His manner was that of a pedagogue questioning an errant pupil and I was disinclined to say anything of my discovery. I had no proof that this Miles Deakin was in any way involved in the crime. Instead, I mentioned my visit to Margaret Walker and her friends.

He snorted. 'Why, in heaven's name? Those three old biddies won't know anything. All they'll give you is tittle-tattle and gossip.'

'They have some very interesting information sometimes,' I answered defensively. 'Bess Simnel in particular has an excellent memory for her age.' I must remember to warn Margaret and her friends to say nothing to anyone in authority of what I had told them. Not that they would be listened to if they did.

Richard made a dismissive noise but calmed down a little, although he still had a heightened colour. I realized that his anger was really about the fact that I had been ferreting out information on my own and not accompanying the rest of the search party as directed.

'I must go and report to the sheriff on our lack of progress,' he said with a sigh, hauling himself to his feet like a man wearied to the bone. I felt momentarily sorry for him. His Christmas was turning into a nightmare.

'Will you be wassailing tonight?' I asked, following him out to the street door and for once not having to make a pretence of being civil.

He grunted something about chance being a fine thing and went off up Small Street at a rapid pace, meeting Adela coming in the opposite direction. He stopped to speak to her, and I could tell by the way his head kept turning in my direction that he was unburdening himself of his woes.

'What have you been doing to upset Richard now?' she demanded with a sigh as I held the door wide for her to enter. She had a basket on one arm covered with a white cloth and I could smell the fragrant scent of baked apples. With her opposite hand she pulled the little cart on wheels that I had made for Adam and in it Luke sat bolt upright, smiling at everyone. She added, 'We'd better have supper early. As soon as it's really dark, the wassailing will begin.'

By mid-evening I, like most men and quite a few women, was reeling drunk. 'Lamb's wool' is a potent brew and I had had more than my fair share.

We had visited friends and neighbours in the vicinity and further afield, while our own little house had been crammed to capacity by those same friends and neighbours returning our calls. Most people I recognized, but there were quite a few I didn't, animal and bird masks being worn by many, especially the young. And, as I have already said, by mid-evening I was in no state to recognize anybody, being fit only for my bed. Not that I sought it, of course. I remember standing on someone's table, along with a few other choice souls, singing at the top of my voice. (Regrettably, I can't sing because I have no ear for music, and produce the most distressing sounds.) I remember, too, having a fight with Burl Hodge – what about neither of us had the slightest recollection next day – staggering around in the street and eventually falling into the central drain. Even that, and the fact that Burl got bitten on the leg by a rat, didn't sober us. Our enmity forgotten, we just lay there, on our backs, staring up at the starry night sky and laughing inanely like a couple of fools. Finally, members of the Watch, condemned to seeing everyone but themselves get roaring drunk, came and rounded us up, sending us all back to our respective homes to sleep off the results of the wassail and wake to splitting headaches in the morning.

Be sure that Nemesis had her revenge. Retribution was sharp and painful. I do not remember ever having been so ill either before or since.

'I must have been poisoned,' I moaned to Adela halfway through the following morning when, sitting up in bed, white, shaken and very weak, I was myself again and the ghastly consequences of the previous night seemed to be over.

'Nonsense!' she retorted. She was at her most unsympathetic, but I have discovered from long experience that wives usually are where strong drink is involved. 'How could you possibly have been poisoned?'

'Easily,' I snapped, 'if someone's ale had turned sour. Kept in a dirty barrel for too long. I tell you, Adela, I've been sick in the past, and I've had some splitting heads, but never anything like I've experienced tonight. Fortunately, I've always been able to rid myself very quickly of anything bad. My mother maintained that I had one of the most sensitive bellies she'd ever known. I must have eaten or drunk something that was rotten last night.'

'I'm all right,' was the acid rejoinder, 'and I ate and drank everything that you did.'

'You couldn't have done,' I said positively.

I didn't blame her for this lack of sympathy. As is a woman's lot, she had borne the brunt of the clearing up, the emptying of slop buckets, the mopping up of the bedchamber floor, the extra washing and drying of sheets – and this in December – that such upsets entail. Moreover, I had no means of proving my theory, only a knowledge of my own body and, consequently, a growing conviction that this was no ordinary aftermath of drunkenness.

My suggestion of ale which had turned sour was, on the face of it, the most sensible one, but as I lay in bed, listening to the morning household sounds going on below me, the gnawing suspicion that someone might deliberately have tried to kill me gradually tightened its grip. It could so easily have happened. Something dropped in a beaker of 'lamb's wool' which had then been handed specifically to me and the thing was done. There had been such a crowd of people not only in our own, but in every house and cottage we had visited that it would be impossible to guess where or when or by whom such an act was committed.

But who would want me dead? Whose toes was I treading on that he or she might feel it imperative to remove me? Was someone growing afraid that I was getting too close to the truth concerning Alderman Trefusis's murder? If the killer were indeed this Miles Deakin, he could still be in the city in disguise, using another name, waiting to wreak his vengeance on Sir George. Maybe he had already taken his revenge: the knight was certainly missing and no one seemed able to find him. It was a time of year when nobody questioned the wearing of masks; when people ate too much and drank too much, so that sickness and even sudden death were rarely queried.

I dared not share these thoughts with Adela. On the one hand, they would alarm her and, on the other, in order to quell those alarms, she would do as she always did and accuse me of letting my imagination run away with me. And who was to say that she wasn't right? I had no shred of proof that my suspicions had foundation. They were entirely without substance and it was only my instinct that warned me to tread carefully in the near future.

Today was the fifth day of Christmas, and from now until the eleventh day – the Eve of Epiphany or the Eve of Twelfth Night, whichever you preferred to call it – the celebrations abated and normal life temporarily resumed. There would be far less feasting and drinking; indeed, none at all for poorer folk like me and my family. I had plenty of time to recover my health and strength. Happily, I have always had great recuperative powers, and even at the advanced age of thirty-one I was still able to shrug off sickness with comparative ease; far more easily than most people.

Adela knew this as well as I did, so she was not surprised when I tottered downstairs just before dinner. 'It's only pottage,' she said. 'Do you feel you can eat it?'

'I can try,' I answered with forced cheerfulness. 'Is there any news of Sir George? Has he been found yet?'

'Not when I last saw Richard. He called about an hour ago to find out where you were and if you were going to join the search again today. I explained that you were at present laid low, but that, knowing you, you would most likely have recovered sufficiently to join him later.'

The older children arrived and took their places around the table looking rather subdued. They had been kept awake part of the night by the sound of my sufferings and were duly impressed by my capacity for regurgitation.

I wasn't too certain about the pottage; it had a distinctly day-before-yesterday's appearance. However, I manfully swallowed a mouthful and then gave a very loud belch. Luke, tied to Adam's baby chair and being spoonfed by Adela, immediately imitated the noise. His foster brothers and sister were enchanted.

'Do it again, Father,' pleaded Elizabeth, clapping her hands.

'Certainly not!' I exclaimed indignantly. But then another involuntary gust of wind escaped me.

Luke beamed all over his sweet little face and once more repeated the sound. The other three were ecstatic.

'How do you do it, Father?' Adam wanted to know, plainly with a view to practising the art himself.

I frowned at him. 'I don't do it on purpose,' I said. 'It's just wind escaping from my belly.'

My son nodded sagely. 'You were ill in the night. I heard you. P'raps it was because of what that bird man put in your beaker.'

Adela, bending over to wipe Luke's mouth, suddenly jerked upright, while I stared at Adam like someone in a trance.

'What . . . What bird man?' I asked as soon as I could command my voice. I waited while my son emptied his mouth of an over-large spoonful of pottage, then demanded again, 'What bird man?'

'The one who was here last night,' he said. 'Put something in your ale. I saw him.'

I leant across the table and grasped his wrist to prevent him filling his mouth again. 'You mean here, in this house? A man wearing a bird mask?'

'Yes.'

'What sort of bird mask? What sort of a beak did it have?'

'Big one. Like this.' With his free hand, Adam drew a great curve in the air over his own little nose. 'You're hurting my arm,' he added reproachfully.

I released him, recalling as I did so Dame Drusilla's words. 'A bird mask with a great beak.'

Adela was regarding me, eyes wide with fear. 'Roger, do you really think that someone . . .?' She couldn't bring herself to say more.

'It's possible,' I said grimly. I turned back to my son. 'Adam,' I asked sternly, 'are you sure about this? Are you certain that the man in the bird mask put something in my ale?'

'Yes, I'm certain.' Adam stared at me with all the injured air of one whose word is being doubted.

'Here? In this kitchen?'

'I told you! There were some beakers on the table full of that frothy stuff you were all drinking. I saw the bird man drop something in one of them and then give it to you.'

'And I drank what was in it?'

He shook his head. 'I don't know. It was getting awful noisy by then and people were acting very silly. I got under the table with Hercules. But I 'spect you did. You were drinking ever such a lot and acting sillier than anybody else.'

I had the grace to blush at this damning indictment and avoided Adela's look of accusation. Instead, I asked, 'Did you see what it was the bird man dropped in the beaker?'

But Adam was unable to tell me any more than he had done already. I had no doubt at all that it was the truth, for why should he lie? Moreover, it bore out my own suspicions. I thought back, desperately trying to summon up the scene after we had returned from calling on friends and neighbours, when we had acted as hosts; when people had crowded into our little house until it seemed to be bursting at the seams. I had definitely been in the kitchen where a good host should be, dispensing hospitality in the shape of food and drink. But by that time, I was more than a little tipsy and, try as I might, I could recall nothing very clearly. I made a great effort to picture a man in a bird mask, but failed dismally. He had, according to Adam, handed me a drink and had probably wished me, 'Waes Hael!' Had I said, 'Drink Hael!' in return? But I could remember no particular voice, only a cacophony of sounds buzzing in my ears like a swarm of bees.

I had been so lost in thought that I'd failed to realize my family were all waiting for me to speak. I cleared my throat and pushed back my stool. 'You say they're still searching for Sir George?' I asked Adela, and when she nodded, said, 'I'll join them.'

'You've hardly touched your pottage,' my wife pointed out anxiously, and I repressed a shudder.

'My belly's still too upset.' I excused myself.

I was just pulling on my boots, with a little assistance from Bess and Nick, when a knock at the street door heralded the arrival of Richard Manifold. He looked exhausted and Adela fetched him a beaker of ale without waiting to be asked. The two older children vanished upstairs.

'You still haven't found him, then,' I said, not bothering to make it a question.

Richard shook his head before taking a long, steady, grateful draught of ale. 'No.'

I frowned. 'You've searched the crypt under Saint Giles and

what remains of the old synagogue foundations? You know there's a secret chamber at the far end?'

Our guest sighed wearily. 'The answer is "yes" to both questions.'

'And the underground chamber at Saint Mary Bellhouse?'

'Yes, yes! I tell you, Roger, I don't think there's a hiding-place anywhere in this city that hasn't been searched. Empty houses, occupied houses, outhouses, the stews, the inns, the alleyways. We've even armed ourselves and ventured into 'Little Ireland'. We didn't get much cooperation there, as I don't need to tell you, but, in fairness, we weren't obstructed, either. According to them, of course, they're all honest trading folk and I don't doubt some of them are.' He rubbed his nose and sighed again. 'This morning we've searched Sir George's own house from cellar to attic and Dame Drusilla's, next door, as well. The old lady wasn't best pleased and went so far as to say she hoped her brother had finally got what he deserved and was probably at the bottom of the Frome or the Avon. She really hates him, but I can't pretend any of the family members are showing much concern. They all give the impression that if he never turns up again, they won't be shedding any tears.'

'What about Patience? Lady Marvell?'

Richard shrugged and finished the remainder of his ale. 'She seems the least concerned of the lot of them.' He paused, biting a fingernail. 'In some strange way, she seems almost . . . What can I say? Triumphant. Yes, that's the word. Triumphant. Almost as if it was something she had wanted to happen.' He rose to his feet. 'I must be off. If we haven't found Sir George by nightfall, the sheriff has decided to call off the search and assume the knight has either drowned or left the city. As you've said yourself, Roger, it isn't an impossible task nowadays to leave without using the gates with the walls in their present state of disrepair. Will you join the search later or is your belly still giving you trouble?'

I indicated my boots. 'I was just coming to join you when you knocked. The fresh air will do me good.'

Richard grimaced. 'Be careful, then. It's very cold outside.'

Here, Adam, who had not followed his half-brother and -sister upstairs, but remained in the kitchen, a silent listener to his elders' conversation, broke in to remind me that I had promised to take him to see the mummers again that afternoon. His lower lip was trembling pathetically (a trick he had learned very early in life) and his large brown eyes were full of tears. I could remember no such promise, but to deny him would only provoke the kind of scene I felt unable to cope with at the present time.

I glanced at Richard, who was looking disapproving – he thought me far too lenient a father – and said lamely and untruthfully, 'I'd forgotten. But I'll join in the hunt again as soon as the mumming is over.'

He nodded abruptly. 'Go where you like. Covering ground that has already been covered doesn't matter. It's all we can do now.'

TEN

No one else wanted to see the mummers, so Adam and I went by ourselves. After four days, audiences were inevitably growing thinner and we were able to get close to the cart which doubled as a stage and which already stood, awaiting the players, in the outer ward of the castle. To my son's delight the painted curtain, slung between its poles, indicated that the day's performance was to be his favourite play, St George and the Dragon. Indeed, we were so conspicuously close to the edge of the cart that when young Tobias Warrener made his entrance as St George, he singled Adam out for special attention, pretending to be astonished at seeing him in the audience yet again. Heads were turned and smiles exchanged to see the child jumping up and down with self-importance.

I can't pretend that I paid much heed to what was going on. My thoughts were preoccupied by my recent conversation with Richard Manifold and his description of the Marvell family's reaction to Sir George's disappearance. He had described Patience Marvell as having an almost triumphant air about her, and for the first time I began to wonder whether the transaction she had tried to make with Briant of Dungarvon had not been, as I had naturally assumed, to remove either her stepson or step-grandson, but her husband. Perhaps, to begin with, she had revealed neither her own nor Sir George's names, and it was only when, finally, the Irishman had discovered their identities, that he had refused Patience's commission because he suddenly saw his opportunity to avenge Padraic Kinsale himself.

But why would Patience wish to rid herself of her husband? Well, not all marriages were happy and hers might be unhappier than most. Perhaps, too, she knew for a fact that Sir George had left his entire fortune to his son from his second marriage, or even simply to herself, cutting out both Cyprian and James. If this were the case and if she were not fond of her husband, why wait until he died to get her hands on his money? The move from Clifton to Redcliffe, with its proximity to 'Little Ireland', had offered her the opportunity she had needed.

But what of Briant of Dungarvon? He had promised that he would not pursue his vendetta against Sir George, and Humility Dyson had assured me that the Irishman was a man of his word. Set against that, however, was the fact that he was a slave trader and a criminal, even if his trade was blinked at by authority on both sides of the Irish Sea. Could he have changed his mind? After all, when I came to think of it, he had only given me his word that he would not kill Sir George. He had said nothing about abducting him and carrying him off to Ireland. Money was money when all was said and done. Perhaps he had contacted Lady Marvell and renewed their understanding. Perhaps he, and not this Miles Deakin, was the man in the bird mask seen by Dame Drusilla standing outside her brother's house . . .

I pulled myself up short. I was making far too many assumptions and most of them, as usual, without proof. I had no reason to think that Patience Marvell was unhappy in her marriage, except that Sir George was a bad-tempered man, generally disliked. It was true that the little I had seen of them together had implied no great affection on either side, but that didn't mean the lady wished to be rid of her husband. On the other hand, she had wished to be rid of somebody and had been prepared to pay for their removal, arguing with a cold and calculating nature, lacking the more feminine virtues such as tenderness and compassion. But this begged the question: who had murdered Alderman Trefusis? And why? I found it hard to believe that the crime had no connection to subsequent events. And yet, there again, I could be entirely wrong . . .

'Father!' I became aware that Adam was tugging at my sleeve, his face anxiously upturned to mine. 'You're not clapping or shouting. The mumming's over. Didn't you enjoy it?'

I realized with a start that the people all around me were waving their greasy hats in the air or stamping their feet or both, and that the mummers were lined up on the stage, taking their bows.

'You didn't even laugh at the Doctor,' my son added reproachfully. 'It was Master Chorley and he was ever so funny. Is your belly feeling queer again?'

'Yes, yes, that's it,' I agreed, becoming aware that someone was tapping me on the shoulder.

'Master Chapman,' said Tabitha Warrener, still in her guise as the Turkish Knight, 'will you and your son condescend to pay us a visit and drink a beaker of Christmas ale with us? We'd all take it kindly if you would.'

I hesitated a moment before accepting the invitation, but then decided Adela would not be expecting us home for a while, and it might seem churlish to refuse.

'Thank you,' I smiled. 'But if you will forgive me, I'll forgo the ale. I drank too much 'lamb's wool' last night and have been paying for it ever since.'

The old woman looked disappointed, but then laughed. 'A common enough problem this time of year.' She smiled at Adam. 'And did you enjoy the play, young master?'

He nodded, round-eyed and suddenly tongue-tied.

We followed Tabitha into the inner ward and across to the building against the orchard wall, where the rest of the mummers were changing out of their costumes and folding them away into the property chests. I thought Dorcas seemed a little better than she had done two days earlier, but she still looked rather pale and tended to cling to her husband for comfort.

Ned Chorley handed me a beaker of ale which I refused, once again making my excuses. Like Tabitha, he looked disappointed, but accepted my refusal with resignation, merely remarking that illness was a hazard of the season and putting the beaker back on the table.

'Arthur can drink it when he comes in.'

Just at that moment, the door of the outbuilding opened and a head came round the corner; a head wearing a bird mask with a big hooked beak. I heard Adam draw in his breath and felt him jump.

Ned and Tabitha spoke almost together.

'You've found it, Arthur!'

'Where was it?'

Arthur Monkton removed the mask and placed it carefully on the table.

'When I went out to drive the "stage" into the inner ward, it was just sitting there as if it had never gone missing.'

Ned chuckled. 'Someone from the castle borrowed it, I reckon, to go wassailing last night. Someone without a mask of his own and without the money to buy or hire one.' He picked the thing up and turned it around in his hands. 'I'm glad whoever it was had the grace to return it, though. It's one of our best masks, Master Chapman, and when Toby here came to wear it last night, it was missing. We thought someone had stolen it. Never expected to see it again. But here it is, safe and sound. There's honest people in the world, after all.'

'I'd hardly call taking something without permission honest,' I objected. 'As a matter of fact, Adam's been describing someone wearing a mask just like this, wassailing in our house last night.'

'Did he see who it was?' Tabitha wanted to know.

'I'm afraid not. Whoever it was didn't remove it.' Adam would have spoken but I managed to catch his eye and gave my head a little shake. I hoped none of the others noticed. My suspicions of poison I preferred to keep to myself.

'Well, all's well that ends well,' said Ned Chorley comfortably. He poured Arthur Monkton a fresh beaker of ale and I noticed how deftly he managed with his left hand. No doubt he had had years of practise, for the stumps of the two missing fingers on his right looked old and shrivelled, as though they had been lost a long time before. All the same, it was noticeable that he was not naturally left-handed: I had observed on Sunday that he often started to do things with his right hand before recollecting his disability.

After a while longer, I said that Adam and I must be going as I had promised Sergeant Manifold I would help in the continuing search for Sir George Marvell while daylight lasted, and that it would soon be dusk.

'No news of the poor gentleman yet, then?' asked Tabitha, pouring herself more ale.

'No.' I took hold of my son's hand. 'And after today I understand that they're giving up the search. The general belief is that he must have fallen in either the Frome or the Avon and drowned. Although why he left his home during the hours of darkness without telling any of his family where he was going and why is still a mystery.'

The five of them nodded solemnly, then crowded round to

wish us goodbye and thank me again for our hospitality on Sunday.

'Will you be coming to see us perform again before we leave?' Tabitha wanted to know, bending down to give Adam a smacking kiss on one of his rosy cheeks.

'How long are you staying?' I asked.

'Until Twelfth Night.' Ned Chorley patted Adam's head. 'We'll do Saint George and the Dragon once more for you before we go.'

'You'll be glad to get into winter quarters,' I suggested as Adam and I moved towards the door.

Tabitha grunted her assent. 'Especially with Dorcas getting near her time. Let us know, Master Chapman, if anything is heard of the knight.'

Promising faithfully to do so, we took our leave. I walked Adam home before setting out once more, grasping my cudgel firmly in one hand. Heavy-bellied clouds were gathering overhead, pregnant with rain or even, maybe, snow. I had no idea where to find Richard, but that didn't worry me. I had my own goal in mind and, ten minutes later, had crossed the bridge into Redcliffe, making directly for the home of the Marvell family.

Somewhat to my surprise, I was admitted by the steward without hesitation and conducted to a handsome room on the first floor with two fine embrasured windows that looked out on to the river. All the family seemed to be gathered there, Patience Marvell seated in a carved armchair next to a roaring fire which flamed and sparked up the chimney without, so far as I could tell, giving out much warmth. Cyprian's wife, Joanna, was on the opposite side of the hearth in just such another chair, while Cyprian himself stood with his back to the blaze, warming his buttocks in time-honoured fashion. The young men occupied the two window seats, both looking sulky and bored and trying to ignore one another's presence.

'I don't see why we should be expected to help look for Father,' Bartholomew, the slightly younger one, was saying as I entered. His tone was aggrieved. 'He doesn't care two fucks what happens to us.'

Lady Marvell let out a scandalized cry. 'I've told you about using such disgraceful language, Barty! You wouldn't dare say such things if your father were here.'

'But he isn't here,' her graceless son pointed out. 'And maybe,' he added, his face brightening, 'he'll never be here again.'

Cyprian moved at that, striding across the room with his ponderous tread to smack his half-brother around the ears. 'You disrespectful little cur!' he exclaimed. 'It's a great pity you were ever born.'

'Hear, hear!' said James, grinning. 'If, that is, he is Grandfather's son, which I very much doubt.'

It was hardly to be expected that Lady Marvell would let this remark pass unchallenged and she was on her feet immediately, demanding that Cyprian force his son to apologize for the slur on her good name. It was at this point that Cyprian noticed me standing just inside the door and roared at them all to be silent. He hastened forward to greet me.

'Master Chapman, is it not? Have you brought us news of my father? Has Sergeant Manifold or Sergeant Merryweather sent you?'

'I'm afraid not.' Was there a flicker of relief on Patience Marvell's face? 'I'm here to beg some information from you.'

There was a short silence before the older man cleared his throat and said, 'Yes. Yes, of course. Ask us what you like, if you think it will help find my father.'

James slid off his window seat and lounged over to the fire, standing behind his mother's chair and dropping one hand protectively on Joanna's shoulder. Not to be outdone, Bartholomew followed suit, taking up his stance beside Patience.

I addressed my question to Cyprian as temporary head of the household, although I thought it more likely that if anyone had an answer it would be one of the women.

'Master Marvell, I've been told that some three or so years ago a young man – or, at least, a man of about my age – wanted to marry Dame Drusilla.'

I got no further in face of an outburst of laughter from James. 'A man of your age wanted to marry Great-Aunt Drusilla! What nonsense is this?'

Bartholomew sniggered.

'Be quiet, the pair of you!' Cyprian commanded. 'It happens to be true, although I was not aware that the story was common knowledge.' An unbecoming flush spread over his homely features.

'True?' demanded his son incredulously. 'Why did I never hear of it?'

'We were living in Clifton then. There was no reason why you should be told. In fact, the fewer people who knew, the better. The man was a scoundrel and after one thing only: Aunt Drusilla's money. Fortunately, Robert Trefusis found out about it and had the good sense to inform Father of what was going on. Father soon put a stop to the affair, as you may well imagine.'

'Put a stop to it?' James grinned broadly. 'You don't mean the old lady was encouraging this bully-boy?'

'She intended to marry him,' Cyprian replied tersely.

'Well, well!' James's eyes were alight with merriment. 'Who'd have thought the old girl had so much spunk in her?'

Bartholomew sniggered again. For a moment, nephew and uncle were at one.

'What did Grandfather do?' the former wanted to know. 'Pay the young puppy to go away?'

'I believe he took his horsewhip to him.' Cyprian took a deep breath, adding after a moment, 'I'm afraid he half-killed him.' He turned back to me. 'Master Chapman, I hope you have a good reason for resurrecting this very painful episode in my family's past?'

'I wondered, sir, if you, or someone else, can recollect the name of the man in question and where he came from.'

Everyone turned to stare at me. 'Is it important?' Cyprian asked, echoing Margaret Walker's words of the previous day.

I gave him the same answer. 'It might be.'

Joanna Marvell, who seemed quicker-witted than the others, asked, 'Do you think this man had something to do with Alderman Trefusis's murder? That he might have harmed Sir George?'

'God's toenails!' Bartholomew swore, and this time was not reproved by his mother. In fact, Patience's expression was, I thought, a peculiar one. A barely suppressed smirk lifted the corners of her rather thin lips as though, in her opinion, I was making a fool of myself; as though she could tell us all the truth if she chose to. I felt more than ever convinced that the person she had wanted Briant to abduct was her husband, and that in spite of Briant's subsequent refusal, she now thought he had changed his mind and carried Sir George off to Ireland. She was probably waiting, a little nervously, for him to reappear and claim his money.

The rest of them, however, were all exclaiming, expressing either doubts about my theory or hailing it as a possible answer to the mystery.

'Can you remember either the young man's name or where he came from?' I repeated, cutting across this babel.

Cyprian Marvell shook his head and looked enquiringly at the two women. 'Joanna? Stepmother? Can either of you recall his name? As to where he came from, I believe . . .' He paused, obviously searching his memory, then nodded decisively. 'I feel sure he came from Clifton way.'

'You're right,' his wife agreed. 'I think his parents rented one of those smallholdings belonging to the manor.' She sucked in her breath sharply. 'And now I come to think of it, I seem to remember your father saying that he had used his influence with the lord to get them turned off his land.'

If this were true, it was food for thought indeed. 'Do you recall the name of the family, Mistress Marvell?' I pressed.

'Try to recollect, my dear,' Cyprian encouraged her. 'Your memory is so much better than mine.'

I could barely restrain myself from giving her a hint, but I managed to keep a still tongue in my head. At last, however, after what seemed an age, Joanna nodded briskly.

'Yes, I can remember Father-in-law saying that the family's name was Deakin and that the son was called Miles.'

Cyprian slapped his thigh. 'You're right, my love. Now you mention it I, too, recall that that was the fellow's name. Miles Deakin! Do you remember, Stepmother?'

'Yes,' Patience said slowly. 'I do recollect now that that was his name. But why is Master Chapman so sure that this man has anything to do with your father's disappearance?'

'Lady Marvell,' I said, 'I am not sure. Far from it. But the last word Alderman Trefusis uttered before he died was the name Dee. Now, no one seems to know of anyone so called, and it occurred to me that perhaps it was only the beginning of another name altogether.'

'Deakin!' exclaimed James. He regarded me shrewdly. 'You already knew the name, Master Chapman. Someone else has mentioned it to you. Admit it. You just wanted my parents' and grandmother's confirmation.'

'I've told you not to call me by that name, James,' Patience stormed at him, before I could answer. 'I am not your grandmother.'

He grinned insolently. 'Step-Grandmother, then.'

'Be quiet, boy,' his father snapped. He turned once again to me. 'What made you think of this man?'

'It was just a thought, sir,' I answered cagily. 'My wife's cousin, Mistress Walker, had told me the story of Dame Drusilla's quarrel with her brother; the reason for the enmity between them. And her friend, Goody Simnel, told me the young man's name.' Here, Lady Marvell gave a snort and muttered something about 'Redcliffe gossips'. I continued as though she hadn't spoken. 'When I heard that it was Deakin, the thought crossed my mind that maybe that was what Alderman Trefusis had been trying to say. If he had recognized Miles Deakin, it's possible he was trying to warn Sir George.'

Cyprian Marvell was looking as excited as a man of his phlegmatic temperament could do. 'You've informed the authorities of your suspicions, of course?'

'Not yet. I have no proof whatsoever to implicate this Miles Deakin, but now that you and Mistress Marvell' – I nodded at Joanna – 'have confirmed his name I think I should put the suggestion to Sergeant Manifold.'

'You must! You must!' Cyprian was emphatic. 'Indeed, I shall make my own enquiries regarding this Miles Deakin. Do you have any other reason, apart from his name, to believe he might be the alderman's murderer? The man who, possibly, has abducted my father?'

'In all truthfulness, no. Dame Drusilla did mention to me, however, when I called on her yesterday, that, the previous afternoon, she had noticed a man in a bird mask staring up at this house. That same night, Sir George vanished. But who the person was there's no means of telling, nor if he had anything to do with your father's disappearance. At this season of the year, the wearing of masks is commonplace. All the same, I have never liked coincidences.'

'Nor I.' Cyprian Marvell stood for a moment chewing his

bottom lip, then held out his hand. 'Master Chapman, I congratu-
late you. You seem to have discovered more – and made more
use of that discovery – than Sergeants Manifold and Merryweather
put together. I've heard of you, of course, and your reputation
for solving mysteries. I know that you are close to the Duke of
. . . I – I mean, the king.' I made protesting noises, but they
were, as always nowadays, discounted. 'If there is anything else
any of us can do to aid your enquiries . . .'

'There is one thing,' I said. 'Dame Drusilla was unable to
inform me if the man in the mask called at this house. Can your
steward or any of your servants tell me if that was so?'

James was immediately despatched to fetch the steward and,
while we waited, I noticed that Patience Marvell was regarding
me with a warier eye than she had done hitherto. If I knew so
much, what else did I know? I returned her gaze blandly.

The steward, when he arrived, assured me that he was unaware
of any caller at the house on Childermass Day.

'Sunday, was it not, sir? No, I cannot recall anyone coming
to the house. The master and family went to church, but otherwise
there was very little activity. You must remember that yourself,
Master Cyprian. A very quiet day.'

'And none of the other servants can recall anyone coming to
the door?' I asked.

'No, sir.'

Cyprian nodded dismissal and the steward withdrew.

'Could someone be lying?' asked Joanna.

Her husband shook his head. 'I see no good reason why they
should.'

But if no one had called to leave a note or a message for Sir
George, then he had not left the house in response to any
summons. The man seen by Dame Drusilla might not have had
anything to do with his vanishing. Then, just as I was about to
take my leave, another idea struck me.

'Can anyone remember if Sir George left the house at all on
Sunday afternoon?'

There was a general shaking of heads, except for Bartholomew,
who said, 'Father did go out after dinner. I saw him from my
bedchamber window. I don't know how long he was gone because
I didn't see him come back. He was home in time for supper,

although he might have returned well before then. Why do you ask?'

'Because it occurs to me that the man in the mask could have waylaid Sir George and delivered his message, either spoken or written, in person. And now you tell me that your father did go out, I think this may well be what happened. Provided, of course,' I added with a sigh, 'Master Bird Mask has anything to do with the matter.'

I could see that Cyprian, his wife and the two young men were very much inclined to regard the mystery as solved as soon as Miles Deakin could be found and questioned. What Patience Marvell's thoughts were was more difficult to fathom.

'You'll go to Master Sheriff or one of the sergeants now, tonight?' Cyprian asked urgently, shaking my hand as if I were an equal.

'Not yet,' I said and glanced towards the windows. Outside, the sky had darkened as the short December day drew to its close, and the leaded glass panes – a sure sign of money – showed nothing now except the reflected flames of the candles lit by the steward before he left the room. When Cyprian would have voiced a protest, I said, 'I should prefer to consider this idea a little longer, sir. I need to convince myself that it's justified before I drag a man's name in the mud or put him in peril of the hangman's noose.' I didn't add that I guessed Richard Manifold and Tom Merryweather, desperate for a suspect for Alderman Trefusis's murder, would embrace my theory all too eagerly, even if they deeply resented my interference.

The older man would have demurred, but his son came unexpectedly to my aid. 'Master Chapman's right, Father,' he said quietly. 'In fact, before a word is said to anyone in authority about this Miles Deakin, an effort should be made to find him and at least discover if he could possibly be the culprit. And if he can positively prove his innocence, then nothing regarding him need be mentioned. You say his parents had a smallholding rented from the lord of Clifton Manor?'

'But remember I told you,' his mother reminded him, 'that I believe your grandfather used his influence to get them evicted. It's no good looking there. The man is probably somewhere in the city, disguised.'

'Nevertheless,' James argued, 'Clifton seems to me to be the place to start. Someone there might be able to tell us what became of the family.' He looked across at me. 'Master Chapman, would you care to accompany me to Clifton tomorrow morning? Together, we might discover something.'

The honest answer was, 'No,' but I could see what was in his mind. As a Marvell, as Sir George's grandson, as a resident since birth of that now abandoned house on the heights above Bristol, he could probably command answers from people I should hesitate to question. Besides, I was growing to quite like James, in contrast to Bartholomew, whom I felt to be a whining, sulky mother's boy.

'Very well,' I agreed. 'I'll meet you at the High Cross after breakfast and we'll walk up to Clifton together.'

'Walk?' he asked with an incredulous laugh. 'Walk? My dear man—'

He got no further. The door burst open and the steward appeared, his face the colour of old parchment.

'Master Cyprian,' he said, his voice trembling so much that he found it hard to get the words out, 'come quickly! Sergeant Manifold's below. They've just fished a body out of the River Avon.'

ELEVEN

There was a moment's complete silence while we all stood, rigid with shock, staring upon the poor man as if he were holding the head of the Medusa.

I think I moved and spoke first, my voice coming out in a kind of hoarse croak 'Whose . . . Whose body?'

The steward shook his head. 'Sergeant Manifold didn't say, sir. Just . . . just that a body had been found.' He turned again to Cyprian. 'Do come, master. Do come and hear what the sergeant has to say.'

But I was already out of the door before he had finished speaking. Richard was waiting at the bottom of the stairs, his face looking haggard in the flickering light of the fire burning on the hearth of the main hall. He glanced up as I started to descend, a shade of annoyance marring his not unhandsome features as he realized who it was.

'You!' he exclaimed. 'What are you doing here?'

I was saved the trouble of replying by Cyprian's arrival hard on my heels.

'Sergeant Manifold,' he quavered, 'is the body that of my father?'

Richard shook his head. 'I don't know yet, Master Marvell. It was still being hauled out of the water when I left. I thought it right to inform you straight away so that you could prepare yourself for the worst. I didn't wish you to hear the news from anyone else.'

I reflected silently that such an action was somehow typical of the man: earnest, dedicated, anxious to please but never quite getting his priorities right; always prone to do the wrong thing.

James, joining his father at the foot of the stairs, said furiously, 'Then why bother us, Sergeant, until you were certain? The shock to Lady Marvell and my mother has been profound. And may prove to be unnecessary. Where is the body?'

'Saint Nicholas Back,' was the reply as Richard flushed angrily at this rebuke.

'Then we'd better waste no more time and go there at once.' James addressed one of the servants who had crowded into the hall, telling him to fetch his and his father's cloaks. 'The warm ones with the fur linings.' He turned to Bartholomew who, with his mother and Joanna, made a small, huddled group in the middle of the stairs. 'Bart, look after the women while we're gone. Try not to imagine the worst.' He spun round again. 'Master Chapman, I'd be more than grateful if you would accompany us.'

I didn't tell him that nothing on earth would keep me away, merely inclining my head graciously. (I caught Richard's quickly suppressed snort of amusement.)

The cloaks having been brought and I having wrapped myself up warmly in mine, Cyprian and James Marvell and I followed Richard out into the cold December night. The month was ending as it had begun with sharp flurries of wind and sleet.

The four of us half-walked, half-ran through Bear Alley, along Redcliffe Street and across the bridge, turning left into St Nicholas Back, by which time we were having to force a passage through a gathering crowd. News of a dead body found in the Avon had spread fast and people were emerging from their houses, braving the winter weather, to see for themselves. Richard was compelled to use his voice as well as his staff of office to clear a path.

'In the king's name, make way for his officers of the law. Stand aside! Stand aside!'

Jack Gload and Pete Littleman were keeping guard over a dimly visible shape lying at full length on the quayside and smelling to high heaven. A couple of stalwart sailors from one of the neighbouring ships who, by their bedraggled appearance, had evidently assisted in rescuing the corpse, were also helping to keep the crowd at bay. Ripples of light, reflections from the various cressets and torches, turned the surface of the river to molten gold.

Richard stepped forward, holding his own torch high above his head so that the face of the dead man was suddenly illumined . . .

It was not Sir George Marvell.

Cyprian gave a gasp of what could have been relief. On the other hand, it might have been one of disappointment. James gave no reaction whatsoever.

Richard Manifold frowned. 'Does anyone recognize who it is?' he asked.

I drew a deep breath. 'Yes, I do,' I said. 'It's an Irish slave trader known as Briant of Dungarvon.'

The body had been carried into St Nicholas's Church, down into the crypt, and laid out on the lid of one of the larger stone sarcophagi. Most of the crowd had gone home, cheated of their very just hope that another gory murder had been uncovered. Cyprian and James Marvell had also returned to Redcliffe Wharf to reassure Bartholomew and the two women that the drowned man was not Sir George. Before he left, James had reminded me – but, thankfully, out of Richard Manifold's hearing – of our assignation the following morning.

'Meet me at the Frome Gate,' he had said, 'as soon after the dinner hour as you can. I shall hire a couple of nags from the Bell Lane stables. I'm damned if I'm going to trudge up those hills or ride our own decent horses.'

'It wouldn't take much more than an hour's good, steady walking,' I protested, knowing how uncomfortable I always was on horseback.

But he had proved adamant, and noting that Richard was regarding us with suspicion, I reluctantly agreed. At least the lazy young devil had had the sense to postpone our journey until after dinner.

Now, in the light of a flaring torch held by Pete Littleman, I was staring down on the remains of what had, until so recently, been Briant of Dungarvon. And 'remains' was the word for what was left of him. His corpse, stripped of its sodden clothing, was shown to be a mass of bruises and broken limbs. There appeared not to be a whole bone left in his body.

'Somebody made a good job of 'im,' Pete remarked gloatingly. 'Like a rag doll with no stuffing, 'e be.'

Richard Manifold pursed his lips. 'I don't believe any person did this,' he said after a while. 'It's more like he's fallen from a great height. I remember a body we fished out of the Avon some six, maybe seven years ago. A poor fellow who'd been pushed off the top of Ghyston Cliff by his wife's lover into the river below. The other man confessed what he'd done in the end, and was hanged for it. He told us how the first man's body had kept bouncing from one rock to the other as he fell all the way down the side of the gorge before finally ending up in the river. And I reckon that's what's happened to this Irish slave trader of yours, Roger. He was probably carried out seawards by the ebb and flow, then washed back in by the next high tide, right up to Saint Nicholas Back.'

Immediately, I knew that Richard's reading of the situation was right. Briant's body had been battered to pieces. The injuries were greater than any one, or even two, men could inflict. And in order for him to end up in the Avon, a fall from Ghyston Cliff was the most likely answer. But what had he been doing up on the downs? Humility Dyson had told me plainly that Briant had gone to join the Clontarf which, according to his information, had dropped anchor at Rownham Ferry. That would have entailed taking the riverside path around the base of the hills that rose above the city. Why would he have walked up to Clifton perched, as its name implies, high above the gorge? Unless . . . Unless, perhaps, he had seen and followed someone up there. And who was that someone likely to be other than Sir George Marvell, who might also have left the city that same night?

I checked my wandering thoughts. As I was far too prone to do, I was making unwarranted assumptions, bricks without straw. The only two incontrovertible facts were that the knight was still missing and that Briant of Dungarvon was dead.

'What will you do with the corpse?' I asked.

Richard shrugged. 'For the time being he can stay here – decently covered, of course. Then, when the coroner's pronounced him dead of accidental causes, he can be tossed into the common pit.'

This callous pronouncement chilled me to the bone. This was a man with whom I had walked and talked very recently. Now he was nothing but a lump of rotting flesh to be disposed of as soon as possible and with as little dignity as possible, thrown into the common pit along with executed criminals and stray animals. I repressed a shudder.

'What a Christmas this is turning out to be,' Richard grumbled. 'Alderman Trefusis murdered, Sir George missing and now this.' He gave a quick glance around the musty-smelling crypt. 'Well, there's nothing more we can do here until I inform the coroner in the morning. Jack, before you go home find something to cover this thing.' He jerked his head at Briant's lifeless body. 'And make sure the crypt's locked behind you when you leave. Are you coming, Roger?'

I cast one last look at the dead slave trader before following Richard up the steps and into the church. As we stepped outside into the cold and windy dark, he remarked suspiciously, 'You and young James Marvell seemed very friendly.'

'He's easy enough to get along with,' I answered, settling my hat more firmly on my head and turning up the collar of my cloak against a little flurry of sleet. 'Not like the other one, Bartholomew.'

Richard grunted and said no more, but I could tell he wasn't satisfied. Nevertheless, he wished me an amicable goodnight when we parted in the middle of the High Street, he to walk up St Mary le Port Street in the direction of the castle, I to return to Small Street and Adela. Except that I didn't; at least, not immediately. Instead, I ventured into Marsh Street to seek out Humility Dyson at the Wayfarer's Return.

At first, he found it hard to take in the news of Briant's death and even harder to accept Richard's theory of how he met it.

'What would he have been doing up on Ghyston Cliff, Master Chapman, tell me that! It don't make sense. He'd gone to join the Clontarf at Rownham Ferry. He'd not been up on the heights above.' But he lost interest in the cause of death when I told him what was planned for the corpse. His mouth – or what I could see of it, almost smothered as it was by the profusion of his beard – tightened to a thin red line. 'I'll tell the lads,' he said. 'Saint Nicholas crypt, you say?'

'It'll be locked.'

He managed a smile, albeit a wintry one. 'Not after midnight it won't be.'

'Take care. The Watch has been reinforced.'

'We'll manage.' He laid a hand on my arm. 'They won't forget this, Master Chapman. In future, they'll look after you like one of their own. If ever you find yourself in serious trouble and in need of help, just come to "Little Ireland".'

For what it was worth, I thanked him. Finally, I went home.

The last day of December dawned a little brighter than the previous two. It was the Sixth Day of Christmas. We were halfway through.

Neither Adela nor I was at our best: we had sat up late discussing the latest episode in what was turning out to be an all too eventful holiday. Initially, my return had been greeted with the inevitable questions and reproaches as to where I had been and what had taken me so long.

'The search for Sir George was abandoned more than an hour ago,' Adela had informed me angrily. 'Jack Nym called in and told me so. He couldn't understand why you weren't back.' But her tune changed to one of concern once I had explained what had happened. 'Sweetheart, I don't like it. There's something evil abroad, and you're getting drawn, as usual, into whatever is going on.'

I reassured her as much as I could, but the subsequent news that I was riding up to Clifton with James Marvell the following morning very quickly undid all my good work. When we finally went to bed, if we were still on speaking terms, we weren't the best of friends.

The strained atmosphere lasted all through breakfast and hastened the three older children's departure for their eyrie upstairs, where their parents' disagreements were soon forgotten in the games and imaginings of childhood.

I spent the time before dinner coaxing the Yule log to continue burning for the remaining six days of Christmas by piling more straw and small twigs around it. It meant bad luck if it went out before Twelfth Night, and I felt we had had more than our fair share of that one way and another. I blew hard on some still-glowing ashes until they sparked and crackled into a tiny flame, catching the new fuel alight. Next, I cleaned and inspected my boots, making sure that a new patch just above the left heel was watertight, before checking the contents of the water barrel and fetching more logs from the yard. The doing of these ordinary domestic tasks soothed me a little and reminded me that normal life still existed.

Just before ten o'clock, as Adela was laying out the spoons and bowls ready for dinner, Burl Hodge called in to know if we were going to see the mummers' performance that afternoon. He didn't seem particularly disappointed when I said I had other plans; he was too full of news.

'Such a to-do as you never heard,' he told me, 'going on at Saint Nick's. Someone's broken into the church and the crypt during the night and taken away that dead body what was there. The one they pulled out the river last evening.' He chuckled. 'Sergeant Manifold's in a rare taking, I can tell you, wanting to know how anyone knew it was being left there overnight. Berating poor old Jack Gload and Peter Littleman like they was a couple of pickpockets, and both of 'em denying they'd said a word to anybody about it.'

He eventually went on his way, still chuckling.

I wondered how long it would be before my name occurred either to Richard or to one of his henchmen and, once it had, how long before the former realized that he had hit on the truth. Consequently, I hurried my meal, even refusing a second helping of frumenty, some of which still remained from Christmas Day. Adela was plainly suspicious of this abstention, but refrained from comment. Within an hour of first sitting down to table, I was at the Frome Gate, muffled in my good, thick winter cloak and my hat pulled well down around my ears. I hadn't taken my cudgel: it was too unwieldy to cope with on horseback.

A raw, nipping wind made me shiver in spite of being so warmly wrapped up, and I prayed that James Marvell would not keep me waiting long. A sudden thought that perhaps the Marvell family ate at a fashionably later hour than ten o'clock had just determined me to return home if he did not show up soon, when he arrived riding a placid brown cob and leading another on a short rein.

'Master Chapman!' he hailed me cheerfully. 'Well met!' He indicated the horses. 'I hope these fellows meet with your approval. They told me at the Bell Lane stables that you're an uneasy rider.' His grin made me wonder what else had been said to describe my lack of horsemanship, but I thought it wisest not to enquire. He went on: 'So the stable master recommended these cobs. Nice, quiet beasts, he said they are. I hope you approve.'

'Thank you,' I said, mounting the second horse and taking the reins. I noticed James eyeing my patched and mended leather gloves with a slightly puzzled frown. Because of my past association with the king, people always assumed that, if not rich, I at least had plenty of money. Many of them thought the way I dressed a deliberate attempt to mislead them as to my true calling, whatever they believed that to be.

There was no sparkle of frost this morning, only a leaden sky and a threat of snow. The landscape was devoid of colour, a monotonous brown and black and grey, and I couldn't help wondering what it was like to live in one of those countries, described by the foreign sailors, where everything blossomed into light and brilliance under the always shining sun. Native sailors, who had visited these climes, assured the stay-at-homes we wouldn't like it. 'You'd miss the rain,' they said. Or, 'Too much sun and heat can send you mad.' Or yet again, 'You'd be crying out to see something green.' Most of the time I suspected they were right. But this morning, I wasn't so sure.

Having crossed the Frome Bridge, we rode westwards for a little way along the northern bank of the river, then turned northwards by St Augustine's Abbey and began to climb the first of the hills that led eventually to the high plateau of ground known simply as the downs. There had been a time when this had been nothing but wild country watered by the little streams that ran downhill to be trapped by the Carmelites in their great water cistern and then piped to various troughs and conduits across the city. Its only population had been outlaws and vagabonds preying on unwary travellers as they made their way southwards to do business in Bristol or visit family and friends. But for the past hundred years or so the town had spread beyond its confining walls, and by now there were little settlements, smallholdings and even quite substantial farms dotting the landscape all the way up to Clifton Manor. This had itself burst its original boundaries to embrace what had formerly been independent homesteads, in many cases nothing more than a cottage and a bit of land on which to grow a few vegetables and maybe keep a pig or goat. Such, I imagined, had been the Deakins' holding until Sir George had used his influence to get them turned off.

Up there, on the high ground, the wind was bitter, and I was thankful when James suggested we take shelter in the nearest ale-house to warm our numbed feet and hands before making any enquiries. There was a small hostelry close by the main track, not particularly well lit nor particularly well patronized on this freezing Wednesday morning when most people were either working or sleeping off the effects of their Christmas wassail. We were therefore able to sit close to the fire and hold our chilled fingers to the cheerful blaze. A quick glance revealed that, apart from ourselves, there was only one other customer in the place – a tough, wiry little man with a brown beard and complexion to match, seated at a nearby table. As we entered the ale-house, I had noticed outside a handcart piled with sacks, and a few candles spilled from the mouth of one of them.

When we had been served with our ale, I spoke to him. ''Morning, master. Are you the chandler in these parts?'

He raised his beaker to me in salutation. 'I'm a chandler, certainly, and I sell my wares hereabouts as well as elsewhere. Plenty o'money in Clifton.'

He looked as though he would like to enquire what my trade was. He was obviously puzzled by the disparity in the quality of my dress and that of my companion.

'Been selling up here long?' I asked.

'Five year 'n more, I reckon.'

This caught James's attention. 'Then, sir, do you remember a family of the name of Deakin? If my information is correct, they had a smallholding somewhere around here.'

The man sucked some ale thoughtfully through his beard. 'That's right,' he said after a moment or two's reflection.

''T'weren't much of a place and the couple didn't do any business with me. Couldn't afford even tallow candles, as I recall. Made their own rush lights. But I remember 'em.'

'There were three of them,' I said. 'There was a son called Miles.'

'So there was.' The chandler drained his beaker. 'Bit of a braggart and a swaggerer, he were.'

'In what way?'

'Always boasting he was going to do better for himself than work himself to death on a bit o'barren land that was only fit for pigs.'

'And did he?' James asked.

'Did he what?'

'Better himself.'

The chandler shrugged. 'I dunno. The whole family disappeared from hereabouts sudden-like about four years ago. No, I tell a lie. It were three years since. T'were the year Thomas Lloyd and John Jay set sail to find the Isle of Brazil and were lost at sea for so many weeks everyone thought they were drowned.'

'Has anything ever been heard or seen of them since?' James wanted to know. 'The Deakins, I mean.'

The chandler shook his head. 'I wouldn't know, master. Not by me, they haven't, but you'd need to ask around the manor. I'm only up this way once a month. At the time, the story was that the old couple had been turned out on account of something that feckless Miles had done, although no one knew for certain what. It was said that that Sir George Marvell – him that used to live in that great house near Ghyston Cliff – was behind it.' The man's eyes narrowed suddenly and he leant forward, peering more closely at James. 'Here! I recognize you, don't I? You're one of 'em. The Marvells. You're one of the two young lads I used to see about when I called at the house. Wax candles only your housekeeper bought. Nothing but the best for Sir George and his family.'

James smiled uncomfortably. 'I'm his grandson.'

The chandler looked resentful. 'Living down in Bristol now, I'm told. Leaving that great place to rot and moulder. Cost me half my takings in this part o'the world when you lot moved away.' He called for another beaker of ale, then went on: 'Rumour says people have been seen of late in and around that house.'

'What do you mean?' James asked sharply.

'Just what I say. Mind you, it's only what I've been told by customers. I've not noticed anything, myself. But then, I'm not here that often, am I? And in any case, I don't go that far up nowadays.'

'What sort of people have been seen there?'

Our fellow traveller received his fresh beaker of ale from the landlord and took several gulps before replying.

'Don't know. But there's talk of people and lights having been seen in and around the house only recently. Within the past few days. Some folk are beginning to say the place is haunted. Or else it's being used by smugglers or slavers for their own wicked purposes.'

I laughed at that. 'Smugglers and slavers aren't going to use anywhere this high up,' I protested. 'Who's going to bring goods either up or down Ghyston Cliff? It's absurd.'

'All right! All right!' the chandler said pacifically. 'No call to get heated about it. I'm only telling you what people have been saying. It may all be moonshine. Still, don't alter the fact that it's a wicked shame to let a house like that just fall to pieces. If Sir George don't want to live there himself, why not let his son and daughter-in-law live there?'

'Because he likes to have his family under his thumb,' James said bitterly.

'I've heard that.' The chandler finished his second drink and got to his feet. 'Well, this won't do. Must be about my business. Nice to have talked to you, masters.' He pulled on his hat, wrapped his thick frieze coat around him and disappeared out of the door. We heard his handcart rattling over the uneven pathway.

I looked at James. 'Do you think we should investigate these rumours that people have been seen around, or near, your grandfather's house?'

He grunted. 'I think we must. It'll turn out to be a mare's nest, I daresay, but we ought to satisfy ourselves that no one's broken in. Although it would serve the old man right if someone had.

I'm afraid it will be filthy and infested with rats.' He regarded my old and darned clothes critically. 'But I don't suppose you'll mind that too much.'

I smiled. Adela had urged me to wear one of my decent suits of clothes, but I could see no reason to do so for an expedition such as this.

We left the manor behind, riding even higher up to where the track branched off to the right, going towards Westbury. Instead, we veered left on to rougher ground, past the remains of the ancient hill-fort which local legends reckon was built before the time of the Conqueror by either the Saracens or the Jews. (All nonsense, of course. What did folk imagine a bunch of Saracens were doing in the West Country? And the Jews had come in William's wake.) Others say the fort was built by a giant named Ghyst in the time of the two great giants, Vincent and Goram, who had hewed the gorge through the living rock. Be that as it may, passing the place has always given me a tingle down the spine – an eerie feeling, as of something evil. That day the sensation was even stronger as I looked at the circle of large, upright stones and the smaller ones scattered among them. A vision of human sacrifice flitted into my mind and refused to go away.

The Marvell house – or Ghyston House, as James informed me it had always been known – stood on the flat plateau at the very summit of the high ground before it began to slope away again towards the mouth of the River Avon and the open sea. In the wintry afternoon light it looked forbidding, surrounded by leafless trees and dripping bushes which were starting to run riot for want of pruning. Paths were becoming overgrown with yellowing grass pushing through cracks in the paving stones, while everywhere there was a stench of rotting vegetation. A bleak, lonely and inhospitable place it must have been, I thought, even when the family were living there.

As though he could read my thoughts, James said, 'Miserable heap, ain't it? Cold all the year round, even in the height of summer. I can't tell you how happy we all were three months ago when Grandfather decided to move down to Bristol.'

'Can you get inside?' I asked.

He grinned. 'I don't have a key, if that's what you mean. But

there's a window at the back with a loose shutter belonging
to the bakehouse. Bart and I used to use it for getting in and out
unseen. Just follow this path round . . .'

I interrupted him, gripping his arm. 'There's no need,' I hissed.
'Look! The door's open.'

And just as I spoke, a gust of wind caught the heavy, nail-
studded leaf, swinging it on its hinges.

TWELVE

We looked at one another, a fearful speculation in our eyes. Then James said firmly, 'It must have been forced. Only my grandfather has a key.'

But the door had not been forced. There was no splintered wood, just a slight creaking as it swung again on its hinges. I began very much to wish that I had brought my cudgel with me, inconvenient as it would have been on horseback. Instinctively I fingered the knife at my belt, but recalled uneasily that when I had cut my meat with it at dinner, it had been blunt. I had meant to sharpen it before I left home, but in my anxiety to get away, I had forgotten. Fortunately, my companion, being a gentleman, was wearing a poniard – one of those fancy daggers with an elaborate, gem-studded hilt and a slim, but lethal, blade.

We exchanged another look and James took a deep breath. 'We must tether the horses and go in,' he said.

I nodded.

A minute or so later, the cobs' reins safely wound around the lower branches of a convenient tree, we mounted the low step outside the door, which I pushed open with a cautious hand. Then we both started back with a startled yell as something swooped towards us out of the darkness with a great beating of wings and a long, ululating cry before flying twice around the hall and away out of the door in the direction of the gorge.

'God's flesh!' breathed James, supporting himself against one of the door jambs. 'What was that?'

'Only an owl,' I gasped, trying to laugh but not quite managing it. 'We must have disturbed its slumbers.'

James steadied himself with an effort. 'Sweet Virgin, is that all? I thought it was the Devil himself come to greet us.' He forced himself upright and glanced at the front of the house. 'You know, it's only eleven or twelve weeks ago that I was living here, but for some reason today it feels like a different place. There's something malignant about it that I never noticed before.'

'That's because it's been empty for all this time. Without its furniture it echoes, and there are no welcoming lights.' I squared my shoulders. 'Come on! Let's go in. Standing here quaking at the knees won't help us.' And I resolutely pushed the door open once again.

Our boots striking the stone flags sounded unnaturally loud in our ears, and a drift of dried leaves, blown around the floor in the draught from the door, was like the pattering of ghostly feet. Moreover, as James had predicted, we could also hear the scurrying of rats as they headed for their holes and safety.

The house was built on the old pattern, with the great entrance hall soaring up into the roof and the rafters high above our heads. At the far end was a dais, while a series of doors pierced the walls to left and right of us, leading to other rooms and the staircases rising to different levels.

James shivered. 'There's a strange odour,' he whispered, his voice shaking a little as he spoke. 'Can you smell it?'

'It's only the mustiness of the house, where it's been shut up,' I said. 'Do you think anybody's here? Sir George, perhaps? You did say he's the only person who has a key and the door was unlocked.'

'What in God's name would he be doing here?' James snapped. 'In a cold, dark house with no furniture? Don't be a fool, man!'

I didn't take offence, recognizing his irritability for what it was. The place, in spite of so recently being his home, was making him feel as scared as I was. He was right; there was an unpleasant odour that didn't come simply from neglect and decay. There was something evil in the air. I, too, shivered.

I nodded at the first door on our left. 'What's through there?'

'My grandfather used that as his private room. His and Patience's bedchamber is immediately above it, reached by some spiral stairs set against one wall. The next door opens on to the main staircase which leads up to the women's solar and, above that again, my parents' former bedchamber and mine. The third door on this side is the entrance to the kitchens, pantry, buttery, bakery and so on. Over there' – he nodded to the doors on our right – 'is firstly the main parlour with Bart's bedchamber up above; the second is the door to the counting-house and the last one leads to the servants' quarters, on all levels. You can get to the brewery and the laundry that way, too.'

While he had been talking my eyes had grown accustomed to the gloom, and it was when another gust of wind caught the door, blowing it wide again, that what I had thought to be a pool of shadow at the foot of the dais, at the far end of the hall, suddenly assumed the form of a body. I drew a sharp breath.

'What is it?' James demanded.

I didn't answer directly. 'Is there any chance of finding a candle, or a lantern, or a light of any sort in here?' I asked. 'And, of course, we'll need a tinderbox.'

'Why? What do you want them for?' His voice was becoming shrill. He heard it himself and made a deliberate effort to control his mounting fear. 'I'll go and look in the counting-house,' he said. 'Something may have got left behind.'

He returned within a very few minutes with two lighted candles, each in its candlestick, one held in either hand.

'We're in luck,' he said, adding a little shakily, 'Or if it's not luck, then someone has been here recently. As well as the candles and tinderbox, there are also a couple of lanterns.' He handed me one of the candles. 'Now tell me what this is about.'

'It may be nothing at all,' I answered, trying to sound reassuring. 'But I thought I saw something lying at the foot of the dais.' I moved forward as I spoke, holding my candle aloft. The flame made the shadows leap and race up the walls, assuming grotesque shapes.

'There is something there,' James breathed, pushing past me and also raising his candle. The next moment he gave a horrified, gurgling cry and staggered back, almost falling over me, his free hand pressed to his mouth. 'G-God in heaven,' he stuttered. 'What . . . What have they done to him?' His knees sagged and he fell to the floor, rocking himself backwards and forwards and making a dreadful keening sound as he did so.

Almost afraid to look, I stepped to the sprawled shape on the floor, raising my candle even higher . . .

Sir George Marvell was lying on his back, his throat black with congealed blood where it had been cut from ear to ear, his eyes wide and staring. Or at least, they would have been had the eyeballs not been gouged from their sockets. Had that been all, it would have been more than enough, but his upper clothes had been ripped from his body to expose his chest and into his right breast someone had carved the word 'DIE'.

I don't know how long I stood there, transfixed by this gruesome sight. I was vaguely aware of James getting to his feet and rushing to the door. Then I heard him vomiting outside. My brain seemed to have ceased to function. All I could think of was that however unpleasant a man Sir George had been, he had not deserved to be treated like this.

James's voice jerked me back to reality. He must have re-entered the hall without my being conscious of it.

'Why . . .?' He tried to control the tremble in his voice. 'Why would someone want to mutilate Grandfather like that? Why . . . Why have they carved "DIE" into his chest? What he must have suffered . . .'

I shook my head. 'If it's any comfort to you, he was dead before that happened.'

'How can you possibly know?'

'There's very little blood,' I pointed out. 'Only a bead or two. That means his heart had stopped beating when that was done to him. Otherwise, there would have been far more blood all over his breast. I suspect the same goes for his eyes.'

My companion expelled his breath in a great sigh. 'That's some consolation, I suppose. But . . . But why would anyone want to disfigure him when he was already dead? I mean, why write "DIE"?'

'I don't know,' I said.

I was beginning to regain control of my limbs and breathing, and my mind had started to function in an orderly fashion once more. I led James back to the door where the nipping winter air revived us still further. The sky overhead was leaden and there was no glimpse of the sun, but I guessed it to be well past noon. In three or four hours it would be growing dark. Something had to be done.

'What ought we to do?' he asked at almost the same moment. All his natural confidence had ebbed and I suddenly realized how young he really was.

'You must ride down to Bristol and fetch the sheriff and whatever help is available,' I told him. 'You're a good rider and it's all downhill, so it shouldn't take you that long to get there. It will be a different story, of course, coming back. You must also break the news to Lady Marvell and your parents.'

'What will you do?'

'I shall remain here with Sir George's body until help arrives. We can't, in Christian charity, leave it on its own – not now that we know it's here. The search for Miles Deakin will have to wait until another day.'

James snuffed his candle, putting it down on the floor, and fastened his cloak. The colour was coming back into his cheeks, together with some of his self-assurance now that he had something definite to do. 'Do you still think he's involved?'

'I don't know,' I said. 'I think it's possible.'

I walked with him to where the cobs were tethered and watched him mount.

'Will you be all right?' he asked. 'On your own.'

His concern suddenly made me feel old. 'Yes, of course I will,' I answered with asperity. 'Why shouldn't I be?'

'Well, you've nothing but that knife of yours with you.' He spoke with some disdain, and not without cause, of my plain, wooden-handled meat knife. 'If somebody came back . . .'

'Why in God's name should they?' I snapped. 'Your grandfather has been dead some days. My guess would be he was killed the night he disappeared. Whoever did that to him is long gone. He isn't coming back to admire his handiwork. And now, get going! As fast as you can.'

James dug his heels into the horse's sides and I watched as man and beast disappeared at a gallop. Then I led my own cob around the side of the house in search of the stables. These I discovered at the back, along with other outbuildings and, providentially, still boasting a good supply of straw. There was even a sack of feed, starting to go mouldy, it was true, but my hardy mount seemed to find nothing amiss with it and began to eat as soon as I put some in a manger. Satisfied that I had done my best by the animal, I retreated to the front and went back into the hall.

My candle had by now gone out and I had to grope about on the floor until I found the tinderbox where James had dropped it. On the dais was a broken-down armchair which had obviously not been considered worth taking when the Marvell family moved house. Carefully avoiding the body on the floor, I lowered my bulk into it, expecting the worst. But, rickety as it was, the thing held.

I wondered how long it would be before I could reasonably expect to see anyone. If he could keep up his initial pace, there was a good chance that James might reach Bristol within half an hour or so. But after that, who knew? People had to be roused and acquainted with the facts, arrangements had to be made and then the long climb back uphill accomplished. I feared I was in for a long, cold wait. It crossed my mind that I would have done better to have sent James to the Clifton manor house for assistance, but it was too late to consider that now. Neither of us had been thinking very clearly.

I switched my thoughts back to the mutilated corpse lying at the foot of the dais. 'DIE'. But why, when the victim had already been killed? Moreover, something about the arrangement of the letters, all crowded on to the right-hand breast, bothered me, although for the moment I was unable to say why. In spite of myself, my eyes were drawn instinctively to that dark shape on the floor and, in the end, suppressing a natural feeling of revulsion, I picked up my candle, which I had put down beside me, and went to have another look at it.

This time, knowing what to expect, the shock was not so great and I was able to view the body with a certain amount of detachment. I couldn't help wondering how a man who had been a soldier, and who must also have been alerted to a certain degree of personal danger by the murder of his friend, Alderman Trefusis, had allowed himself to walk into an ambush. For his murderer must have been lying in wait for him; if not inside the house, Sir George having the only key, then probably among the trees and bushes which surrounded it. What message could possibly have persuaded him to leave his home in the middle of the night and, at his age, walk the five or so miles uphill to the crest of the downs in the biting winter cold at the end of December?

It was at this point, kneeling beside the body, that I noticed something I had missed earlier in the first horror of seeing it. Sir George's right hand was also partially mutilated with cuts and slashes across the base of the first two fingers. And when I lifted the hand to peer more closely at it, I noticed a knife lying at a little distance as though it had been dropped in a hurry. Had the perpetrator of the crime been disturbed before he had finished his ghoulish work?

For the moment, I was too tired and too distressed to pursue the idea, but I stored it away in my mind. My thoughts returned to the word 'DIE' carved into the knight's right breast while I tried to fathom out why it puzzled me. Whoever killed Sir George certainly hated him with a venom that was almost akin to madness, so perhaps the mutilation was nothing more than an added expression of that hatred. Maybe it was nothing more than that.

I was by now too cold and weary to think any more about it. My brain felt numb with fatigue and horror, so I wrapped myself in my cloak, returned to the chair and waited, half waking, half drifting on a sea of sickly dreams, for James to return with the necessary reinforcements.

It was not really until the following morning, the first day of January, that I fully recovered the tone of my mind. The events of the previous afternoon and evening had passed in a sort of daze; a blur of noise, of people's voices raised in horrified exclamations, of the clatter of feet as Richard Manifold, Sergeant Merryweather and their minions tramped in and out. And I had a vague recollection of the sheriff's appalled face as he stared down on what had once been a man. His attempts to question James and myself met with little success: we were both too tired and still too shocked to make any sense. I remembered James saying that he had persuaded his father not to accompany the rescue party, and thinking he had been wise to do so.

Two men had come with a stretcher and the knight's body had been tenderly lifted on to it and decently covered with a cloak. At the time, it had not occurred to me to wonder what had happened to his upper clothing, but now, in the early morning, lying in the comfort of my bed with Adela breathing quietly beside me, I was amazed to think that I had overlooked such a simple fact and that no one else had thought about it, either. Had the murderer taken it away with him, and if so, why? Or was it still lying in some dark corner of that bloodstained hall? And was it important enough for me to make another visit to the

Marvell house later today? I had an uncomfortable feeling that it might be.

I rolled on to my right side and snuggled into Adela's back. At least, when I finally returned home the previous evening, I had been spared her reproaches for my tardiness. Long before the sheriff's sad party made its entrance through the Frome Gate, almost everyone in the city had learned of the terrible discovery made by James and myself and had turned out of doors, braving the winter cold, to see the solemn procession pass by. Adela had been one of the first to greet me as I straggled, exhausted, in its wake, and had insisted that I go straight home to bed. She would brook no refusal on my part.

'You're worn out, Roger. If all the rumours flying around are true, you've had a very nasty experience. If anyone wants to question you, they can do so tomorrow, but for now you need sleep. You're coming back with me.'

I was too tired to argue with her, and indeed, such was the turmoil of my mind, I was glad of someone to tell me what to do. And as Small Street was so close at hand, I found myself indoors within a very short space of time. Elizabeth, with Luke clutched in her arms, and the other two were gathered together in the hall and greeted us in wide-eyed silence, aware that something terrible had happened and that I was somehow involved in it, but not quite certain how. Grumbling, they had been packed unceremoniously off to bed, Luke being further committed to his foster sister's care. And, early as the hour was, once I had been given supper I had followed them not long after. Adela had asked no questions – obviously a sufficient amount of the murder's gruesome details were already well enough known to make them unnecessary – and I had been tenderly assisted up to our room where, naked and unwashed, I had fallen asleep almost as soon as my head touched the pillow.

Much to my surprise, my slumber had been undisturbed by any dreams, fair or foul, and now I was awake and refreshed, staring over Adela's shoulder at the early morning light rimming the shutters and feeling fit to face whatever the day might bring. I kissed the nape of Adela's neck and she stretched and murmured something, but did not wake. Gently, I eased myself into a sitting position, hugging my knees under the blanket, and considered the previous day's events as dispassionately as I could.

Many people had disliked Sir George Marvell – even, I suspected, his own wife – but someone had truly hated him, and the only person I knew of who had reason to loathe him enough to want to desecrate his dead body was Miles Deakin. The knight had not only horsewhipped him, deprived him of an extremely rich old wife (who might have been expected to die very shortly, leaving him a wealthy man), but he had also had the young man's parents turned off their land, robbing the family of its livelihood. But then again, what did I really know of Sir George's past life and how many other enemies he might have made? If he could treat one young man in such a brutal fashion, what might he have done to someone else?

It was the words 'young man' that suddenly brought me up short. Sir George, it was true, had been over seventy by several years, but he had been strong for his age and active. It would surely have taken more than one man to bring him down and cut his throat. I found it difficult to believe that the knight, summoned to an empty house in the middle of the night, would not have been on his guard against trouble of some sort. And the more I thought about it, the more I was convinced that there must have been more than one person . . .

I became aware of Adela steadily regarding me. She had rolled on to her back and was wide awake, her brown eyes holding a look of loving resignation.

'Why does it always have to be you?' she sighed. 'You and Trouble are twins, joined at the hip. If he's there, you're there, unable to keep away.'

'I don't do it on purpose,' I pleaded. 'These things just happen.'

'No, they don't,' she answered tersely. 'They happen because you're incapable of keeping your nose out of other people's business.'

It was the old cry that had followed me throughout my life and, in fairness, I had to admit that such an accusation was probably justified. From childhood, I could never resist a riddle or a mystery.

I tried to look apologetic which made her laugh, but when I would have taken her in my arms she pushed me away.

'You stink, Roger. Go and wash under the pump and then put on some clean clothes. By that time your breakfast will be ready.'

I did as she bade me, but when I finally sat down to eat – having also performed my daily chore of tending to the Yule log – my thoughts had reverted to the death of Sir George. I had swallowed a bowl of porridge and munched my way through two oatcakes without really tasting anything, when I had a sudden idea. Springing to my feet, I handed Adela my knife and stretched out full length on the floor. The children stared at me in fascination, obviously of the opinion that I had finally gone mad, while Hercules, interpreting the move as the prelude to a new and delightful game, hurtled across to throw himself athwart my chest and frantically lick my face.

I pushed him aside and indicated the knife Adela was now holding.

'Sweetheart, I want you to imagine that you have just murdered me and you're going to carve the word "DIE" into my chest. Show me how you would do it.'

My wife flung the knife from her. 'I refuse to do anything so horrible,' she declared. 'It's disgusting. I don't know how you can ask it of me.'

'I'll do it,' breathed Adam excitedly, scrambling down from his stool. 'I have my little knife.'

I sat up abruptly. 'Don't let him touch me!' I yelled. 'He means it!'

Adela did more than prevent him: together with Elizabeth and Nicholas, she bundled Adam out of the kitchen and sent them all to play upstairs until it was time for their morning lessons. Once we were alone – except for Luke, who was too young to appreciate what was going on – she told me exactly what she thought of my ghoulish behaviour. 'And in front of the children, too! It's enough to make them ride the nightmare. I despair of you, Roger!'

'Sweetheart,' I begged, 'bear with me. I agree I shouldn't have asked you when the children were present, but I got carried away. Adela, this is important. I feel sure you must have been told the details of Sir George's murder before I got back yesterday, so it hasn't come as a shock to you. If you were the murderer and you were going to mutilate my body with the word "DIE", how would you do it?'

She could see that I was in earnest and made an effort to

overcome her repulsion. Picking up the knife again, she advanced towards me as I lay down once more. Even then, she hesitated.

'Go on,' I urged. 'How would you do it?'

Adela took a deep breath. 'As he – the killer – did, I suppose.' And holding the knife point downwards in the air, she drew an imaginary letter D above my right breast, a letter I following the line of my breastbone and an E over my left breast. Then she tossed the knife back on the table and burst into tears.

'It's too horrible to think of,' she sobbed. But I knew she wasn't picturing Sir George Marvell as the victim. She was seeing me.

Hurriedly, I got to my feet and folded her in my arms. 'My love, forgive me! Forgive me! I shouldn't have made you do it.' I wiped her eyes tenderly with the edge of my sleeve.

When she was quieter, she asked, 'Did it do any good? Did it tell you anything you wanted to know?'

'Yes.' We sat down, side by side, on the stools and, still with one arm about her, I poured her some more ale from the jug on the table. 'You see, you assumed, as I think anyone would have assumed who only knew the facts without having seen the body, that that was what the murderer had done. You spaced out the letters right across my chest.'

'And it wasn't like that?'

'No. All three were crowded on to the right breast, close together.'

'So?'

'So . . . So perhaps it was just the beginning of another, longer word which was never finished.'

'Why not?'

'Because the killer, or killers – and I feel certain there must have been more than one – were disturbed before they could finish. There was a knife flung down on the floor, half-hidden by the body, and . . .' My voice tailed off as I remembered the mutilated hand with one of the fingers partially cut through.

I caught my breath. Suddenly I felt certain that the murderers had indeed been interrupted before they could complete their ghoulish work. And I felt equally certain that I knew the name of the man who had disturbed them. None other than Briant of Dungarvon.

THIRTEEN

The more I thought about it, the more certain I was that I was right.

Briant had left Marsh Street to make his way to Rownham Ferry where, he had been informed, the Clontarf had dropped anchor. Avoiding the Watch, which was a fairly simple matter as you could hear them coming a mile off, he had made for one of the gaps in the city wall, probably the one nearest the Frome Gate. Once across the Frome Bridge, he would have taken the westward path which skirts Brandon Hill and leads eventually to the ferry. But somewhere, during the early part of his walk, he must have seen the familiar figure of Sir George Marvell ahead of him, climbing one of the hills that lead to the summit of the downs.

I could imagine how intrigued he must have been; how curious to know where the knight was going and why. It might even have crossed his mind to renege on his promise not to harm Sir George. He hated him and bore him a lasting grudge which he had nursed for many years. And here was Fate throwing the man in his way on a dark night when he was flouting the law of curfew and when it might be expected that some robber or footpad would find him easy prey. His murderer would never be found – nor, for that matter, diligently sought – and Briant himself would never be suspected. He could return to Bristol whenever he pleased and continue his calling,

But, if my theory were correct, curiosity must have got the better of any murderous impulse. So, keeping a discreet distance, Briant had followed his quarry all the way to the Marvell house perched high above Ghyston Cliff, only to bear witness to Sir George's gruesome murder. I closed my eyes and pictured the scene. Briant had watched as the knight had unlocked the door, but then started in surprise as two figures – I was by now convinced that there must have been two – rose from the concealing bushes on either side to follow him in. He must have heard the victim's yells for help as he was set on and then the awful silence that succeeded them. Perhaps Briant had waited several minutes while he debated whether to enter and find out what was going on or to take himself off and let discretion be the better part of valour. It was, caution must have whispered, the wisest course.

But in the end, an overwhelming desire to know what had happened to his enemy, to know that justice had finally caught up with Sir George, prompted him to go in. And the scene which met his eyes must have horrified even him: the sprawled, half-naked, mutilated body, the gouged-out eyes, one murderer with a knife scoring something into the bare flesh while the other sawed at the fingers of the knight's right hand. Did Briant let out an involuntary gasp or shout out in protest? He must surely have revealed his presence in some way for one man dropped both knife and hand to rise up in pursuit of the unwelcome intruder, while the other also left his handiwork to join in the chase. Did the pair catch Briant and throw him over the cliff into the river below to silence him? Or did he lose his way in the darkness and blunder over the edge himself? That, I felt, was something I might never know. But one thing was certain, for whatever reason, the murderers had not gone back to finish what they had begun. Maybe a sudden revulsion had seized them, or maybe the shock of being observed had warned them to get out while the going was good . . .

'Roger! Roger, are you all right?' Adela's concerned voice brought me back to reality with a jolt to find that I was still seated at the kitchen table, my arm around her shoulders. 'You were miles away,' she accused me.

'I'm sorry, sweetheart,' I said, giving her a squeeze. 'I – I was working something out.'

'Bricks without straw again?' She sounded sceptical.

'No!' I was indignant. But then honesty forced me to admit, 'Perhaps.'

She laughed and freed herself from my embrace. 'I must clear away the dishes and then give the children their morning lessons.' She picked up Luke and took a clean, dry loincloth from the washing basket. 'But first, I must see to our foster-son. He's soaking. What will you do this morning? Will the sheriff want to see you, do you think?'

The words had hardly left her mouth when there was a brisk knocking on the outer door. There was no doubt it was made by someone in authority. Our friends and neighbours would never knock so loudly.

It was Richard Manifold, come to escort me to the sheriff's office and barely able to restrain himself from asking a hundred and one questions as we walked the short distance to the Councillors' Hall between the Tolzey and All Saints' Church. There was a strange atmosphere abroad in the city. All the Christmas cheer of the past few days seemed to have evaporated, leaving the populace at large tense and frightened. Rumours of the state of Sir George's body had already got out and were being wildly exaggerated. Evisceration, beheading, a limbless torso were, Richard told me, just some of the stories circulating in the town. He glanced sideways at me, obviously hoping to draw me out, but I didn't respond. I was too busy deciding what, if anything, I should mention of my own theories, and it didn't take me long to decide to say nothing. I would stick to the facts of what had happened and that was all.

James Marvell, still looking very pale, was already with the sheriff when I arrived and I was called upon to do little more than confirm his story. As to why we had visited the old house at Clifton, the sheriff accepted without demur James's explanation that he had gone there on a sudden impulse to check that no one had broken in during the weeks it had been standing empty, and that he had asked me to accompany him.

'Master Chapman's a good, strong companion to have in a fight,' he added, 'although neither he nor I really expected to find anything amiss.'

Of Miles Deakin, he made no mention, so, when it came my turn to be questioned, I followed suit. I agreed with everything James had said and we were both soon dismissed. Once outside the Councillors' Hall, the young man took my arm and led me into the Green Lattis.

There was a sudden awkward hush as we entered. All eyes were on my companion and several people made as though to rise and offer some sort of condolences. But without exception, each one thought better of it and sank back on to his stool, averting his gaze.

James grinned wryly at me. 'Grandfather wasn't popular. People would like to feel sorry for me, but they can't. I'm sure most folk think of his death as a good riddance. They're shocked and horrified at the manner of his murder, of course, and perhaps a little frightened, but in general, they're glad he's gone.' I murmured a half-hearted protest, but my companion shook his head. 'There's no need to feel embarrassed. He wasn't a nice man, although there were times – rare, I admit – when I felt a sort of fondness for him.' He added in a burst of confidence, 'I don't know how my own grandmother felt about him, but Patience had certainly grown to hate him. I can't say I blame her. He treated her abominably. My father may be the only person alive who had any rag of affection left for him.'

The pot boy arrived, took our order and departed.

'What about Alderman Trefusis?' I asked. 'Sir George seems to have had one friend there, at least.'

James grimaced. 'I've been thinking about that. It was a very odd friendship because I would have sworn that they didn't really like one another. But they seemed bound together by the fact that they had both soldiered in France. Both had fought under Talbot of Shrewsbury and Grandfather had been knighted in the field. Yet neither ever talked about that time. If ever I enquired about their exploits, Grandfather would shut me up.'

'Modesty?' I suggested as our beakers of ale were placed before us.

James snorted. 'Neither of them was what I'd call a modest man. But what worries me is that they both met their end in a similar way. Both had their throats cut and it's my belief that if you hadn't interrupted the attack on Robert Trefusis, the same mutilations would have been perpetrated on his dead body.'

I sipped my ale. 'That thought had occurred to me.'

My companion nodded. 'I had an idea it might have done. And as far as I can see, the link between them is this Miles Deakin. Trefusis was the one who informed Grandfather of what was going on with Deakin and Great-Aunt Drusilla. And he did try to say the name before he died.'

'I've been giving that some thought,' I said. 'Also the word cut into Sir George's chest.' And I explained my concern about the letters being cramped together on the knight's right breast. I went on: 'Just as I believe the alderman's "Dee" was only half a word, I think the same might apply to "DIE". How do we know how Miles Deakin spells his name? It could be D-e-e-k-i-n or D-e-a-k-i-n—'

'Or even D-i-e-k-i-n,' James interrupted eagerly. 'Yes, you're right. We have to find him.'

'You didn't mention anything about him to the sheriff.'

'No. His Honour will be even more desperate now, after Grandfather's murder, to find a scapegoat. If the man were discovered, he wouldn't stand a chance. I want to satisfy myself of his guilt before I hand him over to the authorities. Are you willing to ride up to Clifton with me again?'

'Today?'

To my relief, he shook his head. 'No, I must stay with the family for a while. The funeral has to be arranged and the will obtained from Lawyer Heathersett.' He finished his ale and rose. 'I'll let you know. It may not be until after Twelfth Night, when Christmas is finally over.'

This arrangement suited me very well as I had plans for visiting Clifton by myself to do a little investigating of my own. Consequently, once dinner was over, I pulled on my boots, took my cudgel from its corner and said that I needed to go for a walk, if only to clear my head.

Adela looked pointedly at my pack, but I said quickly, 'People won't be buying again yet awhile. Not until the twelve days are over.'

'Then you can take Hercules with you,' she said. 'He needs to stretch his legs.'

Elizabeth put her head around the kitchen door. 'Grandmother and her friends are at the top of the street,' she informed me. 'I've just seen them from the attic window.'

Of course they were! The only wonder was that they hadn't arrived earlier. They must only just have learned that I was involved in the discovery of Sir George's body and were hastening to get the story so that they could lord it over their friends as having the only true account. Silently, Adela handed me the dog's rope collar and lead, but I didn't stop to put them on him. Snatching Hercules up in my arms, I hurriedly quit the house, turning sharp left in the direction of Bell Lane and feigning deafness to the frantic shouts of 'Roger!' which pursued me until I disappeared from the good dames' view. I felt a stab of pity for Adela, who would bear the brunt of their frustration and vexation.

A watery sun was struggling to appear from behind the clouds and there was a nip in the air, dispersing the chill dampness of the past few days. As I climbed towards Clifton, thankful to be on my own two feet again instead of in the saddle, I felt reinvigorated, glad to be by myself once more, unencumbered by other people. I filled my lungs with fresh air while Hercules ran about chasing imaginary rabbits, fell into streams and sniffed and barked at everything that moved, his tail wagging like a pennant in the breeze.

By midday, we had reached the summit and in a very short space of time, were standing outside the Marvell house not far from the edge of Ghyston Cliff. I wondered suddenly if the door were still open or if someone had managed to close and secure it the previous day. But I need not have worried. As I tentatively pushed it, it swung inwards with the same creaking of its hinges.

At once, Hercules drew back, shivering and whining. For a moment, I was afraid someone might be in there and gripped my cudgel tighter; but then I realized that it was the lingering smell of death that was disturbing the dog. I picked him up and held him in my arms. He whimpered again, but the trembling ceased.

I made my way to the counting-house where James had found the candles. He had also mentioned lanterns and, sure enough, there were two with horned panes ranged with the candlesticks along one wall. Dust lay thick everywhere and, without furniture, the room echoed eerily, like the sound of the tide in an underwater cave. I put Hercules down, found the tinderbox and lit both lanterns. With one in either hand, I then proceeded to search the hall.

I knew what I was looking for and found it before very many minutes had passed. The knight's hat, cloak, gloves, his belt and pouch, together with the shirt and tunic ripped from his upper body, had been thrown into a corner beside the dais, concealed from view by the shadows. Yesterday, everyone had been too shocked and horrified by the discovery of Sir George's mutilated body to think about his missing clothes, but before long somebody – Cyprian, perhaps – would remember them and either come in person or send someone else to find them.

I sat down on the floor, my back against the edge of the platform, the lanterns and Hercules beside me, and opened the pouch, a strong affair of ribbed leather looped on to the belt. At first, to my great disappointment, I thought it was empty, but then I realized that the silk lining was torn and a scrap of paper had got between it and the leather. Carefully, with fingers that shook a little, I prised it free, unfolding it and spreading it out flat on the floor.

It was a piece of rag paper about three inches square, but there was writing on it, so I moved both lanterns closer and tried to make out its message. The ink was of poor quality, probably blackberry juice mixed with blood, and the writing difficult to read. The letters were shaky and badly formed, but not illegible: the sender had been taught to write, although not well and not fluently. Still, it was more than many folk could do.

Within a few minutes I had worked out what it said.

Must see you. The old house. After midnight. Tonight. Alyson.

That was all. But it had been enough to bring Sir George hurrying up to Clifton on a bitter winter's night at the end of December. The note smacked of a secret tryst, and having learned from Briant of the knight's past infidelity, it seemed the most likely answer. But who was Alyson? That was something I had to find out. I put the note back in the pouch and, together with the rest of the clothes, returned it to the corner where I had found it. Then I restored the lanterns and tinderbox to the counting-house, having first blown out the flames, called to Hercules and considered what to do next.

The cliff path leading to St Vincent's chapel and the neighbouring hermitage was as perilous as ever. It was nearly three years since I had last traversed it and, during that time, it seemed to have become even narrower and more overgrown with vegetation. The rope railing had, in at least two places, come adrift from the cliff face to which it was attached and, with Hercules tucked under one arm, I trod as cautiously as possible. Nevertheless, I could still hear the rattle of pebbles and dirt as a little more of the pathway slipped into the gorge below.

The hermit, who lived in the cave next door to the tiny chapel and who was seated on the ground hunched over a fire of smoking twigs, glanced up as I entered. His manner was belligerent and I remembered him as a miserable fellow with a seeming grudge against his fellow men, particularly those who disturbed his meditations. But I had forgotten his antipathy towards dogs.

'Get that mongrel cur out of here,' he snapped.

Hercules growled and bared his teeth.

'Why?' I sneered. 'Are you afraid he'll foul your cave? He stays here with me. That path's not safe.'

The man smoothed down the few strands of hair that covered his bald pate and blinked his watery eyes. Then he scrambled to his feet.

'I know you,' he said. 'You've been here before. And that animal.'

'You've a good memory,' I applauded him. 'It's nearly three years ago. The year of the war with Scotland. Back then, I was looking for a woman named Emilia Virgoe. Now, I'm trying to find someone called Alyson. I don't know her other name.'

I half-expected him to shrug his shoulders and say that, in that case, he could do nothing to assist me. Instead, 'Oh, I know it all right!' he exclaimed scornfully. 'It's Carpenter! Alyson Carpenter! A little whore, if ever there was one.'

'She's young, then?'

The hermit curled his lip. 'She ain't seen more'n fifteen, maybe sixteen, summers, I reckon.' He paused to cough as the smoke caught the back of his throat, and the spittle dribbled down the front of his frayed and stained brown robe. 'Good, God-fearing parents,' he went on, 'but what sins they've committed to have a trollop like her for a daughter, the saints alone know. She's the scandal of Clifton. Anything in breeches she's after. Her poor father's beaten her black and blue, but it does no good. She's after anything that's got two legs and a prick in between.'

I'm no prude, far from it, but all the same, it jolted me to hear a holy man speak so bluntly.

'What about Sir George Marvell?' I asked. 'A man old enough to be her grandfather at the very least. Even her great-grandfather, maybe. Would she have fancied him?'

'I've told you!' he exclaimed irritably. 'That girl would chase anything with two—'

'Yes, yes,' I interrupted hastily. 'But Sir George? Would he have encouraged her advances?'

'That randy old goat couldn't keep his hands off anything in skirts. What his poor wives must have put up with, I can only guess. One of the girls he was fucking was murdered, but that was years ago.' The hermit's watery eyes gleamed with a cruel satisfaction. 'And now he's been murdered himself. Most gruesomely, too, if all I've been told is true.' His yellow teeth were bared in a sudden, unaccustomed smile. 'Did young Alyson have something to do with it?'

'No, no!' I disclaimed hastily and realized that it was time I took my leave. I backed out of the cave. 'This Alyson Carpenter, does she live on the manor?'

'Goram Lane. Last cottage in the row nearest the cliff edge. But—'

Thanking him hurriedly, I transferred the dog to my other arm and beat a retreat up the cliff path as fast as possible, clinging to the rope railing with my free hand for very life. One false step and Hercules and I would have hurtled to our deaths below.

Goram Lane was simply a single row of one-storey cottages right on the edge of Clifton Manor, each with a plot of ground at the back which would support a few vegetables and perhaps either a goat or a pig. Such animals as I glimpsed looked sufficiently well fed, but none of them fat enough to support a family. The men who lived here were workers on the manor estate. My guess was that Alyson's father followed the trade which his name implied and, at this time of day, would be away from home. I walked to the last cottage in the row, the one nearest the cliff edge, and knocked on the door.

A plain-looking woman with a harassed expression answered it. 'Yes?'

'I'm a poor traveller, mistress,' I lied, 'and I've had no dinner today.' My stomach was fairly bursting with one of Adela's stews, but I did my best to look hungry. 'Could you spare me a beaker of ale and a slice of bread and cheese?'

She looked uncertain, eyeing me up and down with some misgivings. The reason for this was immediately apparent when the door was pushed wider and a young girl joined her.

This, I knew at once, could be no one but young Alyson. She was, as the hermit had told me, no more than sixteen years of age. A tangle of soft brown curls was confined beneath a three-cornered kerchief, while a pair of bold blue eyes appraised me from head to foot. She evidently liked what she saw, for she held the door wider still and gestured me inside. The older woman made a protesting noise, but was plainly unable to control her daughter. She had a faintly surprised air about her, like a duck who has given birth to a swan, and I suspected Alyson could twist her mother around her finger. It was clearly left to the father to try to control their headstrong offspring.

'We can give you bread and cheese and ale, can't we, Mother? Come in.'

I nodded towards a wooden bench pushed up against the outside wall. 'I'll have it here if you don't mind, mistress, if you'll bring it out to me, and perhaps some water for the dog.'

'Won't you be too cold?'

'Hercules and I like it out of doors,' I said, blatantly ignoring the dog's attempts to enter the cottage.

Alyson giggled. 'I won't be long,' she promised.

She was as good as her word and before five minutes had passed came out with a tray on which reposed a huge hunk of rye bread, a slab of goat's milk cheese, a brimming beaker of ale and a bowl of water. She had wrapped herself in a thick cloak which, despite the winter chill, she allowed to fall open to reveal the trim figure beneath.

As she placed the bowl of water on the ground for Hercules, she glanced up at me with a provocative smile.

'You did that on purpose, didn't you?'

'Wh-What?' I stammered.

She straightened up. 'Asked to have the food out here, so that you could talk to me alone.' She tilted her head to one side. 'But I'm not sure why. I'd like to think it's because you want to kiss me, but somehow I don't think it is.'

She was as shrewd as she was pretty and far too old for her years. No man would ever get the better of her. I decided there and then that deception was no use: only complete frankness would do.

'I wouldn't mind kissing you,' I admitted, 'but no, you're right. I want to talk to you about Sir George Marvell.' Her eyes widened and she caught her breath. 'Mistress Alyson, were you . . .? I mean, did you . . .? What I'm asking is . . .'

'I know what you're asking,' she said, suddenly serious. 'Is it true what everyone's saying about his murder? That whoever did it had cut him up?'

'Not exactly,' I hedged. 'Someone . . . Well, never mind that. Mistress, did you write him a note asking you to meet you at the old Marvell house four nights ago? The night of Childermass Day?'

She gasped and some of the colour left her cheeks. 'No! No, of course I didn't! Why would I? I – I may have granted him a favour now and then in the old days, but it never meant anything.' She must have noticed my expression and made haste to excuse herself. 'He was quite handsome still and vigorous for his age. Besides, he gave me very nice presents: a necklace and a bracelet which I have hidden where my parents won't find them. I'll sell them one day when I'm ready to run away. But since he went down to live in Bristol, I've not even thought about him until now. Who says I wrote to him? What note?'

I explained as briefly as I could what I had found. Alyson was aghast and vehemently denied all responsibility for the letter.

'I didn't write it, I swear! You must believe me!' She was no longer a precocious little minx, but a frightened child. I put an arm about her.

'It's all right. I do believe you,' I said.

But it suddenly occurred to me that others might not. What James Marvell had said about Miles Deakin could equally well apply to this girl. Law officers, desperate to solve the murders of two prominent citizens, might seize on any clue to lead them to the murderer. Yet surely not even two blockheads like Jack Gload and Peter Littleman could imagine that this frail child could cut throats and mutilate a body without help. No, I was being foolish. Nevertheless, it might be safer to destroy the note before anyone else could find it. I must return to the house and do so. It would be removing what could be vital evidence, but I had done worse things than that in the past. I wasn't going to let it worry me.

I told Alyson what I intended doing and she gave a shudder of relief.

'Oh, thank you,' she gasped and put up her mouth to be kissed.

I laughed and obliged, but in a brotherly way. She pouted, already regaining her self-assurance, and tried to kiss me again. I gently turned her head aside.

'Do you recall a young lad who lived in these parts called Miles Deakin?' I asked.

Alyson tossed her curls. 'Oh, him!' she exclaimed dismissively. 'He was a fool, he was. I don't suppose he could read or write. I'm not sure, mind. But why would anyone have taught him? He was always boasting how one day he would marry a rich wife. He thought he was so handsome that he'd only have to crook his little finger to get one. Why do you want to know?'

'Have you any idea what happened to him and his parents? They don't live on the manor any more, do they? Do you happen to know where they went?'

'No. Why should I? They meant nothing to me.' Her face clouded and she laid an urgent hand on my arm. 'You will go back to the house, won't you, and destroy that note? You promised.'

I laid aside the tray, the bread and cheese uneaten, although I had drunk the ale. 'I'm going now,' I said and whistled up Hercules, who had wandered off on some business of his own.

I think she would have detained me further, but she suddenly breathed, 'My father's coming,' and, picking up the tray, vanished indoors.

At the end of Goram Lane, I passed a worried-looking man carrying a basket of carpenter's tools. He appeared careworn and, thinking of his daughter, I decided he had every right to be.

The Marvell house was still silent and unoccupied. No one had as yet arrived from Bristol to investigate further.

I pushed open the door and Hercules and I went in.

FOURTEEN

This time, I didn't bother to light either a candle or a lantern. There was sufficient daylight from the open door to see my way across the hall to the dais and I knew exactly where to find the discarded clothing.

The same disquieting odour still hung about the place; a mustiness compound of dirt, decay and the peculiar sickly-sweet scent of blood. Hercules whimpered a little but did not hang back, trotting ahead of me, although his tail was drooping. Suddenly he stopped, one paw raised, head to one side, listening. I paused also, straining my ears to hear what he had heard, but the silence, except for the whisper of the dead leaves scuttering across the floor, was as profound as ever.

'What is it, lad?' I asked.

He gave a single bark, but then proceeded on his way, making straight for the end of the hall. A bird fluttered amongst the rafters high above us and then resumed its slumbers. I told myself I was getting jumpy for no good reason.

I found Sir George's clothes where I had dropped them earlier, and yet it seemed to me that the sad little pile was not quite where it had been. I plunged my hand inside the pouch, my fingers groping for the paper . . .

It wasn't there. The pouch was empty.

At first, of course, I refused to believe it, thinking the note must have slipped under the lining again and ripping at the silk until I had torn almost all of it away from the leather. Nothing. Then I decided I must have fumbled when I put the paper back and dropped it on the floor, so I went down on my hands and knees, feeling all around me in an ever increasing circle. Finally, I was forced to fetch and light a lantern from the counting-house and make a more extensive search. But there was still no sign of any note.

I sat down on the edge of the dais and closed my eyes, trying to recall my actions of an hour or so ago. And with sudden clarity,

I could see myself pushing the paper down inside the pouch and then fastening its flap. The note which had summoned Sir George to his death had definitely been there then. Now it was gone. There was, therefore, only one conclusion to be drawn. It had been stolen.

This meant that someone had been here during the time that I had been visiting the hermitage and Goram Lane; someone who, perhaps, had seen me arrive and who, most certainly, had seen me depart. Someone who, even now, might still be watching me. I felt the hairs lift on the nape of my neck.

I stood up slowly and blew out the lantern, my uneasiness communicating itself to Hercules, who began to tremble. He raised his head, sniffing the air while I grabbed my cudgel, swinging it gently to and fro, feeling the comfort of its weighted end. I could do a lot of damage with my trusty 'Plymouth cloak'.

I walked forward a pace or two, keeping my eyes on the two lines of doors, one on each side of the hall, which gave access to the other parts of the house. Then I told myself I was being foolish. Whoever had been here in my absence would not have expected me to come back – I had not expected it myself – and had probably gone on his way. No one was lying in wait for me. The best thing I could do was to return home and say nothing about today's events. I could not mention the note without either implicating young Alyson Carpenter or revealing my intention to destroy evidence, but at least I now knew how Sir George had been lured to his death.

A door softly opened and closed somewhere behind me, and I realized with a shock of dismay that I had forgotten the door which invariably opened into and out of the back of any dais; a door which allowed the head of the household to make his entrance or exit after or before everyone else. I swung round, but was a fraction too late. A cloak descended over my head, muffling me in its folds.

Hercules was barking like a fiend and I could hear his jaws snapping as he tried to tackle my assailant. I dropped my cudgel as I sought to free myself from the thick, all-enveloping wool and the hands which were seeking to choke the life out of me through the cloth. But I was at a disadvantage in that the fellow had seized me from behind and so I was unable to use my legs to knee him in the groin. I heard him curse violently as Hercules bit him somewhere tender, but his grip didn't slacken. Half-throttled, half-stifled, I was beginning to lose consciousness and fought even harder to get my arms free . . .

A girl's voice shouted, 'What are you doing to him? Leave him alone, you brute!' The hands were suddenly removed from about my neck and I was pushed to the floor. There was a flurry of movement and the next moment the cloak was removed from about my head and shoulders and Alyson was kneeling by my side while Hercules danced around us, pausing occasionally to lick my face. There was a trace of red on his chin. My attacker had obviously drawn blood.

Alyson smoothed the hair back from my forehead. 'Are you all right?' she asked.

I nodded weakly, putting up a hand to my mangled throat. I made a sort of croaking noise and then, to my shame and horror, I fainted.

When I came to again, my saviour was bathing my brow with the edge of her cloak which she was dipping in a small basin of greasy-looking water.

'Where . . . Where did you get that?' I wheezed.

She smiled. 'From the kitchen. There's still some water in the barrel. It's a bit slimy, but it won't do you any harm. The bowl's rusty and has a small hole in the bottom, so it must have been left behind as useless.'

I sat up abruptly, feeling extremely foolish, and fended off any further ministrations.

'How long have I been unconscious?'

'Not many minutes.'

I doubted this, calculating how long it must have taken her to go to the kitchen, find the bowl and water and return. Five minutes? Ten? Fifteen? There was no hope now of overtaking my attacker who must, by this time, be well away. I leant forward, taking Alyson's wrist in an urgent grip. 'What did the man look like? You must have seen him. Describe him to me!'

She shrugged her slender shoulders. 'I would if I could, but he was masked.'

'Masked? What sort of mask? Was it a bird with a big, hooked beak?'

'No. A dog with a silly, flat sort of face.' She sat back on her heels, regarding me. 'Are you all right now?'

I scrambled to my feet, unhappily aware that I must cut an undignified figure. 'Yes, of course I'm all right. I can't think how I came to faint like that. It must have been the shock of the assault.'

She nodded gravely. 'And you're not a young man.'

For a moment, I was speechless. Finally, 'And I'm not in my dotage, either,' I snapped. She would have spoken again, but I forestalled her. Any attempt at explanation on her part would, I felt, only make matters worse and shatter my self-esteem completely. Besides, another thought had occurred to me. 'Why did you come after me?'

Alyson also rose to her feet, putting the bowl down on the dais and wiping her wet fingers in her cloak. She looked a little apprehensive. 'Are you going home to Bristol now?' she asked.

'That is my intention. Unless,' I added grimly, 'I get ambushed by my assailant on the way. But this time I shall be on my guard. He won't get the better of me again. Why do you want to know?'

'Then will you please take me with you?' Her face was eager. 'I can't risk the journey on my own.'

'Do your mother and father know of this request?'

She gave me a pitying look. 'Of course not, stupid.'

'In other words, you're running away from home. The answer is no, I won't take you.'

'Oh, please!' She was reproachful. 'I've just saved your life.'

I sighed. 'Don't think I'm not grateful. I am. Very. But I won't help you deceive your parents. Anyway, why do you want to go to Bristol?'

'I heard the mummers are playing there during Christmas.'

'There are mummers, certainly. But they're a very small troupe.'

She nodded eagerly. 'I know. They stopped to give a performance in Clifton before going on to the city. But the girl who plays the Fair Maiden, Toby's wife' – she coloured slightly as she spoke his name – 'is with child. She won't be able to perform much longer. I could help them out.'

That all-betraying blush made the situation perfectly plain. She fancied young Master Warrener and intended to seduce him.

She would probably succeed. Maybe she had succeeded already. I felt a sudden surge of anger on Dorcas's behalf.

'You know Tobias Warrener, do you? You made friends with him?'

My tone was dry and she lifted her chin defiantly. 'We talked after the performance, that's all.'

'But you'd like to know him better, is that it?' She refused to reply, her mouth setting in a mulish line. I went on: 'My answer is no, mistress, I won't take you to Bristol with me. I won't help you to deceive your parents, nor will I help you to come between a man and his wife. The mummers are friends of mine. I'm truly grateful for all you've done for me, but no!'

I picked up my cudgel and Hercules began frisking around me in joyful anticipation of moving at last.

'I'll follow you,' she threatened.

I shook my head. 'You won't be able to keep up. I have a very long stride.'

'I hate you,' she said. 'I wish I'd let that man kill you. It would have served you right.'

I couldn't help laughing, which made her angrier than ever and she lashed out at me with her little fists. I decided it was time to be gone. I gripped her by the shoulders.

'Sweetheart,' I said, 'you're a very pretty girl who could make a good match if you'd just learn to behave yourself. Forget about men like Sir George and young Toby Warrener. Look around you for a decent husband and settle down to domestic life and having children. It's what women are for.'

Her eyes narrowed as she scrutinized me carefully. 'You sound just like my father.' She pulled herself free of my grasp. 'Just like all men,' she continued scornfully. 'You're even older than I thought. If you have a daughter, I'm sorry for her!' Then she was gone, her cloak flying out behind her as she vanished through the door.

I stared sadly at Hercules. 'She's right, you know, lad. I used to try to seduce girls, not read them lectures about propriety.' He barked and jumped up at me excitedly, anxious to be on his way. He didn't care for this place with its lingering smell of death. With my free hand, I fastened my cloak at the throat and pulled up the hood, then swung my cudgel once again. 'There's one thing,' I added as we moved towards the oblong of grey daylight at the other end of the hall. 'She needn't feel sorry for Elizabeth. That girl never heeds a word I say. As far as she's concerned, I'm just an eddy of trouble disturbing the otherwise calm waters of her life.'

Although I was on my guard, our return journey to Bristol was uneventful. Such people as we passed were all going about their lawful business and were uninterested in a man and his dog. One or two gave us greetings of the season, wishing me the love of the Holy Virgin and her Babe; others were too busy collecting fresh branches of greenery with which to decorate their houses anew for the great festival of Twelfth Night Eve, now only four days away. This was the night when we would all go wassailing around the orchards, pouring jugs of sweet cider around the base of the tree trunks; libations to the old Saxon gods of the Tree and the Stone. For generations, the Church had tried to suppress such heathenish practices, but to no avail. So they had wisely incorporated it into the Feast of the Epiphany and the coming of the Wise Men to the stable, where they had been shown the Christ Child in his manger, the Hope and the Light of the world. (But the old gods still held their place in people's hearts and refused to be ousted.)

Adela was in the kitchen, putting the finishing touches to her Twelfth Night cake.

'You both look exhausted,' she said, putting down a plate of scraps for Hercules, who fell on them like a ravening wolf. 'You've walked that poor dog off his feet, and in this cold weather, too.' She regarded me thoughtfully. 'You don't look too well, yourself. Supper won't be long, but first, I'm afraid you have a visitor. James Marvell. He's in the parlour, warming his toes.'

He was in fact pacing around, impatient for my return, dressed in funereal black from head to toe.

'Master Chapman,' he said eagerly as I entered, 'I think I may know where we might find Miles Deakin.' He paused, suddenly concerned as I swayed a little on my feet. 'Is something wrong? Shall I call your wife?'

'No, no!' I sank gratefully into one of the armchairs. 'I shall be all right in a moment or two and I don't wish to worry her. Is that a jug of ale I see on the hearth? If you'd be kind enough to pour me some . . .'

'Of course.' He handed me a brimming beaker, then settled down in the chair opposite mine, the fire crackling and sparking between us. 'Has something happened?'

I suddenly changed my mind and decided to tell him everything, holding nothing back. He listened attentively, merely grimacing slightly over the intelligence that his grandfather had bedded a girl young enough to be his granddaughter. But, 'I'm afraid he couldn't leave women alone, and the younger the better,' was his only remark, made with a wry grimace.

Finally, I came to the end of my recital and waited for his further comments. He leant forward, elbows on knees. 'You don't think these Carpenters, this Alyson's parents, could be my grandfather's murderers, do you?'

It was a thought that, until that moment, had not occurred to me, and I stared at him, somewhat shocked that I could have overlooked such an easy and obvious answer. But after a moment or two, the reason for this omission was clear and I gave a decisive shake of my head.

'From what I saw of them, neither is sufficiently strong. Nor would they be even as a pair. You saw your grandfather's body. It was a vicious, brutal murder carried out by at least two people with a desperate grudge. I doubt very much indeed if Alyson's parents would have dared lay a finger on Sir George, whatever their feelings about him. Besides, they know their daughter. According to the Saint Vincent's hermit, the whole district knows her for what she is. They must realize only too well that disposing of one man would in no way prevent her moving on to the next. No, I think we can absolve Master and Mistress Carpenter of the crime with absolute certainty.'

James nodded. 'I think so, too. You say this unknown attacker tried to kill you. You're sure of that? He wasn't just trying to lay you out?'

I swallowed the dregs of my ale and wiped my mouth on the back of my hand. 'It's not the first attempt on my life,' I said, and told him the story of the poisoning.

He frowned. 'And your little son definitely saw someone put

something in your drink during the Saint Thomas Becket's Day wassail? You believe him?'

'Why shouldn't I? I had already suspected poisoning myself, my sickness was so violent.'

'But why? Why should anyone wish to kill you?'

I shrugged. 'You may be aware that I have a certain reputation for solving mysteries.' This was no time for false modesty. 'Perhaps whoever it was is afraid that I'm getting too close.'

'And who is that?'

'The man in the bird mask, obviously. The same man who was seen outside your and Dame Drusilla's houses the afternoon before your grandfather disappeared. The man who must have given him the bogus note from Alyson Carpenter that sent him hurrying up to Clifton in the middle of the night.'

James chewed a thumbnail. 'Which could, of course, have been Miles Deakin,' he murmured.

'Quite so. You say you know where he can be found?'

'Might be found. I've been talking to one of my great-aunt's maids who, if I read the situation aright, was enjoying the young man's favours at the same time that he was paying court to Drusilla herself.'

I pulled down the corners of my mouth. 'An enterprising fellow, making sure of a good lay once he was married to Mistress Marvell.'

James looked sour. 'So I think. I begin to sympathize with my grandfather's view of the matter.'

'And this girl knows where he might be?'

'Yes. She thinks, although, mark you, she isn't sure, that he and his parents went into Gloucestershire, to his mother's sister, who lives near Nibley Green.'

I nodded. 'I know the place. There was a battle there some thirteen years ago. I remember it being talked of when I was a novice at Glastonbury Abbey. I think the village still bears some of the scars.'

My companion grunted. 'It was between the Berkeleys and the Talbots, I believe, to settle some private grudge. I've heard people mention it.' He hesitated. 'I was wondering,' he said eventually, 'if you would be willing to go to Nibley to see if you can ferret out any information concerning the Deakin family.'

He gave a deprecating shrug and indicated his mourning. 'I can hardly leave my father just at this present. So much work has devolved upon him, and Bart is worse than useless. Patience also, and although I hesitate to own it, my mother is little better. Do you think you could see your way to doing me this favour?'

'No,' I answered brusquely. 'To Nibley and back would take the better part of four days and my wife and family would very reasonably be angry at my absence on Twelfth Night Eve. What with the wassailing and the first-footing it's the most important day of the festivities. I'm sorry, Master Marvell, but I must decline. I'll go after Twelfth Night. I have to be on my travels then, in any case. I shall need to be hawking my wares or the family purse will be empty. I can easily journey that way and call at Nibley Green and North Nibley in the course of my work.'

He leant forward eagerly. 'I'll hire a horse for you again from the Bell Lane stables. On horseback, you could get there and back easily in two, maybe two-and-a-half days.'

'Is the matter so urgent? Don't forget that enquiries are still being made by the sheriff and his men and will continue to be, despite the season. Indeed, now might be the time to inform them of our suspicions of this Miles Deakin and leave them to do whatever they think fit.'

James bit his lip, then shook his head decisively. 'No, for the reasons I gave you before. The sheriff was with my father and myself this morning and, as you may imagine, he is being pressed by the mayor and aldermen for an arrest. Two prominent citizens murdered most barbarically! Miles Deakin wouldn't stand a chance.'

'He would stand his trial the same as anybody else.'

'And have you never known an innocent man condemned?'

I said nothing. I couldn't deny it. I wondered if he knew the story of Robert Herepath, who had been hanged for the murder of a man who wasn't even dead, and my involvement in it. 'Very well,' I conceded after a few moments. 'But as I told you, I'll not go until next week. After Twelfth Night.'

'I repeat, I'll pay for a horse if you'll go tomorrow.'

'Why? A few days can make no difference.'

'I can't really explain.' His gaze shifted and he stared into the heart of the fire. 'If the murderer is this Miles Deakin, I want to know. He has a simple, straightforward motive. Revenge.' He shifted uneasily in his chair. 'I'm concerned about my father. Something is worrying him. He denies it most emphatically. Too emphatically. But there is something on his mind which is troubling him. If it is at all possible, I should like the killer found for his sake.'

'You're sure you're not imagining this? Your grandfather's murder, the brutal nature of it, must have shaken you all.'

He raised his eyes to mine. 'No, I'm not imagining it. I know my father too well.'

'Has it occurred to you,' I asked after a moment or two, 'that this Miles Deakin might not be capable of writing his name? In a man's flesh or anywhere else.'

He glanced up, startled. 'No,' he said slowly. 'I hadn't thought of that. You're right, of course. It's quite possible that he couldn't.'

'Moreover,' I went on, 'I'm still convinced that it took two people to commit both murders. Mind you, that doesn't necessarily rule out the fact that it could be Deakin. He might have had an accomplice.'

'And he might be able to write his name.'

'D-I-E-K-I-N.'

'Yes. There are many ways of spelling a name. Grandfather spelt ours several different ways. You said yourself that you thought the despoiling of the body was interrupted.'

'I still think it possible.' I said nothing about Briant of Dungarvon. That was my secret and would remain so.

'Look,' James urged, leaning forward once again in his chair, 'we have to find this Miles Deakin and make up our minds if we think he could be the killer. And the sooner the better, as far as I'm concerned. I tell you, Master Chapman, I truly am concerned about my father. There is definitely something bothering him. For his peace of mind, if it is this Deakin fellow, I want him caught. If, on the other hand, it turns out that he could not possibly be the guilty man, then we must think again.'

'And you have no idea what it might be that is worrying Master Marvell?'

He shook his head.

'Have you asked him?'

'Certainly. But he denies that there is anything wrong. He insists that I'm imagining it. But I'm not.'

'Has any other member of your family noticed anything?'

He shook his head. 'They think his depression is due to the circumstances of my grandfather's death.'

'But that's not your opinion?'

'Partly. Naturally it is. But I also believe that Father knows something about Grandfather's past which may do the old man discredit. Maybe, in a moment of honesty, Grandfather confided some secret to him.' He broke off, shrugging. 'And then again, perhaps it is just my imagination.'

'Let me get this clear,' I said. 'You're hoping that this young man, this Miles Deakin, will turn out to be Sir George's killer for the very good reason that he has a simple, understandable motive. As you said yourself, revenge. Revenge for his beating at your grandfather's hands and revenge for his parents' loss of livelihood. Am I right?'

'Yes.'

'And you also think that such an outcome would relieve your father's mind of whatever it is you fancy is bothering him?'

'Yes,' he said again.

I sighed. 'Very well. Hire me a horse from the Bell Lane stables and I'll set off first thing tomorrow morning. But if I find that the Deakin family has moved on further north than Nibley Green, I'm not going after them. I intend to be home for Twelfth Night Eve come what may. Is that understood?'

James got to his feet and wrung my hand in gratitude. 'Thank you, Master Chapman. I shan't forget this. If ever I can do you a good turn, just let me know. The horse will be waiting for you in the stables tomorrow morning from first light. Once again, I thank you most sincerely.'

I grimaced. 'You wouldn't care to come and explain things to my wife, I suppose? She is not going to be pleased.'

Adela, however, when I told her over supper, appeared more resigned than angry, merely remarking that she had always known how it would be. 'For the fact is, Roger, that from the moment I heard the news of Sir George's murder, I knew you would be unable to keep out of it; that you would be poking and prying about, if only to annoy poor Richard.'

I protested at this calumny as well as I could through a mouthful of apple dumpling, much to the amusement of the children, who were convulsed with laughter.

'You're like the dog!' shouted Adam. 'You're like the dog when he tried to bark with his mouth full of sosinges.'

This remark was kindly translated for me by Elizabeth, who explained that Margaret Walker had taken her, Nicholas and Adam to see the mummers that afternoon; a farcical comedy about the Sultan of Morocco and his dog, Ali, whose job it was to bark every time his master was in danger, but who also had a passion for sausages which he stole from the Sultan's kitchens.

'And he couldn't bark,' Adam reiterated, banging his spoon in ecstasy on the table, ''cause his mouth was full up with sosinges.'

'The dog was played by Master Chorley,' my daughter added. 'You can always tell it's him by his missing fingers.'

'And Mistress Tabitha was the Cook and Tobias was the Sultan,' my stepson said, passing his plate for a second helping of dumpling. 'Master Monkton wasn't there today. I expect he'd drunk too much and was having a rest.'

This idea made us all laugh, and the subject of the mummers and their plays lasted us very well until bedtime. Adela insisted we all retired together.

'For thanks to your foolhardiness,' she told me, 'in agreeing to this jaunt, you've a tiring few days ahead of you.'

FIFTEEN

In the chill, grey dawn of the following morning, just as the wintry sun rose like a smoking orb over the city rooftops, I approached the Bell Lane stables. I strode out freely, unencumbered by my pack, it having been agreed between Adela and myself that I would simply ride to Nibley Green, make my enquiries and return immediately whatever the outcome. I would waste no time trying to sell my wares, but make all haste home in time for Twelfth Night Eve, my daughter having added her voice to her stepmother's in demanding my presence for this culmination of the Christmas festivities.

Adam, too, had added his mite. 'If you don't come home you'll be a Bad Man and I shan't love you any more.'

It was small wonder, I reflected, that friends and acquaintances regarded me as too lenient a father. Most of the men I knew ruled the roost in their own households. I never seemed to have mastered the art.

As I neared the recently opened gates of the stable yard, I saw a recognizable figure approaching from the opposite direction, emerging into Bell Lane from the narrow alleyway leading from the castle. I touched my cap and called out, 'Good morning, Mistress Warrener. You're abroad early.'

Tabitha was dressed very much as she always was when not performing. The same wide strip of faded cloth was tied around her head, wisps of grey hair escaping from beneath it. The nondescript skirt was kilted about her knees revealing a pair of strong, manly-looking legs in woollen hose and two large feet in wooden clogs. A thick shawl draped around her broad shoulders was her only concession to the biting cold and her raw, red hands were deformed with chilblains.

She nodded as soon as she realized who it was had hailed her and bade me, 'Good day.'

I followed her into the stables, where she was greeted by the head stable man.

'Master Monkton saddled you with the task of visiting the horses today, then?' He grinned as he uttered the word 'saddled', proud of what he considered to be a witticism. (He was a simple man, easily pleased.)

Tabitha grunted, not seeing the joke. 'Arthur's hurt his hand,' she said. 'He needs some salve, so I'll trouble you for an apothecary's direction as soon as I've looked at the animals. They're going on all right, I suppose? There's no need for this daily visit as far as I can see, but Arthur insists on doing it. I don't know if he told you, but we'll be leaving on Twelfth Night. We're giving our last performance on Twelfth Night Eve, then we'll join in the first-footing and the wassailing round the castle orchard before getting underway first thing next morning. I'll settle up with you the previous day. Mind you render your account to me as I'm the only one of 'em as can read and write.'

The stable man nodded. 'Don't fret yourself, Mother. Master Monkton's explained everything to me already. What's he done to his hand?' Before Tabitha could reply, however, he turned to me. 'Your mount's ready and paid for, Roger. I've given you that same brown cob as last time.' He grinned broadly. 'He shouldn't prove too much for you, but if he does, my advice would be get off and let him ride you instead. It'll probably be quicker.'

The stable boys were sniggering fit to burst their laces. I gave my most long-suffering smile, but resisted the temptation of a riposte. (This was just as well, as it happened, as I was unable to think of one.) Instead, I addressed Tabitha Warrener.

'You're off, then, next Tuesday, mistress? We shall miss you.'

She twitched a straw from one of the mangers and began to chew on it. 'Aye, we're off,' she agreed. 'It's Sweetwater Manor and winter quarters for us before the worst of the weather sets in. And Dorcas is getting near her time.' She bit off the end of the straw and spat it out. 'Before you go, are they true, all these rumours about the knight that's been murdered? That the body was mutilated by someone carving letters into his chest?'

'Yes, quite true,' I said. 'Sir George's grandson and I found the body.' The head stable man and stable boys had stopped making jokes at my expense and drawn closer in order to hear the better. 'His throat had been viciously slashed and the word

"DIE" cut into his right breast. Also, his eyes had been gouged out.'

The stable boys looked slightly green about the gills. Even the stable man swallowed rather hard. Only Tabitha showed no emotion.

'Why "DIE",' she asked, 'when he was already dead?'

I shrugged. 'Nobody knows. There seems to be no answer to that question.'

I wasn't about to proffer my own pet theory. For the moment, that was a secret between James Marvell and me.

Tabitha didn't labour the point, merely jerking her head in the cob's direction. 'You don't usually ride,' she said. I made no answer. 'Although,' she went on, 'I can see you haven't your pack with you, so I would hazard a guess it's private business that you're on.'

I grunted, which she could take as a yea or nay as she pleased, and climbed awkwardly into the saddle, disposing of my few necessities in one of the saddle-bags. There then followed the usual difficulty of arranging my cudgel, one of the stable boys eventually solving the problem by couching it, like a lance, at my side. I thanked him and gave him a groat, which he had the impudence to bite just to make sure it was good. Finally, with everyone grinning like idiots, I dug my heels into the animal's sides and the horse started forward with a jerk which nearly unseated me. As I rode out of the stable yard into Bell Lane, I didn't dare look behind me. I didn't need to. Their shouts of merriment pursued me all the way to the Frome Bridge.

Once free of the surrounding hills, I felt bold enough to urge the cob to a canter. I was feeling more nervous than I would admit, facing the realization that I had rarely ridden a horse on my own before. Nearly always in the past, I had had a companion who could come to my rescue if necessary. Furthermore, it was winter and the ground in many places hard as iron. There had also been a frost overnight and treacherous patches of ice occasionally made the cob almost lose its footing. I cursed myself roundly for having agreed to the expedition.

As the day wore on, however, it grew a little warmer and the sun rose higher in the heavens, sparkling on meadow and forest and streams alike, turning everything into a world of faery. When my stomach told me it was dinnertime, I stopped on the edge of some woodland at a charcoal burner's cottage and persuaded the goodwife to sell me bread and cheese and ale. Afterwards, much refreshed, I continued my journey in better heart, even spurring my sluggish mount to a short gallop on a stretch of flat, open ground between two belts of trees. But for the most part, we went at a comfortable canter.

Nibley Green lies north of Bristol by some fifteen to twenty miles and so, on horseback, could be reached in the better part of a day. Nevertheless, it was growing dark when, following a friendly shepherd's careful directions, I reached the scatter of outlying cottages leading to the main street and the village green. Many of them still bore evidence of the battle fought in the area some thirteen years earlier when the Berkeleys fought the Talbots in a private dispute over land. There was one ale-house with a bush of holly outside that looked clean and seemed not too rowdy and, moreover, had an outhouse where I could stable the cob. I dismounted, unhitched my saddle-bag and cudgel and went inside.

A quarter of an hour later, I was comfortably ensconced in front of a blazing fire, making short work of one of the landlady's beef and oyster pies and drinking her health in a beaker of exceptionally fine ale.

'You keep this place on your own?' I queried.

She was a big, full-bosomed creature with the very dark hair and eyes that indicates Celtic blood. And, indeed, we were not far from the marches of Wales.

She shrugged. 'Since my man died twelve years ago come next Eastertide. It's not unusual. Many women keep ale-houses and inns.'

I tapped my plate with my knife. 'This is splendid fare.' I glanced around me at the empty benches and stools. 'You should be doing a better trade than this.'

She laughed. 'It'll fill up again after Christmas. But nobody has money to spare at this season of the year. People stay indoors with their families. Besides, it's early yet. A few will drift in later and sup their Christmas ale.' She seated herself opposite me and watched me eat. 'You're a stranger in these parts. Where are you from?'

'Bristol.' I wiped the gravy from my chin with the back of my hand. 'You say you've been here twelve years?'

'Longer. I said my man died twelve years since.' She eyed me shrewdly. 'Seeking information, are you?'

'I'm looking for a family called Deakin. It's possible they came here about three years ago to live with Goody Deakin's sister after they were turned off their holding in Clifton Manor.'

The landlady bit her thumbnail reflectively. After a while she nodded. 'Yes, I do recollect them: a mother, father and a good-looking son.'

'Was the son's name Miles?'

'Yes. Now you remind me of it, I believe it was. When he first came here he was in a sorry state. Someone had beaten him badly. Almost, I would say, to within an inch of his life. I never got the full story from Agnes Littlewood, nor from the old man, her father. But my belief is that there was a woman in the case. Some irate husband had given that lad a beating that had very nearly killed him.'

'Not a husband,' I said. 'A brother. And the lady in question was more than eighty years old.'

She stared at me in disbelief for several seconds, then, realizing I was in earnest, started to laugh. 'I don't think Agnes ever knew that. She would have found it too great a joke not to share.'

'This Agnes Littlewood, she was Miles Deakin's aunt?'

'That's right. His mother's sister.'

'Do the Deakins still live here?' I tried to keep the eagerness out of my voice.

My hostess shook her head. 'Well,' she amended, 'Agnes and her father, old Alfred Littlewood, do, but the Deakins moved on again after a year or so. I fancy the two women didn't get on.' She settled herself more comfortably on her stool, her dark eyes bright in the firelight. 'Tell me about young Miles and the eighty-year-old woman and you shall have another piece of pie free of charge.'

This was an offer too good to resist. Besides, there was nothing secret about the history of Drusilla Marvell and her swain, so I told the tale with a few imaginary embellishments of my own to make it even more interesting and amusing. But I stopped short of recounting recent events, afraid that they might alarm the landlady into sending a warning message to the Littlewoods.

'So why are you looking for Miles Deakin?' she asked when I had finished.

'Dame Drusilla's brother died recently,' I answered truthfully.

My companion laughed. 'So the lady feels free to find him again, eh? And has commissioned you to do so.' I didn't reply, letting my silence tell the untruth for me. 'Well, as I say,' she went on, 'Miles and his family have long gone, but Agnes might know where and be able to point you in their direction. I'll show you her cottage in the morning. Meanwhile,' she added as the ale-house door opened and a couple of the villagers came in, 'we have company at last. And by the look of that powdering of snow on their coats, it's settling in to be a miserable evening. Make yourself comfortable and I'll bring you that second slice of pie.'

I awoke next morning to a light fall of snow which had turned streets and rooftops white, and for several moments was afraid that I might not be able to get home again the following day in time for Twelfth Night Eve. A quick foray out of doors, however, showed that the fall was not deep – a sprinkling merely – and I was able to enjoy my breakfast of fried herring and freshly cooked oatcakes with an easy mind. The bed I had occupied overnight had been clean and comfortable and I had slept well. I felt refreshed in mind and body.

My hostess indicated a cottage at the end of the village street as that belonging to Agnes Littlewood and her father, Alfred, and when I considered sufficient time had elapsed for them to have eaten their breakfast, I set out. The cottage was typical of others I could see, being one-storeyed, made of daub and wattle and thatched with moss and twigs. A rough patch of ground to one side suggested that in the summer months an attempt was made to grow a few herbs and vegetables, and it was possible that one of the pigs in the common sty at the end of the street was theirs. I could also hear the bleating of a goat somewhere about.

My knock on the door was answered by a very thin woman

in coarse, homespun clothes with a narrow face and two faded blue eyes that, once she realized I was not one of her neighbours, regarded me with suspicion.

'Yes?' Her voice was sharp and I could see her looking for any clue that might suggest my calling.

'Mistress Littlewood?' I smiled ingratiatingly. 'The aunt of Miles Deakin?'

This was the last thing she had expected and she paused in the act of closing the door in my face.

'Who are you?' she demanded.

'I – I'm trying to discover the present whereabouts of Miles – er – Deakin,' I faltered, suddenly finding it more difficult than I had anticipated to think up a reason for my enquiry. 'A – er – a lady in Bristol is anxious to see him again.'

It sounded feeble even to my own ears, so I was astonished when the woman sighed and said, 'You'd better come in.'

Inside, it was extremely dark and cramped, with the only light coming from a small window at the far end of the room and a rush light burning on the table. A fire on the central hearth belched smoke through a hole in the roof and bedding was rolled up against one wall. I realized why the Deakin family had left and was only surprised that they had stayed as long as they had. Five people crowded into such a confined space must have made life well nigh impossible.

Agnes Littlewood closed the door and took the bellows to blow up the fire. A flame or two appeared before it died down once more to a sullen glow. She didn't ask me to sit down although the room boasted two three-legged stools as well as a rickety chair with arms pulled up close to the hearth. 'Well,' she said abruptly, 'who is this woman who wants to find my nephew?'

'A lady,' I corrected her. 'A very wealthy lady. She knew Miles when he was in Bristol some three years back and now wants to meet him again. Her . . . Her patronage could be greatly to his advantage.' The lies were starting to stick in my throat.

'You mean the old woman, do you? The one whose brother broke nearly every bone in poor Miles's body and got my sister and her husband turned off their land?'

'Yes,' I admitted, feeling suddenly ashamed that I had shared this story with the landlady of the ale-house the night before, and treated it as a joke. I added, 'The brother's dead now.' What I didn't say was that I was searching for Miles because I thought he might be that brother's murderer and the killer of yet another man. The burden of guilt was almost overwhelming and I was beginning to wish heartily that I had never let James persuade me into undertaking this mission.

Agnes Littlewood shrugged. 'It's no good coming to me. Miles left two years back. Never said where he was going – or even that he was going. Went out one day and never returned. My sister and her man waited another six months, but when he didn't reappear, they moved on to our other sister at North Nibley, where they still are today. But I can save you a journey if you're thinking of going there. I visited them all only last week, and they know no more now of Miles's whereabouts than they did on the day he disappeared.'

'You're sure of this?'

She threw me a look of contempt without deigning to reply.

'Thank you, mistress,' I said eventually. I felt certain she was telling me the truth. There was nothing more to stay for. 'I'll take myself off then.'

I turned towards the door but as I did so, I heard her take a breath as though she would add something. I turned back, raising my eyebrows.

She hesitated, then said, 'Someone who knew Miles did say he thought he'd seen him in Bristol three months ago. It was someone who lives down that way and was passing through North Nibley on his way to Gloucester. He recognized my brother-in-law in the street and stopped to talk to him. Mind you, he wasn't at all sure it was Miles he'd seen, but he thought it might have been.'

'Three months ago,' I repeated and Agnes Littlewood nodded. 'But the man was uncertain?' She nodded again. 'Who was the man? Do you know his name?'

'I think my sister called him John Cleghorn and said he was a baker by trade. But she didn't set much store by his having seen Miles. She remembered Cleghorn and thought him a bit of a liar.'

'Why would he lie about such a thing?'

Again came the shrug. 'Why do people lie about anything? Why are you lying to me now?'

I was taken aback. 'Am I?' I managed to get out.

'Yes.' She was unequivocal. 'But you're not going to tell me why, so I'm not going to waste my breath asking.'

Before I could gather my wits together and decide whether or not to tell her the truth, the door opened once more and an old man, leaning heavily on a stick, came in, pausing just inside the doorway. This, I guessed, must be Alfred Littlewood, but the light of the snowy scene outside was behind him, and I could not immediately see his face.

'There's someone here,' he said, raising his head and turning it from side to side. 'A stranger. I've warned 'ee, Agnes, about letting in strangers.' He sniffed. 'An' I reckon it's a man an' all.'

It was then I realized that he was blind.

His daughter pulled him inside and shut the door. 'You're letting all the cold air in, you silly old fool.'

'Who is it? I'll not be kept in the dark.'

The irony of the remark seemed to strike neither of them. Agnes removed his hat with an impatient gesture and pushed him down into the chair.

'It's only a nice young fellow asking about Miles. There's nothing to be afraid of. He's going now.'

I was at last able to get a good look at Alfred Littlewood, an old, bent man with wispy grey hair and a weather-beaten skin. Round his head, covering his eyes, was a dirty bandage which sank into his eye sockets as if there was nothing behind it. And with a shock of distaste, I knew suddenly that the sockets were empty: the eyes had been torn out. At the same moment, I remembered yet again something I kept thrusting to the back of my mind; the removal of Sir George Marvell's eyes from his dead body. The bile rose in my throat.

I saw Agnes look at me sharply and with contempt. She had noticed my expression of revulsion, although she was wrong in thinking her father was its cause. But before I had time to say anything in my own defence, the old man lost his grip on his stick and it dropped with a clatter. I stooped quickly to pick it up while he groped around ineffectually with both hands. And it was then I suffered a second shock. The first two fingers of his right hand were missing.

Without thinking about what I was doing, I grabbed his right wrist.

He let out a yell that demonstrated his lungs, at least, were in good working order.

'What's he doing? What's he doing? I warned you, Agnes, about letting strangers into the house. He's going to murder the pair of us.'

'Don't be foolish, Father,' was the acid retort. 'All the same,' she added, addressing me, 'I'd like an explanation of your conduct. And come to think of it, you haven't yet told me your name.'

'I beg your pardon,' I said, releasing the old man's wrist and restoring his stick to him. 'My name's Roger Chapman. Master Littlewood,' I went on, 'this Christmas we've had a troupe of mummers to entertain us in the castle yard at Bristol. One of the men, the older one, a man of maybe your age, has injuries just like yours except that he's not blind. But one of his eyes has terrible scarring around it and the first two fingers of his right hand are missing.'

Alfred Littlewood at once became very excited. 'What's his name? What's his name, young fellow? Do you know it?'

'Ned Chorley.'

Alfred's face fell and he shook his head. 'Thought I might've known him, but I don't. However, I'll tell you this. Your mummer was once an archer in the French wars, like me. We were the cream of the army, we were. We were the English Goddams them French bastards feared the most. And if they caught us, do you know what they did to us? First, they hacked off our bowstring fingers, because without the first two fingers of your right hand, you ain't never going to be able to pull a longbow again. Then them devils gouged out our eyes and cut off our balls. Finally, if you were lucky, they finished you off with a dagger thrust or strangled you with a rope.'

'And if you were unlucky?'

'They turned you loose to wander about until you died.'

'That happened to you?'

He nodded. 'But I was found by two of our scouts who'd got into the French camp in search of information. They guided me back to our own lines.'

'And this Ned Chorley?'

The old man sucked on one of his few remaining teeth. 'He must've been rescued before they really pushed out his eyes. He were more fortunate than me, then. But his days as an archer would've been finished.'

I stared ahead of me blankly, getting my thoughts in order. So Ned Chorley had been a soldier, an archer. The idea had never occurred to me, and yet I realized that it should have done. I remembered suddenly his talking about King Richard and what a good strategist he was, his glowing admiration for his military skills in the way only an old soldier would appreciate. And the missing fingers, the scarred eye, were now explained. At some time in his life he had been taken prisoner by the French, but rescued before they could really wreak their vengeance on him.

I brought my attention back to Alfred Littlewood. 'You're quite sure you never met him, master?'

The old man shook his head impatiently. He was beginning to lose interest in the subject. 'Where's my dinner?' he whined.

'It's not dinnertime for a while yet,' Agnes snapped. 'You've only just had your breakfast, you greedy old villain. Sit there and warm yourself at the fire while I see Master Chapman out.' She opened the cottage door again with a gesture it was hard to ignore. As I huddled my cloak around me and stepped out into the still lightly falling snow, she asked, 'Will you go on to North Nibley?'

'No. I must be home in time for Twelfth Night Eve,' I said. 'I've promised my wife and children to be there. Besides, I doubt if your brother-in-law could give me any more information than he's given you. If this John Cleghorn lives in Bristol or in Clifton Manor, I'd do better trying to find him myself. Though from what you say I don't suppose he'll have anything of interest to tell me.'

I moved away and heard the door shut behind me before I had gone more than half a dozen steps.

I saw no reason to linger in Nibley. The journey had not been entirely fruitless, but I doubted I was going to learn anything more. Also, the snow might increase and I had no wish to be stranded. If I left now before conditions worsened I could be much more than halfway to Bristol by nightfall, which meant that, although I never liked travelling on a Sunday if I could help it, I might very well be home by dinnertime the following day. So I said farewell to my hostess, who seemed genuinely sorry at my decision to leave, fetched my reluctant horse from his cosy stable and set off southwards, comforted by the thought that I had something, at least, to report to James Marvell and that the journey had not been a complete waste of my time and his money. There was now at least the possibility that Miles Deakin might be somewhere in Bristol. If we could find a baker called John Cleghorn, maybe he would be able to tell us more.

SIXTEEN

It was not until I was riding across the Frome Bridge the following morning, all the church bells of Bristol ringing in my ears, that I realized with a jolt that of course I knew Baker Cleghorn. Or, at least, if I didn't know him personally, I knew of him. Burl Hodge's son, Dick, was his apprentice and Adela bought her sweet dough at his shop. I must be getting old that I had not immediately made the connection. My mind was working more slowly nowadays. It was very worrying.

I remembered also that the baker had his shop in St Leonard's Lane. I would visit him as soon as I could and find out what he had to say concerning his possible sighting of Miles Deakin three months earlier. But for now, my one thought was to get home out of this biting cold, for Sunday had come in with a bitter wind blowing and the last phase of my journey had been uncomfortable in the extreme. I had made good progress all day yesterday, or what remained of it after I had taken leave of my hostess at Nibley Green, my sturdy cob making a steady pace southwards, some instinct telling him he was returning home and urging him on. The result was that I had been able to break my journey and stop for the night only a few miles north of the city when the darkness and freezing conditions made it certain that I could not continue. That morning, in spite of the weather, I was up betimes, barely pausing long enough to eat my breakfast, with the result that I was within the city gates just as the bells began to ring for Tierce.

I didn't stop to bandy words with the Frome Gate porter, although he did his best to start a conversation, inquisitive to know where I had been at such an early hour. I heard him muttering indignantly to himself as I rode away, and at any other time I might have obliged him, knowing him to be chilled and bored with his own company. But Small Street was only a street or two away. First, however, I had to return the cob to the stables in Bell Lane.

They had not yet closed for the hour or so necessary for the head stable man and his assistants to go to Sunday Mass, and I rode in through the gateway just as Ned Chorley arrived to carry out the mummers' daily inspection of their horses. I slid thankfully from the saddle and hailed him.

He smiled briefly and said, 'Good-day to you, Master Chapman,' before turning to speak to the lad who had come forward on seeing him.

I clapped him on the shoulder.

'You've been hiding your light under a bushel, sir. You didn't tell us you had been a soldier. And not just a soldier, but an archer. Nor that you had been captured and tortured by the French.'

The stable lad was regarding him goggle-eyed, but Ned himself was looking red and uncomfortable.

'There was no call to tell you, Master Chapman,' he muttered, adding, 'it was all a long time ago. Who told you?'

'A man I met yesterday had the same injuries as yourself except that he was blind. His eyes had been gouged out. He said that he had been an archer – a longbowman – who had been taken prisoner by the French and explained what they did to bowmen taken alive.'

Ned Chorley was interested in spite of himself. 'Then how is it he's still here to tell the tale?'

'After his captors had castrated him as well' – I saw the stable lad wince – 'they turned him loose to wander about until he died. As I understood it, two of our scouts who had penetrated the French camp found him and led him to safety.'

Ned Chorley nodded. 'It happened sometimes,' he grunted.

I waited a few moments, but as he seemed disinclined to say more, I asked him outright, 'And is that also what happened to you?'

Again he nodded, then vouchsafed, 'I was rescued, yes. But I was luckier than your informant. Those French devils had only just started to get to work on me.' He shivered suddenly, but whether from the cold or disturbed by his memories it was hard to tell. He turned away abruptly, seizing the stable lad by the elbow. 'Let's take a look at the horses, then I can tell Master Monkton that they're safe and well.' He gave a snort of laughter. 'That man's a worrier.'

As I watched the cob being led off to his stall by another of the stable lads, I asked, 'How's Master Monkton's hand? I understood from Mistress Tabitha that he'd injured it.'

Ned looked annoyed at this further interruption, but answered civilly enough, 'It's on the mend but still a bit red and swollen. Dog bites are nasty things and can be dangerous. The animal might have been rabid. However, it seems he was lucky and the wound's mending cleanly.'

'I'm glad of that,' I said. 'Shall we see you tomorrow night at the wassailing?'

'In the castle orchard? Yes, indeed. We give our last performance in the afternoon. Will you and your family be coming? It's Saint George and the Dragon. Young Adam's favourite.'

'I daresay,' I said with a laugh. 'Your performance as the Doctor is what he really comes for. He'll miss you when you go.'

The old man nodded but showed no particular sign of pleasure. He seemed less friendly than he had been and I found myself wondering if we had offended him in some way. He disappeared in the direction of the stalls and, a moment later, I heard him talking in dulcet tones to his horses.

I took myself off to Small Street, where my arrival was greeted with greater delight than was usually accorded my return. Adela threw her arms about my neck, saying, 'Roger! This is a pleasant surprise. We didn't expect you until tomorrow!' Hercules danced around me, barking like a fiend and nipping my ankles, while even the children came downstairs to welcome me without the customary demand to know what I had brought them. They were obviously stuffed full of Christmas sweetmeats, which was just as well, as for once I had nothing for them.

'You're just in time to see to the Yule log,' my wife informed me with relief. 'It's almost out.'

It was indeed looking black with only wisps of smoke curling up from the bed of straw on which it was lying, but a session with the kitchen bellows gradually coaxed it back to life and induced a few small flames to make a reluctant appearance. I reflected with relief that there were only two more days to go before it could be left to smoulder into ashes.

'Is there any news on the murders?' I asked Adela as she stood watching my efforts with the log.

She shook her head. 'I think the sheriff and his men are baffled. Did you learn anything useful on this trip to Nibley Green? Was the journey worth it?'

'One or two things,' I admitted, getting to my feet and regarding the struggling flames with satisfaction. 'I must see James Marvell.'

'Not today,' my wife said firmly. 'It's Sunday. Dinner is almost ready and this afternoon you can help me put the final touches to my Twelfth Night cake.'

'I thought you'd finished it,' I grumbled.

'No. I didn't, after all, put the pea and the bean in when I made it. I thought you and Elizabeth could have the honour of doing that. You can push them in through the sides of the cake so we'll be certain of getting them in separate halves. You can very well postpone seeing Master Marvell until tomorrow.'

So much for Adela's plans. We had barely finished our meal when a knock at the street door heralded the arrival of James himself, come to discover if I had gleaned anything of importance during my trip.

'You made good time,' he said as I followed him into the parlour and waved him to a chair. 'I didn't expect to see you until tomorrow. But someone at church told me he'd seen you riding through the Frome Gate earlier this morning, so I came round as soon as I could. There have been no developments here during the two days you've been away.'

Adela came in with a couple of beakers and a jug of ale on a tray, which she placed on the hearth where a small, very desultory fire was burning. Her annoyance at James's intrusion was palpable, but he didn't seem to notice. He was too intent on getting an answer to his question.

'So, do you have anything to tell me?'

I poured us both some ale and settled in the opposite chair before giving him such information as I was able.

He sat forward eagerly when I mentioned Baker Cleghorn and his belief that he might have seen Miles Deakin in Bristol three months earlier. 'He told Miles Deakin's father this? How long ago?'

I shrugged. 'Recently, I assumed, when he was passing through North Nibley on his way to Gloucester.'

'And has Master Cleghorn returned to Bristol yet?'

'I don't know,' I said. 'I'll ask my wife.'

Adela, when consulted, said she had spoken to the baker only the previous day when she had visited his shop.

'Then we'll call on him at once.' James, pausing only long enough to swallow the dregs of his ale, rose purposefully to his feet.

'It's Sunday,' I demurred, hoping to restrain him. I had no desire to go out into the cold again and was looking forward to the rest of the day by my own fireside.

'So he won't be engaged in trade. We shall be assured of his whole attention.' James picked up his cloak and wrapped it around him. 'Where does he live? Behind the shop?'

Once again I was forced to consult Adela, who confirmed that Master Cleghorn's house was also in St Leonard's Lane. 'You're not going out?' she asked reproachfully. 'You've only just got home.'

I was apologetic, but found that my earlier reluctance to brave the elements had vanished. I was suddenly as anxious as my companion to discover what the baker had to say.

St Leonard's Lane was only a step or two away, being the next street along in a westerly direction, running from Corn Street at one end and connecting with Bell Lane at the other. The dwellings here were substantial residences built, as were most Bristol houses, of wood and plaster and tiled with stone. The ground floors of a few, like Baker Cleghorn's, were shops with the families living on the premises in the upper two storeys. The one we wanted was halfway along on the right-hand side proceeding from Bell Lane and was easy enough to find, a sign depicting a loaf of bread hanging above the door. This was located to one side of the shop front, now raised and bolted shut, and James had no compunction in banging on it loudly, disturbing the Sabbath peace.

We had to wait a while for someone to descend from the upper floors, but eventually the key scraped in the lock, the door was opened a crack and a voice enquired cautiously, 'Who's there?'

'Master Cleghorn?' James asked.

'Aye. Who wants him?'

It took James some time to convince the baker that we were

genuine callers and not a couple of bravos out on a Christmas
jaunt, frightening elderly citizens. Our lack of masks was to our
advantage and we were eventually admitted to the house and
conducted to a room on the first floor. This was richly and comfortably furnished, arguing a degree of wealth which easily explained
the baker's caution. It transpired that he was a childless widower
living alone except for a sister who kept house for him, but who,
today, was absent on a visit to a friend.

'So you gentlemen will, I'm sure, understand my reluctance
to let you in,' our host explained, at the same time indicating
two cushioned chairs and inviting us to sit down. 'This season
of the year particularly.'

We assured him that we did and accepted his offer of wine,
which he served in some very fine silver goblets. The bakery
trade was obviously thriving.

'And what can I do for your honours? Master Chapman I
know,' he added. 'Your wife, sir, is a good customer of mine.'

He seemed unaware of James's identity, which was all to the
good. We had no desire to rouse his suspicions concerning the name
of Deakin, which a connection with the Marvell family might
possibly do. Instead, James claimed Miles as an old acquaintance
whom he was trying to find after a lapse of some years. He then
glibly explained that I had recently been peddling my wares in
Nibley Green and had been told by Mistress Littlewood of her
brother-in-law's meeting with himself.

'And Mistress Littlewood,' I added, 'said that you, sir, claimed
to have seen Miles Deakin here, in Bristol, not three months
since.'

The baker shook his head. 'No, no! I only thought it might
have been him. But I was by no means certain.'

'You are acquainted with the Deakin family?' I asked.

'Yes. They were some sort of distant kinfolk of my late wife.'
He spoke apologetically, plainly ashamed of such low
connections.

'And where did you think you saw Miles, Master Cleghorn?'
James asked.

'I've told you, I'm not sure . . .'

'I understand that. But whereabouts?' my companion insisted.

The baker hesitated. 'It was only a fleeting glimpse and in the most unlikely of places.' Again he paused, adding, 'It's that really which convinces me I was completely mistaken.'

'Where, Master Cleghorn?' James spoke through clenched teeth. He was beginning to lose patience.

For a long moment there was silence, then the baker resolutely shook his head. 'No, I refuse to say. I'm sorry, gentlemen, but I realize now that I was totally in error. That it could not possibly have been Miles. I therefore prefer to keep my own counsel.' And he got to his feet, making it plain that our visit was at an end. 'I'll wish you good day.'

In the face of so pointed a dismissal, we had no choice but to leave. Our host's face had set in rigid lines. He was not to be bullied or persuaded.

Once out in the street again, James gave vent to his anger. 'The old fool! Why did he suddenly put a clamp on his tongue like that?'

'I don't know,' I said slowly. 'But I have a feeling that all of a sudden he recognized you. I may be mistaken and I can't think of anything you said that would have made him suspicious. As I say, it's just a feeling.'

James hunched his shoulders angrily. 'Oh, well! It can't be helped, but if you're right, he has to know of the connection between Miles Deakin and my family. What was your impression, Master Chapman? Do you think Baker Cleghorn believes he saw our man or is now convinced that he was wrong?'

I shivered and drew my cloak more tightly around me. It was getting even colder and I had no desire to stand talking in the street. Nevertheless, I gave his question my due consideration.

After a few moments reflection, I said, 'I think I do believe Master Cleghorn saw a man he thought to be Miles Deakin. But for some reason of his own is now unwilling to tell us where.'

'For what reason?'

'I don't know.'

On this unsatisfactory note we parted, he to return to Redcliffe and I to walk the short distance back to Small Street. I was growing frustrated with a situation that yielded so few answers and which had marred a Christmas I had looked forward to with some eagerness as a time to spend quietly with my family and do little else except enjoy the festivities. The last two years, as I have already said, had been both gruelling and dangerous, dominated by King Richard's seizure of the throne. It occurred to me that my use of the word 'seizure' was more revealing than I knew. He would say that he had claimed his birthright, but was that how I really saw it? In spite of that secret mission I had undertaken for him to France the preceding year, and in spite of what I had learned there, I nevertheless found in myself a growing dismay at what he had done and an ever-increasing foreboding for the future. 'Stirring up a hornet's nest' was a phrase that, for no apparent reason, flashed into my head, and I told myself not to be so foolish. All the same, I arrived at my own front door in no very happy frame of mind.

Here, however, a pleasant surprise awaited me.

Elizabeth answered my knock and as soon as she saw me went scurrying back into the parlour. I heard her whisper loudly, 'He's here!'

Adam gave vent to one of his shrill giggles.

I pushed open the parlour door with some apprehension, wondering what the three children were up to; an apprehension which, I'm ashamed to admit, turned to annoyance when I became aware of Margaret Walker's presence. Luckily, before I had time to make some caustic remark, Adela came forward, smiling all over her face.

'Roger,' she beamed, 'come and see what Cousin Margaret's brought you. Just look at this!'

'This', spread out over one of the chairs, was a splendid dark blue woollen cloak, held together at the throat by a smart brown leather tie.

'Grandmother made it for you,' my daughter announced, taking my hand. 'Isn't she clever?'

I stared blankly for a moment, then asked stupidly, 'For me? You made it for me, Mother-in-law?'

'Oh, for Our Sweet Lady's sake!' she exclaimed impatiently. 'You'd think I'd never given you anything in your life before.' To be honest, I couldn't think of many presents I'd had from her, but I refrained from saying so. 'I spun the yarn myself and paid Master Adelard to have it woven and dyed. The cutting and sewing I had done by a tailor who has rooms in Tucker Street.

And a very good job he's made of it, too. Here! Try it on instead of just standing there, staring at it.'

She and Adela divested me of my old cloak and draped the new one around me. It had that faintly sour smell of newly treated wool and its folds were wonderfully warm and soft.

'B-But why?' I stuttered ungraciously.

'Oh, for Jesu's sake, does there have to be a reason?' Margaret demanded irritably, adding with a half-laugh, 'I'm fond of you, Roger. Always was in spite of the fact that you're like most men, utterly selfish and boorish. Moreover, I'm tired of seeing you in that old grey cloak of yours. The hem is rubbed and the wool is wearing thin in places. It might have been all very well when you were in a duke's employ, but now that Richard is king . . .'

'Margaret,' I began, but then stopped. What was the use of saying yet again what I had said so many times in the past? I had never been in the duke's employ, nor was I now that he was king. I had done favours for him from time to time, but had rarely been paid, preferring to keep my independence. (Although it's true to say that favours for royalty are tantamount to commands.) My former mother-in-law liked to believe differently: it was then a connection that gave her added importance in the eyes of her friends.

I took a deep breath. 'Margaret,' I said again, 'it's beautiful and I thank you with all my heart. I shall be the grandest man in church today and every Sunday.'

'Oh, no!' she answered firmly. 'That cloak is not just for Sundays and holy days, to be put away in a chest the rest of the time. It's for everyday use, to smarten you up a little. Adela, you must see to it. Give that old grey thing away so that he won't be tempted to wear it. I know what men are, Roger especially. He's never happy unless he looks like a – a –'

'Pedlar?' I suggested ironically. 'Mother-in-law, I can't go tramping round the countryside in this. It will be stolen in a trice.'

Margaret sniffed. 'No, it won't. Not the way you treat clothes. You'll have it looking like something Hercules has made his bed on before many days have passed, just you wait and see.'

It was no use to argue with her. I thanked her again with genuine warmth – indeed, I was deeply touched by this unlooked-for gesture – and at the same time made up my mind to keep my old grey cloak for common use, wearing the magnificent new blue one for those occasions when I thought it appropriate.

But for me to make a decision is simply throwing down the gauntlet to Fate.

We all went to St Giles's in the afternoon – I wearing my new cloak, needless to say – then I escorted Margaret home to Redcliffe, Adela having been unsuccessful in her attempt to persuade her cousin to stay for supper. It was after I had seen Margaret safely into her cottage that I had the notion, as I was so close, to call on young Dick Hodge. It crossed my mind that perhaps Baker Cleghorn might, just possibly, have said something to his assistant concerning his sighting of Miles Deakin. I considered it unlikely, but it was worth the effort of visiting Burl's cottage near the Rope Walk to find out.

Jenny answered my knock and was pleased to see me, as always. 'Burl's not here, Roger,' she said. 'He and Jack have stepped out for an hour, but if you care to come inside and wait . . .'

I thanked her, adding, 'It's not Burl I've come to see. Is Dick at home?'

She looked surprised, but held the door open at once. 'Yes, he's here,' she said, calling over her shoulder, 'Dick! It's Master Chapman. He wants a word with you.'

The inside of the cottage, cramped and dark and overcrowded, reminded me forcibly of the one Adela and I had once shared in Lewin's Mead, and I realized with a shock that, with four children as well as ourselves, this is how we would be living, had Cicely Ford not willed her house in Small Street to me. I realized also something of the reason for Burl's jealousy and resentment at my undeserved good fortune over the past few years.

Dick was seated at the table, trying to learn his catechism, one forefinger laboriously tracing the words, his lips silently forming them as he made out each one. Jenny looked on proudly. Neither she nor Burl could read or write, but she had insisted – much against Burl's wishes as he thought it a waste of time and money – that the two boys be taught their letters.

Dick looked up as I sat down on the stool facing him, obviously glad to have an excuse to leave his reading. 'What can I do for you, Master Chapman?'

Jenny put a stoup of her homemade ale in front of me and went off to stir the pot over the fire which contained their supper. (It smelled good, whatever it was.)

'Dick,' I began, but then hesitated, not quite sure how to proceed. He regarded me stolidly and waited. Life had no urgency for the younger of Burl's two sons. 'Dick,' I said again after a pause, 'has Baker Cleghorn recently mentioned to you that he'd seen, or might have seen, an old acquaintance who – er – who perhaps had returned to the city after several years' absence?'

Dick slowly shook his head. 'No,' he said.

I saw Jenny throw me a curious glance, but it would never occur to Dick to ask me why I wanted to know. He was not interested enough to pry into other people's affairs. He had never had an enquiring mind.

'You're quite certain?'

He smiled his sweet, unworldly smile. 'Certain, Master Chapman. He's a good master, but he doesn't have much to say.'

Jenny laughed. 'It's you who doesn't have much to say to Master Cleghorn, more like,' she chided him. I saw her eyeing my cloak. 'That new, Roger?'

I explained about Margaret's gift and she grimaced.

'Master Adelard must be giving her plenty of weaving to do. Mind you,' she added generously, 'Margaret was always clever with her fingers. She's one o'the best spinners in Redcliffe.'

I finished my ale and stood up. 'I must be going, Jenny. It's getting dark. Thank you for the ale. Mind you lock up after me and don't answer the door to anyone until Burl and Jack get back.'

'No, I won't. No one's been taken for these dreadful murders yet, I suppose?' I shook my head, but as I moved towards the door, she left stirring the pot and came to see me out. 'Roger,' she said diffidently, 'what . . . what are you doing with your old cloak?'

I hesitated. 'If you want it for Burl, Jenny, you know he wouldn't take it. Not from me. Anyone else, perhaps, but not me.'

She flushed painfully. 'No, I know that, Roger. We've had

words about it many times these past few years. He knows envy's a sin, but somehow or other he can't seem to rid himself of it. But I wasn't asking for Burl. It's Dick.' She glanced sideways at her son, but he had returned to his catechism and wasn't listening. 'His winter cloak's as good as worn out. I wouldn't ask, but . . .' Her voice tailed away and she looked as if she might burst into tears.

I stooped and kissed her cheek. 'Jenny,' I said, 'it's Dick's. And I shall be jealous every time I see him wearing it. You know how I hate new clothes.' She smiled mistily at me. 'Adela will be at the market in the morning. I'll give it to her to bring to you there. Now, lock the door behind me. There's evil abroad in the streets this Christmas. I'll see you tomorrow at the wassailing.'

SEVENTEEN

The Eve of Twelfth Night, or the Eve of Epiphany, whichever you prefer to call it, dawned with clear skies and the
sparkle of frost on rooftops and the rays of a thin winter
sunlight piercing the clouds. The children were up betimes,
excited by the prospect of their last visit to see the mummers,
of being allowed to stay up late to go wassailing with the adults
and, Nicholas and Elizabeth in particular, at being king and queen
of the feast. Usually this was not known until the Twelfth Night
cake was cut, when the man who found the bean in his slice was
named the king and the lady who discovered the pea in hers the
queen. Adela, however, had cheated this year by allowing the two
older children to push the pea and bean into the cake after it was
baked.

Adam had protested loudly to begin with, but a promise that
he should be king of the feast the following year had pacified
him with surprising ease. In spite of all that had been going on
around him, he, at least, had enjoyed his Christmas, the ignorance
and self-absorption of childhood protecting him like a magic
cloak. The climax of this, the penultimate of the twelve days of
Christmas, was to be his visit to the castle for the mummers'
final performance. And it was to be his favourite play, St George
and the Dragon.

When I had returned home the previous afternoon, I had told
Adela of my visit to Burl's cottage, although not the reason for
it, and of my promise to Jenny that Dick should have my old
grey cloak. This had met with her full approval and so, when
she set out for the Tolzey that morning, it was folded up in her
basket, ready to give to her friend.

The children, including Luke in his box on wheels, and
Hercules had gone with her and I was attending to the
Yule log, thanking heaven that tomorrow I could finally let it
go out, when there was a knock on the street door. Wiping

my grimy hands down the sides of my jerkin and cursing under my breath, I opened it to find James Marvell standing outside.

'Master Marvell,' I murmured politely, struggling to keep the annoyance out of my voice, 'what can I do for you?'

He gave a faint smile. 'I've disturbed you,' he said, making it obvious that I had been unsuccessful at hiding my feelings. I made a feeble protest, which he ignored, and continued, 'I thought I should tell you that my father had a secret visitor last night, and now seems more depressed and downhearted than ever.'

'You'd better come in,' I invited and led the way into the kitchen. My hands were black from the Yule log ashes and I knew I dare not risk entering the parlour in such a condition. I had too healthy a respect for Adela's temper if she found filthy fingermarks in this holy of holies.

I poured myself a bowl of water from the water barrel and, with the help of a piece of rough grey soap, began to scrub them clean. My uninvited guest sat down on a stool and watched me curiously. (I assumed that in the Marvell household a servant would have been summoned to provide the soap and water.)

'You say this visitor of Master Cyprian's was secret. So how do you know about him?'

James put his elbows on the table and propped his chin in his hands.

'I couldn't sleep,' he said. 'All that's happened in the past two weeks kept going round and round in my head; thoughts of Grandfather's mutilated body, the death of Alderman Trefusis, Father's growing depression, as if he knows something the rest of us don't. I ate and drank my All-night, hoping that a full belly would help me sleep, but it didn't. In fact, it had the opposite effect. It made me even more restless and full of energy. In the end, I got up, took my candle and started to go downstairs. I'd descended one flight and reached the head of the staircase that leads down into the hall when I heard a knock on the street door. I remember thinking how stupid it was of anyone to call at such an hour when the servants would all be in bed – I'd heard the Watch cry two of the clock some little while before – and also that in the present circumstances no one was going to risk opening a door at that time in the morning, when to my utter astonishment

Father came out of his private room, candle in hand, and did just that.'

'Opened the door, you mean?'

'Yes. He didn't hesitate and was plainly expecting someone. I quickly extinguished my own candle and drew back into the shadows, waiting to see what happened and to rush down to his assistance if it should prove necessary.'

'But it didn't?'

'No.' There was a pause. 'He simply let the person in and they both disappeared into his room.'

'So?' I demanded impatiently, wiping my hands dry on the piece of sacking we kept for that purpose. 'Did you recognize the latecomer?' My excitement was mounting. I was finding it hard to breathe.

'It was a man,' he said at last, 'but I couldn't see his face. He was wearing one of those head masks that people wear at Christmas. A dog's head.'

A dog's head mask! Someone had talked recently of such a thing, but I was unable to remember who or when or where. I cudgelled my brains, but to no avail. What was even more infuriating was the vague recollection that I had had this same feeling even earlier. When whoever it was had mentioned the dog mask, I had experienced a jolt of recognition, a sensation that I had heard the phrase before. And I was certain it was not all that long ago.

James must have seen something in my face for he asked eagerly, 'Does it mean anything to you, Master Chapman?'

I shook my head. There was no point in raising hopes that I might not be able to fulfil.

'Have you asked your father about his visitor?' I queried.

'Yes. He flew into a rage, which is very unlike him – he is normally the most unemotional of men – and told me to mind my own business. "It's nothing to do with you!" he said. And then added, "You're better off not knowing." Naturally, I couldn't accept that, especially not when he looked so haggard, and told him so. He had calmed down a little by then – he cannot sustain anger for very long – but still refused to say more. I would, however, have continued to press him, but just at that moment Bart came looking for me on some pretext or another. I forget what and it doesn't really matter. He was just snooping. That twitchy nose of his had told him that something was up; that Father and I were having a private conversation, and he had come to find out what was going on. I think, for once, Father was relieved to see him, said he wanted to talk to him about the will and marched him off to his private sanctum, so I came to see you to find out if you had any ideas to offer.'

I perched on the edge of the table, frowning. 'Last night,' I said, 'or early this morning as it really was, when your father and his visitor went into his private room, was all quiet? Did you hear raised voices at any time?'

'No. Not once. And I stole downstairs and listened at the door for several minutes. There was a low, sustained murmur, but that was all.'

'Do you think money changed hands?'

James shrugged. 'That I'm unable to say. But I know for a fact that Father keeps a locked casket in the cupboard because I've seen it. Whether or not it contains money I've no idea. It used to be Grandfather's room, but since his death Father has taken it over, now that he's head of the household.'

He looked at me hopefully, as if expecting me to come up with some sudden and brilliant insight as to the identity of the unknown guest, but I was obliged to disappoint him. No flash of inspiration illuminated my somewhat clogged and dull early morning mind. In fact, if the truth were told, I was growing weary of the whole unpleasant business and wanted nothing more than to forget it and enjoy what was left to me of Christmas. Tomorrow, with the Mass celebrating the coming of the three wise men to the stable in Bethlehem and the showing to them of the Christ Child – the Epiphany – the days of celebration would be over. Life would return to its normal, humdrum course until the next feast day. The twelve days would be gone and I should have spent them searching for a sadistic killer. No doubt Richard Manifold felt the same way, but that, after all, was his job.

Some of these thoughts must have conveyed themselves to James Marvell, for he rose abruptly from his stool, saying, 'I'm sorry to have troubled you, Master Chapman. I realize that there is nothing either of us can do without knowing Dog Head's identity, but I needed to tell someone and you are the only person I could think of. I cannot talk to either my mother or Patience or Bartholomew, and if my father refuses to confide in me—' He broke off looking lost, then went on: 'I hate to see him look so unhappy. He's a good man who has had much to vex him in his life.' He took a deep breath. 'I have a feeling that this business must touch the family honour. Father has always been proud of our name.'

As he moved towards the kitchen door, I asked, 'Do you think Master Marvell's unknown visitor might have been Miles Deakin?'

He paused, his hand on the latch. 'The thought has occurred to me, I must admit. The knowledge that Baker Cleghorn thinks he saw the man in Bristol not so long ago makes me feel sure the rogue is indeed hiding somewhere in the city and is threatening to make known his affair with Great-Aunt Drusilla. Father would find that hard to stomach and may well be paying him to keep his mouth shut.'

I considered this for a moment, but almost immediately dismissed the theory.

'Master Marvell looks to me to be a sensible man,' I said. 'He must know that the story is common knowledge already in the town, among certain members of the population, at least. I heard the tale from my former mother-in-law and her cronies, one of whom supplied me with Miles's name. The fact that no one mentions the story to your father doesn't necessarily mean ignorance on the part of the general populace – only that they have too much respect for him to do so. And I don't suppose anyone would have dared to throw it in your grandfather's face.'

That brought a momentary smile to his lips, but then he frowned. 'So what are you saying to me? That if the unknown visitor was Miles Deakin, he must have a stronger hold over Father than anything we already know of?'

'I'm saying that Master Marvell is surely too practical a man to pay good money to suppress a story he must realize is common currency. So, yes, I suppose if his visitor was Miles Deakin then the rogue must have some other hold over your father.' I unhooked my leg from the corner of the kitchen table and stood upright. 'But this is all pure speculation. The sad truth is that we know nothing definite. After twelve days and two murders we are just as far from the truth as we were at the beginning. Perhaps it's time we shared our suspicions concerning Miles Deakin with the proper authorities. Let the sheriff and his men find him – if, that is, he is to be found.'

But James would still not permit it. His scruples forbade his great-aunt's former suitor being thrown to the wolves, as he put it, until we had more proof of his guilt than we had at present. I thought him overscrupulous, but when he had gone, I decided he was right. My own desire to be free of the whole unhappy business was clouding my judgement.

I tried to forget about it for the rest of the day and, to a large extent, succeeded. When dinner was over, we had our own cake-cutting ceremony. Nicholas and Elizabeth were duly crowned with trailing wreaths of greenery as king and queen of the feast after finding the pea and the bean in their slices carefully given to them by Adela.

'Cheat! Cheat!' cried Adam, but without any real rancour. He was too excited by the prospect of going to see the mummers' last performance that afternoon and of being allowed, for the very first time, to take part in the wassailing that evening. On previous occasions he had been regarded as too young and had been looked after by Margaret Walker who, this year, would come to take care of Luke. Our son was puffed up with self-importance at no longer being the baby of the family.

The townsfolk had turned out in force to see the mummers' final presentation of St George and the Dragon. We got to the castle early and consequently managed to find places beside the waggon, which served as the stage. We had barely taken our places when we were joined by Jenny Hodge and her boys, Jack and Dick trying not to look too eager now that they were grown-up men of the world, but failing dismally. The latter was wearing my old grey cloak and looking very smart. I felt a pang of envy and wished I had never agreed to part with it.

'Burl not coming?' I enquired.

Jenny shook her head, her lips tightly compressed, and I saw the two lads glance at one another.

'Trouble?' I asked.

She nodded. 'He found out about the cloak.' She drew an angry breath. 'Oh, I could shake our Dick, I really could. I'd dinned it into his silly noddle not to tell his father where it came from. Say it's from one of the neighbours, I said. And he promised faithfully to do so.'

I smiled. 'But being Dick . . .' I left it there.

'But being Dick,' Jenny finished for me, 'with a head full of dreams and cobwebs and about as long a memory as a newborn gosling, he lets the cat straight out of the bag. "It's Master Chapman's old one," he says. "He has a new one and doesn't need it any more, so Mam asked him if I could have it and he agreed." Well, you know how Burl feels about you, Roger, and no one's sorrier for it than I am. You could have heard him shouting three streets away.'

I grimaced. 'But Dick's wearing it, for all that.'

Jenny's eyes lit with laughter. 'It's one thing that can be said for Dick. He may be a bit slow-witted but he can be obstinate. He's a will to match Burl's own when it comes to it. He wasn't going to part with that cloak, not if Burl ranted and sulked until Doomsday. Burl threatened to whip him, but Dick's bigger than he is now. He just took the whip out of his father's hands and threw it out of the door. After that, Burl realized there was nothing he could do. And Jack took Dick's side, of course. He always does. So, here Dick is, wearing your old cloak.'

Jenny looked round for her younger son as she spoke, but Dick had drawn back into the crowd behind him. He never relished being an object of attention.

'Well, I'm glad he stuck up for himself,' Adela chimed in from Jenny's other side. 'He's grown into a fine young man, Jenny, and you should be proud of him.'

Jenny's reply was lost in the sudden braying of the mummers' trumpets as they made their appearance from the inner ward of the castle. Ned Chorley was dressed as the Doctor, and Adam began to jump up and down with excitement in anticipation of

the comic scenes to come. But first, of course, there was the
more serious business of St George slaying the Dragon, rescuing
the Fair Maid and then being slain himself by the wicked Saracen
Knight.

But, finally, Good triumphed over Evil, St George was restored
to life by the Doctor, the wicked Saracen Knight was slain and
it was time for the mummers to make their final bow. They did
so, to much cheering and loud applause, and Toby Warrener made
a speech thanking the citizens for their warm welcome and
hospitality throughout their stay.

'We shall remember you kindly,' he finished, 'and we shall be
joining you in the wassailing tonight. Thank you and God keep
you all.'

The two carts were then driven back into the castle's inner
ward, the gates closing behind them, while the rest of us began
to disperse.

'Will we be seeing you tonight?' Adela asked Jenny just before
we parted. 'Will you come to share the remainder of our Twelfth
Night cake before we join the crowds in the streets?'

Jenny sighed. 'Nothing would give me greater pleasure, my
dear, though in Burl's present state of mind I doubt it. But we
may meet by chance.'

And on this hopeful note we parted, Jenny, escorted by her
protective sons, one on either side, to make her way home to
Redcliffe, Adela, the children and I walking the shorter distance
back to Small Street. Here we found Margaret waiting for us,
carrying a basket containing her night shift – for she was to stay
the night – as well as some Christmas fairings.

'These will be the last,' she warned as eager hands reached
for the proffered treats. 'I wonder you haven't all been struck
down with the bellyache.'

The streets were crowded. Torches flared everywhere, held high
above the excited mob as we pushed and shoved and shouted
our way towards the castle, where all the gates stood open to
allow us through into the inner ward and the castle orchard
beyond. Without the town walls, on the hills above the city, we
could see the bonfires flaming against the winter sky. Those
people who lived in the outer suburbs would now be converging

on the orchard of Gaunts' Hospital with their barrels of cider, just as we, who lived within the walls, were converging on the castle. And further out again, in the countryside, farmers and smallholders everywhere would be joining forces to wassail the apple trees, pouring their libations to the old gods and tying their ribbons and corn dollies to the branches in order to ensure that the coming harvest was a good one, even better than that of the preceding year.

We jostled our way across the barbican and in through the castle gates to find the civic dignitaries already there before us with two great barrels of cider, standing on a platform in the inner ward from which we could fill our flagons and jugs. And, to everyone's delight, the mummers had prepared one last surprise for us as the hobby-horse, with a loud neighing and tinkling of bells, came galloping into the orchard just as the mayor was about to' pour the first libation. Toby Warrener was 'riding' him, propelling the great wicker body forward and making the head rear up and down. The other mummers, too, appeared in wassail garb, with laces tied around their knees and knots of ribbon on their shoulders. The crescendo of noise rose to fever pitch, all of us shouting and clapping and cheering. Adam, held tightly in my arms, was very nearly sick with excitement.

When some sort of order had been restored, the procession began, the mayor and aldermen leading, around the orchard, in and out of the trees, watering them with the cider in our pots and hanging up lumps of toasted bread among our other offerings. Someone started to chant the age-old song 'Hail to thee old apple tree' and soon we were all singing at the tops of our voices. The air was thick with the smoke from the torches and the bonfires, and I knew a moment of panic when I suddenly lost sight of Adela and the two older children. Then the smoke cleared and there they were again at my side, singing and laughing, safe and sound.

But, at last, even the most exuberant had had enough and we began to think longingly of our beds. Adam had fallen asleep in my arms, his head resting on my shoulder, and Adela had a supporting arm around Elizabeth. Even Nicholas, valiantly endeavouring to play a man's role, was unsteady on his feet.

The singing had died away to a mumble, except for a few pot-valiant youngsters in the crowd, determined to prove they could outstay their elders. The mayor and sheriff, together with their ladies, led the way out of the orchard and the rest of us followed wearily. But it had been a good night – one of the best – and the apple crop secured for next autumn.

We reached home to find a bleary-eyed Margaret waiting up for us to report that, in spite of all the hubbub in the streets – 'enough to waken the dead,' she complained – Luke hadn't stirred all night.

'Then you've been luckier than I am,' Adela retorted acidly. 'Usually, by this time of night when I'm into my first sleep, he's awake and ready to play.' She smiled fondly, belying her tone of voice, and I marvelled once again at how easily she had accepted my nephew – my half-nephew, to be accurate – into her life and heart. I saw Margaret Walker grimace to herself and, knowing my former mother-in-law as I did, expected her to pass some remark. Fortunately, the other three children were beginning to grizzle with fatigue and both women went upstairs with them to assist with their undressing, hear them say their prayers and tuck them up in bed. By the time they returned to the kitchen, where I was helping myself from what little remained of the Christmas food, washed down with yet more cider, Margaret had forgotten whatever she had intended to say. Besides, she found a diversion in me.

'You eat too much,' she said, briskly removing the piece of Twelfth Night cake I was consuming. 'You'll get fat. Adela! Speak to him!'

But my wife was too tired and only wanted her own bed. While we were undressing, she asked sleepily, 'Did you catch sight of Jenny and the lads?'

I fell between the sheets stark naked, too tired even to don my night-shift.

'I did think I saw them a couple of times,' I admitted, 'but I may have been mistaken. There was such a crowd.'

Adela frowned. 'I do hope Burl didn't stop them from coming. I'm beginning to dislike that man. I've never been very fond of him . . .'

But her voice died away as the cider fumes and genuine

tiredness took their toll. I was floating gently, weightless, and for the first time in some days untroubled by unpleasant dreams, the only irritation being a distant banging as though someone were hammering on a door . . .

Adela was shaking me by the shoulder. 'Wake up, Roger,' she hissed close to my ear. 'Somebody's knocking on the street door. Can't you hear them? Wake up!'

Her insistent whisper was reinforced by the sudden appearance of Margaret in her night-shift, holding aloft a lighted candle in one hand.

'Roger! Someone's banging the door and that dog of yours is barking like a demented fiend. If you don't get down there and see who it is, the children will be awake again and, in consequence, all as sulky as bears tomorrow.'

Even as she spoke, Luke began to stir in his cot next to Adela. Grumbling furiously and feeling like death, I heaved myself out of bed, wrapped my nakedness in an old bed gown which had once belonged to Margaret's husband and had now seen better days, seized my cudgel and staggered barefoot downstairs. As I unlocked and unbolted the street door, the colourful words with which I had intended to greet the intruder died on my lips.

Jenny Hodge pushed her way past me into the hall. 'Roger!' she gasped, clutching my arm, 'have you seen Dick? He isn't – he isn't by any God-given chance with you, is he?'

I put an arm around her and felt her trembling. 'Jenny, what do you mean? No, of course Dick isn't here. It must have turned midnight some time ago. Isn't he with you?' (People ask silly questions in the agitation of the moment, and I am no exception.)

Jack, whom I had not noticed until then, also stepped into the hall just as Adela and Margaret arrived on the scene, carrying lighted candles. My wife handed hers to her cousin and took both of Jenny's hands in hers.

'Jenny, what is it? What's this about Dick?'

Jack said abruptly, 'Dick hasn't come home.' Then, realizing his mother's voice was suspended by tears, went on: 'He came with us to the wassailing at the castle, and for a while we were all three together. But Dick met some friends and went off with them. We didn't see him again, but naturally thought he'd come home when the wassailing was over. When we got home and he wasn't there, we didn't worry overmuch at first. We thought he'd come rolling in drunk, and Father – he hadn't come to the wassailing with us – was getting ready to give Dick a taste of his belt for being so late. But,' Jack added simply, 'Dick's not come home and it's nearly dawn. You can see the first rags of brightness in the sky.'

'I shouldn't worry,' I said bracingly. 'As you say, he's probably lying drunk somewhere in the street.'

'If that were so, he'd have been taken up by the Watch,' Jack said bluntly. 'And Father's approached the sergeant of the Watch. They've arrested nobody tonight.'

'He's more likely to be lying in the castle orchard,' Margaret said in her down-to-earth fashion.

It seemed such an obvious answer that I could have embraced her; something she would have disliked intensely. But I know we all breathed a sigh of relief. Even Jenny dried her eyes on her sleeve and managed a watery smile.

'Of course, that'll be it,' she said with a sniff. 'What fools we are, Jack, not to have thought of it for ourselves. As soon as the castle gates are unlocked tomorrow morning – I mean, this morning – he'll come ambling home full of remorse for the fright he's given us.'

'And so he damn well should be,' Jack retorted with what, for him, was strong language. (Jack Hodge was one of the least aggressive men I think I ever met.)

Jenny apologized profusely for having disturbed our rest on what, thanks to Margaret, she now realized had been a fool's errand.

'Burl always tells me I act first and think afterwards,' she muttered.

'He didn't think of the orchard, either,' I pointed out as she and Jack took their leave.

Adela, regardless of her night-shift, ran after them. 'Send us word of Dick's safe return, won't you?' she urged, clasping Jenny's arm.

'Of course.' The latter smiled mistily. 'Just as soon as he arrives home.'

But Dick Hodge never returned home. His body was found in the castle orchard later that morning. Someone had slit his throat.

EIGHTEEN

We were getting ready to go to Mass when we first heard the news. Margaret was still with us, having decided, once she had eaten her breakfast, to stay and accompany us to St Giles's. A loud knocking on the street door, just as we were about to set out, took us all by surprise.

'Now, who can that be?' Adela demanded of no one in particular. She had just picked up Luke and was endeavouring to bring some order to his tussle of copper-coloured curls. 'Margaret, my dear, you're nearest. Would you please see who it is? Tell them . . .'

She got no further as Richard Manifold, his face ashen and lined with fatigue, pushed past Margaret to stammer out the terrible news. For several seconds there was a silence of total disbelief. It was as if Richard were speaking, but in a foreign tongue which none of us could understand.

He repeated the words again. 'Dick Hodge's body has been found in the castle orchard amongst the long grasses at the far end. His throat has been cut.'

'But . . . But who would do such a thing?' Margaret asked. 'Everyone liked him. I wouldn't have said he had an enemy in the world.'

Adela thrust Luke into my arms. 'I must go to Jenny,' she said in a shaking voice. 'That poor woman! That poor, poor woman!' And she began sobbing wildly.

Margaret put her arms about her cousin, tears coursing down her wrinkled cheeks, and rocked her to and fro.

'Hush, my dear, hush,' was all she could think of to say. Elizabeth and Adam, not quite sure what was happening, began to cry in sympathy, while Luke, normally so cheerful, suddenly became aware of the overcharged atmosphere and started to yell. I sat him down on the floor, with instructions to Nicholas not to let him crawl anywhere near the Yule log, and pushed Richard Manifold into the kitchen where I poured us both a beaker of ale from the breakfast jug still standing on the table. My hand was unsteady and I spilled some.

I asked, 'There's no mistake, I suppose?' A stupid question to which he did not even bother to reply. 'But Dick Hodge!' I went on, dazed. 'Why? He never hurt anyone. Everyone liked him. I've never heard a soul say so much as an unkind word against him. It doesn't make sense.'

Richard gulped his ale as though in desperate need of it and shook his head. 'You're right. No one can understand it. If asked, I should say he was one of the best-liked people in this city.'

'Burl and Jenny know?'

He nodded. 'The sheriff went himself to tell them. Took his lady with him. They're beside themselves with grief, as you can imagine.'

'And Jack?'

'Not saying much by all accounts, but grim-faced and ripe for vengeance. Ready to act on the slightest suspicion and ask for proof afterwards. We'll have to keep our eyes on him to prevent him doing something foolish.'

It had been in my mind to flout James Marvell's wishes and tell the sergeant of our thoughts concerning Miles Deakin, but at these words, I held my peace.

'Have you no idea at all who might have done it?'

'No.' Richard drained his beaker and set it down on the table with a snap. 'How do you begin looking for the killer of someone everyone liked? The only suggestion so far is Sergeant Merryweather's, and that is that Dick has been mistaken for somebody else.'

My beaker was halfway to my lips, and there it remained, poised in mid-air. 'Oh, sweet Jesu and all the saints in heaven,' I breathed.

Richard, turning to speak to Adela, who had just appeared in the doorway, swung back towards me. 'What?' he demanded eagerly. 'What do you know?'

'Dick Hodge was wearing my old grey cloak,' I said, and proceeded to tell him the story.

Adela stood as though turned to stone, one hand, childlike, covering her mouth. Richard Manifold, too, stood looking at me for several long moments before taking a deep, shuddering breath.

'It seems as though Tom Merryweather might be right,' he said slowly. His gaze narrowed. 'What have you been up to, Roger? What have you discovered that might put you in that sort of danger? You've been in the thick of this affair since the very beginning but, knowing you, I doubt you've shared all your knowledge with either me or anyone else in authority. So what is it? And who would want to kill you?'

'How would I know?' I asked feebly. I, too, drained my beaker. My one thought now was to get to Redcliffe and the Marvell house as soon as possible, but without arousing suspicion. I had to consult with James on what was best to do.

I became aware of Adela shaking my arm. 'Roger,' she implored, 'if you know anything that might account for this terrible deed, you must tell Richard at once.'

'I know nothing of any consequence,' I lied. And, to deflect further questioning, asked, as if it were of some importance, 'When was the body found?'

'Early this morning,' Richard answered impatiently. 'One of the castle reeves was making his usual rounds to make sure that no irreparable damage had been caused by last night's revellers or the mummers—'

'They've gone, then?'

'At first light, apparently. As I was saying, one of the reeves found the body in the long grass by the outer wall.' He pulled himself up short, suddenly conscious that he was wasting valuable time. He added severely, 'Roger! I charge you straitly that if you have any information you think the law should know you must tell me on pain of imprisonment.'

'Never mind the law,' Adela said, clutching my arm even tighter. 'Roger, for Jenny's and Burl's sake, you must help them find Dick's murderer.'

There was no church for any of us that morning, although it behoved us to go and pray for Dick Hodge's soul. Margaret offered to stay and take care of the children while Adela went to visit the grieving family. I also announced my intention of going out, a decision that was greeted with silent suspicion on my former mother-in-law's part, but before I could leave the house another knock at the door heralded the arrival of Baker Cleghorn.

He looked ill and his eyes were red-rimmed from weeping. His hand shook as it clasped mine. 'Master Chapman,' he said urgently, 'I must speak with you.'

I invited him into the parlour, to Margaret's great annoyance. She sniffed loudly and shepherded the children upstairs to change out of their better clothes which they had donned for the Epiphany service. They had all calmed down by now, and Luke waved a chubby fist in valediction as he was borne up the stairs in Margaret's arms.

I shut the parlour door. 'Well, Master Cleghorn?'

'This is a terrible business,' he moaned. 'A terrible business!' He sat down limply on one of the chairs. 'That dear, sweet boy! Murdered!' He glanced up. 'Master Chapman, tell me honestly! Do you truly believe that Miles Deakin might have done this dreadful thing?'

I frowned. 'Master Cleghorn, I can't give a positive answer to that question because I don't know. But it's possible.'

He gave another groan and twisted his hands together in his lap. I guessed what was coming, so held my tongue and waited for him to continue.

After a few more seconds, he raised his head to look into my face. 'I was loth to say anything when you and young James Marvell came to visit me on Sunday, but the reason for my reluctance . . .' He paused.

'Yes?' I asked, trying to curb my impatience.

He gave a dry cough and then went on: 'The reason for my reluctance was because of where I thought I had seen Miles Deakin. You see, I thought I saw him – if it was him, that is – coming out of Dame Drusilla's house.' Having once made this admission, he proceeded with greater ease. 'It was over three months back, towards evening when it was growing dark; that dusky, autumnal half-light that you get at that time of year. I was returning from visiting a friend in Redcliffe and was passing Dame Drusilla's on the opposite side of the street. As I did so, her door opened and a man came out. I have to admit that he was well muffled up in a cloak and hood, but the hood had fallen back on his head a little and a wall torch had been lit above the doorway. Its light fell directly on his face for a moment or two, and I recollect thinking to myself, "Miles Deakin, by all that's holy!" As I told you, the Deakins were related to my wife and at one time we visited them regularly, much against my will. I also knew, of course, about the scandal three years back when young Miles wormed his way into the old lady's affections.' The baker paused once again before adding, 'But it was only a glimpse. The man adjusted his hood almost immediately to cover his face. I could well have been mistaken. I was, and still am, not at all certain that it was Miles.'

'You were certain enough to tell his father that you'd seen him when you encountered Master Deakin in North Nibley. At least, so Agnes Littlewood told me.'

Baker Cleghorn was indignant. 'I was surely not so positive as that. I said I might have seen him.' The tears filled his eyes again. 'But that's no matter. All that matters now is to discover the murderer of that dear boy.'

'And both the other murders,' I added grimly.

He looked startled. 'Of course. One forgets . . . What will you do now?'

'I shall consult with Master Marvell directly. In fact, I was on my way out to see him when you called.'

'Then I won't detain you.' The baker got unsteadily to his feet and wiped his nose on his sleeve. 'Whoever did it, may he rot in hell.'

I nodded. 'You won't be the only person wishing that, Master Cleghorn. Dick Hodge was much liked in this town.'

This was very true, and there was a sombre atmosphere lying like a pall over the city as I made my way across the bridge into Redcliffe. More than one person stopped me to discuss the dreadful news, tears unashamedly running down their cheeks, and several expressed the wish to lay hands on Dick's killer.

'He wouldn't even reach the scaffold, Master Chapman, I'll tell you that! The hangman wouldn't even be able to see where his head was to put it in the noose. It'd be screwed up between his legs.'

James and his family were at church when I arrived at the Marvell house, but I was given a seat in the hall to await his arrival. Fortunately, I was still wearing one of my decent suits which I had put on to attend St Giles's, so I looked less of a disgrace than usual. I also had with me my new blue cloak, which now I could hardly bear the sight of. If only I hadn't let Jenny persuade me into giving Dick my old one! For I felt quite sure that Sergeant Merryweather's suggestion was correct. In the general darkness and confusion of the wassail, and recognizing the grey cloak as mine, someone had mistaken Dick for me. It was not a comfortable thought, and I hoped Adela would not refine too much upon it.

It was less than half an hour later that the Marvell family returned from Mass, and as soon as the steward indicated my presence, James hurried to greet me.

'Master Chapman, have you heard the terrible news?'

I lowered my voice. 'That's why I've come. I've had a visit from Baker Cleghorn.'

He drew a sharp breath. 'And?'

'I can't tell you here.' I glanced over his shoulder to where the other family members were regarding us, openly curious. 'We must be private.'

He took my arm and marched me out into the street, offering no explanation to his indignant relatives. It was very cold and trying to snow again. I shivered and pulled my hood well down about my ears.

I gave him my news, including Sergeant Merryweather's theory that someone other than Dick Hodge had been the intended victim.

'With which I agree,' I said, and gave him the history of the two cloaks.

'Dear sweet Jesus,' James breathed. 'You mean you think the murderer thought young Hodge was you?'

'Yes.'

'But why?'

'Because our killer thinks I'm getting too close to the truth.'

'Miles Deakin?'

'That is what we have to find out.'

James turned towards Drusilla's door, outside which we were standing. 'Then there's no time like the present,' he said and, raising his hand, rapped smartly on the big iron knocker. And when his knock was not immediately answered, he rapped again, even louder.

An indignant porter opened the door. 'Impatience! Impatience!

Oh, it's you, Master James. You can't see the mistress now. She's just about to eat her dinner.'

My companion pushed the man aside and indicated that I should follow.

'My aunt's dinner can wait,' he replied brusquely. 'Where is she? In her usual room?'

He was heading for the stairs but the porter said tetchily, 'Dame Drusilla's in the little solar at the back of the house. It's warmer there. But she won't want to see you, my young master, I'll tell you that. I'll be standing ready to show you out again.'

James ignored the man and brushed past him to open a door on his left. 'This way, Master Chapman.'

The little solar was indeed warm. It was a small, cosy room, its walls hung with tapestries depicting the story of Esther and Mordecai, and a great fire blazing on the hearth. A table was drawn up close to this and spread with a fine white cloth, silver dishes winking in the firelight. Dame Drusilla was seated at the head of it, knife in hand, but no food had as yet been served.

She glanced towards the door expectantly as we entered, then frowned. Today, she had again abandoned her colourful garb and was dressed all in black, but with a great ruby cross hung about her neck on a golden chain, and with sapphires and emeralds studding her girdle.

She stared angrily at her great-nephew. 'James, what is the meaning of this intrusion? Who let you in? Don't you know it's my dinnertime? Go away and come back later.' She noticed me and her frown deepened. 'And take your friend with you.'

'Where's Miles Deakin, Aunt?' James asked.

The old lady froze in her seat. Only her eyes seemed alive in the wrinkled face. 'I don't know what you're talking about,' she said as soon as she could command her voice.

James strode up to the table and stood over her. 'Don't lie. He's been seen coming out of this house by someone who knows him well.'

'Who?'

'Never mind that,' snapped her undutiful great-nephew. 'He's here, isn't he? Living secretly under your roof.'

For a moment I thought she was going to continue denying

it, but her temper got the better of her. 'And what if he is? What's that got to do with you? Or with your father, if he's the person who's sent you? My dear brother's dead now, and good riddance! He can't interfere with my life any more. And neither can you or Cyprian.'

James lowered his head towards hers. 'But the law can,' he hissed, 'if your precious Miles is the man who's been committing these dreadful murders.'

There was a sudden silence so profound that the crackling of the logs on the hearth sounded like the raging of some great forest fire. Dame Drusilla stared open-mouthed at James, every bone of her emaciated face showing clearly beneath her parchment-like skin. I found I was holding my breath, waiting for her furious denial . . .

Instead, she leant back in her chair and began to laugh, not defiantly nor in a forced kind of way, but with genuine merriment.

'Oh dear, oh dear!' she gasped as soon as she could speak. 'Whoever put that ridiculous notion into your head?'

'Why ridiculous?' James demanded. 'Miles Deakin had cause enough to hate Grandfather and Alderman Trefusis, if anyone did.'

Dame Drusilla stopped laughing and her face twisted viciously. 'Oh, I'll grant you that,' she spat. 'More than enough. If I'd been a younger and fitter woman, I might have done the murders myself. But I didn't. And neither did Miles.'

James gripped the old lady's shoulder. 'What makes you so sure of that? He's here, in Bristol, isn't he? How long have you been giving him shelter?'

She looked up at him defiantly, her mouth set in a thin, bitter line. 'I should tell you to keep your nose out of my affairs. But since you've made this ridiculous allegation against the poor man, I'll make you free of the truth.' Here there was an interruption caused by a servant with her dinner dishes on a tray trying to enter the room. Drusilla waved him away impatiently, saying, 'Later!' and turned back to James. 'Miles Deakin has been sheltering in this house for six months or so, long before George and the rest of you moved down from Clifton. He came to me in the summer in a terrible state, ill, diseased and in rags. I took him in and my people have nursed him back to health.'

'Why didn't he go home to Nibley, to his parents?' James asked contemptuously. 'Or is it that the living's softer where there's plenty of money?'

The old lady seized hold of the stick leaning against her chair, and for a moment I thought she was going to strike him. Then, with an obvious effort, she controlled herself.

'He stayed at my request,' she said. 'I've always been fond of him.' She hesitated. 'I've always loved him,' she amended. 'People like you and your grandfather think that people of my age are incapable of those sort of emotions, or that they are indecent in someone over eighty.' Dame Drusilla's hand shot out and she grasped her great-nephew's wrist. I saw him wince. 'Well, one day, if you live as long as I have, you'll find out your mistake.' She released him and sank back in her chair, breathing heavily. 'Miles stayed because I asked him to, and because he was happy to oblige me.'

'Of course he was,' sneered James. He indicated the luxury around him. 'Who wouldn't prefer such riches to his parents' poor hovel?' He took a deep breath. 'And while he was lying low here, Deakin plotted his revenge. He must have been over-joyed when Grandfather came to live next door. It must have made things so much easier. He could get to know the old man's habits. Follow him around.'

Dame Drusilla made no answer to this except to jerk herself forward and ring the little silver bell which stood on the table next to her plate.

The servant who had entered before must have been lingering within earshot, waiting for the summons, for he appeared imme-diately, again bearing the tray in his hands.

'No, no!' his mistress exclaimed irritably, once more confusing the poor man. 'Take the food back to the kitchen and tell the cook to keep it hot. Then find Master Deakin and bring him to me.'

The fellow withdrew and Dame Drusilla leant back again in her chair, pointedly closing her eyes and compressing her lips, an indication that conversation was at an end until such time as her orders were obeyed. James stared down at her in bafflement, while I pondered uneasily on her last command. 'Find Master Deakin and bring him to me.' 'Bring him' I noted, not 'send him'.

The room was becoming insufferably hot and the sweat was beginning to stick my clothes to my back. I had a sudden sinking feeling in the pit of my stomach that for the past two weeks I had been wasting my time following a scent which had been cold from the very beginning. And my worst fears were confirmed from the moment I saw my quarry standing in the doorway, the servant's guiding hand beneath his arm.

Miles Deakin was blind.

James and I stood gawping at him for several seconds, both of us, I think, trying to convince ourselves that the blindness was a sham. At least, I know I did. But a second, closer look at those filmy eyes shattered the hope completely. I had seen that vacant stare too often in blind people not to be convinced. The eyes were half rolled up in their sockets and there was an opaqueness that could not be feigned.

Drusilla got to her feet and held out her hands. 'Come to me, Miles,' she said gently. 'I'm standing by the table near the fire. You can feel the heat. Try, my dear, and later we'll have dinner together.'

He took a few stumbling steps towards her, then stopped, head cocked to one side, listening. 'There's somebody here,' he said.

'Only my great-nephew and his friend.' She sent us a mocking glance. 'They won't hurt you. They're going now.'

'How long have you been blind, Master Deakin?' James asked.

The man's head turned as he tried to locate the voice. 'About a year, sir. It came on me sudden-like. One day I could see all right and then the next morning, I woke up blind. I could see nothing but shadows. After a while, I couldn't even see those.'

It flitted through my mind that we could question the servants and ask them to confirm Miles Deakin's condition six months ago, when he first sought sanctuary with Drusilla. But even as the thought occurred to me, I knew it was pointless. I could recognize genuine blindness when I saw it and, furthermore, the murders had only been committed in the past two weeks. I looked across at James.

'We might as well go,' I said quietly. 'We know now that the truth lies elsewhere.'

The old lady gave a snort of laughter. 'Some common sense at last, thanks be to God!' She gently led the blind man to a chair at the opposite end of the table and seated him in it. He lifted his sightless eyes gratefully towards her.

James, however, still hesitated. 'How does Deakin go out alone at night, if he's blind?' he asked. 'And don't deny it, Aunt. Baker Cleghorn saw him.'

Drusilla stood with one hand protectively on the back of the man's chair and regarded her great-nephew with a contempt as chilling as his own.

'If Baker Cleghorn' – her tone was as scorching as the heat from the fire – 'had bothered to look harder, he would have noticed one of my servants just behind Miles. He never goes out unaccompanied, but he naturally prefers night to day. The darkness makes him less aware of his blindness. And now, perhaps you and Master Chapman would go and leave us in peace. I've always been reasonably fond of you, James. You and your father have seemed to me the best of an unpleasant bunch. But I am fast changing my mind. And from there,' she added darkly, 'it's a very short step to changing my will.'

While James was absorbing this threat, I stepped forward and asked, 'Dame Drusilla, are you sure you don't have any idea who the man in the bird mask might have been that afternoon? The one watching your or your brother's house on Childermass Day?'

She stared at me for a second or two, then threw back her head and laughed. 'You thought that was Miles, did you?' Her great age hadn't dimmed her wits. 'Oh dear, oh dear! You have been wandering all around the churchyard and getting nowhere fast, haven't you? Even the dead must be laughing. No, my lad, I'm sorry to disappoint you, but I've no idea at all. As I told you at the time, Christmas is the time for young idiots to put on masks just for the sheer pleasure of frightening people.'

I thanked her politely and then, without waiting for James, turned and left the house. He caught me up a minute or so later to find me, oblivious of the cold, leaning against the wall beside the street door, staring into space. I was not even aware of him until he shook my arm.

'Master Chapman! Are you all right?' His voice eventually penetrated my dark and swirling thoughts.

'No,' I said, 'I'm not all right. I'm sick to my very guts.' I turned on him savagely. 'Do you realize that I've wasted two weeks blindly' – and how appropriate that word was – 'following a trail which has led me nowhere. All around the churchyard, as Dame Drusilla phrased it. Small wonder she thought even the dead were laughing.'

'There's no need to blame yourself. It always seemed possible it might be Deakin.'

'Possible!' I repeated angrily. 'But there's the rub. I turned "possible" into "probable" and then into almost a certainty. I've been the stupidest fool in Christendom. I! I, who should know better!'

And what were you doing, God, I thought bitterly to myself, that you didn't nudge my elbow to bring me to my senses? He'd let me make an idiot of myself, but perhaps, I reflected uneasily, he'd been right to do so. I'd been getting too set up in my own conceit and, because of that conceit, young Dick Hodge was dead. I couldn't remember at any time during the past twelve days asking for God's guidance. I suddenly felt I had been humbled and, what was more, that I deserved it.

'What do we do now?' James asked miserably.

I opened my mouth to say that I didn't know, that we now had no choice but to leave it to the sheriff and his men, but found myself saying something quite different.

'We must go to see your father,' I said. 'You must persuade him to tell us who it was who came to see him, wearing the dog mask.'

NINETEEN

D og mask! As soon as I uttered the words it was as though a great mist which had been clogging my brain for days had been suddenly lifted.

Alyson Carpenter had told me that my attacker at the Clifton house had been wearing a dog mask and Adam had described to me a play about the Sultan of Morocco and his dog which the mummers had performed. I remembered, too, the jumble of masks they had in their possession, including several depicting birds – one of which they claimed had been stolen and then returned, a statement I had never thought to query; at least, not until now.

'They'll all be at dinner,' James said, 'and I should be with them. We won't get Father alone till after the meal. And, indeed,' he added, 'you must be wanting your own dinner, Master Chapman. Come back later and we'll confront him together.'

He was right. I realized that I was very hungry, but was loth to go home. Adela would probably have returned from seeing Jenny and Burl by now and I wondered what sort of state she would be in; whether or not she would even have prepared a meal. Then I recollected that Margaret was there and would have taken charge.

All the same, I postponed my arrival at Small Street by going round by the castle and asking to speak to whoever it was who had found Dick Hodge's body. I had no authority to do this, and was faintly surprised when one of the castle reeves came through from the inner ward, wiping his mouth on his sleeve, an indication that he had left his dinner in order to see me. I couldn't help reflecting that there were times when my reputation as being in the king's employ had its uses, however misleading it might be.

'Master Chapman.' The man nodded curtly to me, but his tone was civil enough. All the same, it was not his duty to attend upon the whims of a pedlar and I could tell he was resentful of his fear of offending me. 'How can I help you? There's nothing further I can say about finding poor Dick's body than what I have already told Sergeant Manifold and the sheriff, information which I'm very certain the whole town must know by now.'

'I'm really more interested in the mummers,' I said. 'I was informed they'd left.'

'At first light.' The reeve shrugged. 'In fact, the carts were loaded and they were waiting to get away before the gates were open. One of them fetched the horses from the Bell Lane stables last night in order that there should be no delay from that quarter this morning. They should be well on the road by now. They were extremely anxious to get back to Hampshire and their winter lodgings before the weather worsened, which it very often does after Christmas. And the younger woman is, of course, in a delicate condition. So I'm afraid if you were wishful to speak to them, you're unlucky. It would take a fast horse to catch up with them now.' A slight smile touched his lips: he obviously knew the stories about me and horses.

'Their winter quarters, I think Mistress Tabitha told me, are at Sweetwater Manor, between Winchester and Southampton, belonging to a Master Tuffnel.'

The reeve nodded. 'Yes, that's right. A Master Cyprian Tuffnel.'

'Cyprian?'

My tone was so sharp that he looked at me curiously. 'Yes, so one of them told me. Not a common name, I grant you, but a saint's name for all that.'

'It's Master Marvell's name, chosen presumably by his father, Sir George.'

The reeve fingered his chin. 'So it is,' he said. 'Do you think it has some particular significance?'

I didn't reply to his question because I wasn't sure of the answer – not yet, at any rate. But I did feel a growing conviction that God had come back to me and was once more directing my footsteps.

I thanked the man for his help and left him staring after me, a puzzled frown creasing his brow. He was probably trying to work out what help he had given me. In spite of the bitter cold and my gnawing hunger, I went and sat on a wall close to the Mint. (I could hear them hammering away inside, fashioning the new coins needed for King Richard's reign.) With a concentrated effort of memory, I recalled Tabitha saying that her father had been warrener to Master Tuffnel's father, and that she and he had grown up together. Which meant that Cyprian Tuffnel was a man of roughly her age and of an age with Sir George Marvell and Alderman Trefusis. Had he, too, been a soldier in the French wars? Had the other two known him? Had they been companions? Could that possibly be why Sir George had given his son the name of Cyprian, in memory of an army friendship?

I took a deep breath. I was rushing ahead too fast again, letting my theories outstrip the facts, jumping to conclusions. It was my besetting sin, but this time I could not rid myself of the feeling that I was justified. A recollection of Tabitha saying that Master Tuffnel had been good to her and Ned Chorley when they most needed it rose to the surface of my mind. Also that Cyprian Tuffnel had been some years older than herself – which would make him even closer to George Marvell's age . . .

A sudden blast of icy wind blowing up from both of Bristol's rivers made me shiver violently and get hurriedly to my feet, grabbing my cloak around me. It was time to go home and find out what was happening there. But as I walked through the icy streets and the church bells still ringing out for the later Epiphany Day services, I had a sudden vision of the terrible injuries inflicted on Ned Chorley and Alfred Littlewood by the French, and then of those perpetrated on George Marvell; the lopped off fingers and the gouged-out eyes. The word that kept going around and around in my head was 'retribution'.

Margaret Walker had not failed us. Luke was on her lap and she and the children were all seated at the kitchen table quietly getting on with the pottage she had heated. Adela was there, too, her eyes red-rimmed and swollen, but only making a pretence at eating. I saw her hand shake as she lifted her spoon.

'Ah, here you are at last,' my former mother-in-law remarked grimly as I made my entrance. 'Sit down. Elizabeth, get your father his dinner.'

My daughter heaved a martyred sigh, but nevertheless rose from her stool and filled a bowl with stew from the pot over the fire.

I braced myself and addressed my wife. 'How are Burl and Jenny?'

'You may well ask!'

The picture was immediately clear to me. I was to be the
scapegoat. I was to bear the burden of being to blame for Dick
Hodge's death. No matter that it was Jenny and even Dick himself
who had persuaded me – more, begged me – to let him have my
old cloak. That wasn't the point and never would be. The point
was that I spent my time poking about in affairs that didn't
concern me so that people wanted to kill me in order to stop my
prying. I sighed. I suppose I might have guessed it.

'Burl's vowed never to speak to you again,' Adela informed
me in trembling accents. 'And, honestly, Roger, I don't know
that I can blame him. He and Jenny are both half-dead with grief.
As for Jack, I wouldn't go near him for a while if I were you.
You're likely to get a bloody nose if no worse.'

To my surprise, it was Margaret who came to my defence.
'Well, I think that's very unfair,' she said stoutly. 'You can't hold
Roger responsible for Dick Hodge's death because he did the
lad a good turn. In fact, if I know Roger, he's too fond of wearing
disgusting old clothes to have parted with that grey cloak unless
he'd been begged to. And so I shall tell anyone who says anything
of the kind to me.'

I think Adela was as dumbfounded by this unlooked-for parti-
sanship as I was and was silenced. Furthermore, she has a sense
of justice and, after turning her cousin's words over in her mind
for several minutes, suddenly said, stifling her sobs, 'You're right,
Margaret, my dear.'

She lapsed into silence, pushing away her almost full plate,
but I no longer felt, at least in my own home, that I was the
object of my family's animosity. True, Adam did murmur his
usual, 'Bad man!' but it was more a term of affection, I felt, than
any sort of reproach.

'Does anyone have any idea who might have killed Dick Hodge
and the others?' Margaret asked me.

I shook my head.

She eyed me shrewdly. 'I really meant do you have any idea?
What about the young man Dame Drusilla wanted to marry?
What did Bess Simnel say his name is? Miles Deakin? I had an
idea you suspected him at one time.'

'You can forget Miles Deakin,' I said shortly.

Margaret raised her eyebrows. 'O-ho! You do know something. Don't try to deny it.'

'I know that he had nothing to do with the murders,' was my answer. I frowned at her and she nodded in reluctant acceptance of the fact that I was going to say no more on the subject.

'What are you thinking of doing now?' she asked, knowing me too well to suppose that the recent tragedy would have made me falter in my search for the truth.

I smiled, feeling an unexpected rush of affection for her and her understanding and loyalty. I must be fonder of her than I knew. 'When I've finished my dinner,' I said, 'I'm going to visit Cyprian Marvell.'

'You think he may know something?'

'I think it possible, but whether or not he will share his knowledge is a different matter.'

'And if he doesn't?'

I hesitated, then, 'It's time I took up my peddling again. This is the last day of Christmas and we must all get back to the workaday world.'

Adela reared her head at that. 'You won't go far in January, Roger? The weather is liable to worsen very suddenly. Remember this past autumn.'

'When you sent me to Hereford on a wild goose chase? No, I shan't forget that in a hurry, nor its consequences.' She had the grace to blush. 'I may go south,' I continued, 'into Hampshire. It all depends.'

'On what?'

'On what I learn this afternoon from Cyprian Marvell.'

Cyprian Marvell was one of those quiet but stubborn men who, once he has decided on a course of action, refuses to budge from it even for the Archangel Gabriel himself.

James and I had bearded him in the little room which had been Sir George's sanctum and which he had now appropriated as a refuge against the other members of his family. He had retired there after his dinner and was deeply displeased by the sudden appearance of his son and myself. He had been moved to use some very forthright and graphic language which had surprised us both, coming from such a normally mild-mannered and temperate man.

Not that we had let it trouble us, I standing with my back to the door to prevent my unwilling host from leaving, while James pressed his father to say who his nocturnal visitor had been and what he had wanted.

At first, Cyprian had refused to answer either question, but eventually, worn down and desperate to get rid of us, he had admitted that the unwelcome guest had asked for money.

'Blackmail?' James demanded brutally.

'If you like.'

'Why? What for? Something he knew about Grandfather? Something to his discredit?'

Cyprian folded his lips, leant back in his chair and closed his eyes. His attitude implied that we could ask from now until Doomsday and we should get no more information out of him. I decided it was time I took a hand.

'Master Marvell,' I said, 'was it one of the mummers?'

His eyes flew open at that and he shot me a startled glance. James, too, turned to stare at me in surprise. There was also something reproachful in his look: he felt that I had been keeping him in the dark.

'Why do you say that?' he asked.

'Because Ned Chorley also fought in the French wars. He was an archer; you can tell that by his injuries.' And I repeated what Alfred Littlewood had told me about the revenge exacted by the French on any of the hated English archers who were captured.

'Dear God!' James exclaimed. 'And you think—?'

'I think he may have known both Sir George and Alderman Trefusis and was aware of something to their discredit, either from personal experience or from some tale told to him by a third person.'

James turned towards Cyprian. 'Father?'

But the older man still refused to say anything further. He folded his hands across his belly and feigned sleep. His son gazed at him with a mixture of exasperation, anger and affection. After a moment or two, he tried again.

'Father, three men have been killed, and brutally killed, and the body of your own father vilely despoiled. An innocent young man, little more than a boy, has been done to death. Don't you want the villain who did this laid by the heels?' Still there was no reply. James sighed. 'Then Master Chapman and I have no choice but to go to the sheriff and tell him what we know.'

Cyprian did open his eyes at that, but when he spoke his voice was calm.

'You know nothing, because I shall deny all knowledge of my night-time visitor. I shall say you were mistaken. If necessary, I shall accuse you and Master Chapman of trying to make yourselves important. I shall say it has been your weakness since childhood, that nowadays you wish to score against Bartholomew and that is your sole motive for these accusations. As for Master Chapman, there are plenty in this town who resent him and would be only too ready to believe such a claim.'

James looked at me despairingly. 'He means it,' he said, 'but we'll go anyway.'

'No.' I shook my head. 'Leave it. There's nothing to be gained by falling out with your father. Family quarrels are the very devil, and take longer to heal than other disagreements.' I smiled reassuringly. 'I'll go and leave you to make your peace with Master Marvell.'

Cyprian was suddenly uneasy and was regarding me with misgiving. This abrupt climbdown had obviously aroused his suspicions. I decided to give his thoughts another direction.

'Master Marvell,' I said, 'a word in your ear. I know for a fact – and I am willing to swear to this as I hope for the life hereafter – that your stepmother has had dealings with the Irish slave traders in the city. I saw her in company with one of them, myself. Now, what her business with him was I've no idea, but if I were you I should be on my guard. You and your son.'

And with this, I took my leave, bowing to Cyprian, nodding to James, and left them gaping after me.

I had walked the whole length of Bristol Bridge when suddenly I stopped and retraced my steps halfway to the chapel of the Virgin Mary which spanned its centre. Inside, the chapel was deserted and very quiet, there being no Epiphany service there that day. (The clergy were too busy at the dozens of other religious establishments that gave the town its nickname, 'The City of Churches'.) The winter light filtered through the stained-glass window, but it was too thin to throw the usual patterns of colour on the dusty floor. I made my obeisance at the altar, then propped myself against the southern wall and gave myself up to thought.

There were things that needed working out.

If Miles Deakin had not been the man in the bird mask standing outside Sir George's house on Holy Innocents' – Childermass – Day, who had it been? I cast my mind back to that particular Sunday and recalled that the mummers had spent it with us, in Small Street, after Dorcas Warrener had been taken ill during the service at St Giles's. But I also remembered that after dinner, Tobias had been despatched by Tabitha to make sure that their gear was safely under lock and key at the castle and that he had been absent for some little time. Was he then the man in the bird mask who had passed the note, which purported to come from Alyson Carpenter, to Sir George?

The mummers would have known about her because of her friendship – or more than friendship – with Tobias when they were performing in Clifton before Christmas. Had they gone there deliberately in the hope of finding the knight? Had they known that was where he lived? Somehow I doubted it or, if I was right in attributing the murders to them, they would have sought him out earlier. I decided, therefore, that they had first heard of his living in Bristol from Alyson. No doubt she had boasted of her conquest to Tobias and he had conveyed the information to the others. The discovery that Alderman Trefusis also lived in the city had probably been a happy accident, at least for them.

To Alyson, too, I attributed the mummers' knowledge of the empty house at Clifton. I had little doubt that if, indeed, she had managed to seduce young Toby, then they had made use of it for secret meetings. But a note had been written to the knight, a fact which made me hesitate until I suddenly remembered being told that Tabitha could both read and write, perhaps not well, but probably as well as the younger woman. It was more than likely that Sir George had never seen Alyson Carpenter's writing – there was, after all, no reason why he should have done – so he would not have queried if it were her hand or no. In any case, it had done all that was required and sent him off to Clifton on Childermass night to meet with his murderers. Had he recognized them before he died and known why they exacted vengeance?

The thought pulled me up short as I remembered with a jolt that I had spent that same night in the mummers' company while Dorcas took my place beside Adela at home. So was it possible that two, or maybe three of them, had been able to leave me sleeping and make their way to Clifton and back again without my being aware of their absence? It's true, I sleep soundly, but not so sound that at some point during the hours of darkness I don't wake up and become aware of my surroundings. I would say that at least once a night I'm roused by a full bladder and either make use of the chamber pot or piss out of the window if I feel in need of a breath of air. Why, therefore, would the night of Holy Innocents' Day have been any different?

But even as the thought entered my head, I recalled the remains of the poppy seed and lettuce juice lozenges on the battered tin plate that I had found beneath my bed. Tabitha had claimed that burning them through the night helped them all to sleep while on the road, the strong perfume making them oblivious of uncomfortable beds in strange places. No doubt she was right, and if you put them directly underneath a sleeper's bed the fumes would probably render him very nearly unconscious until morning. I remembered, too, a nagging headache that had troubled me throughout the following day.

Tabitha had been awake, dressed and sitting up when I had finally managed to open my eyes that morning. But she had looked tired. Had she been keeping guard over me while the menfolk had gone to lie in wait for Sir George? But what was it precisely that he had done to them? And why had they carved the word DIE into his chest when he was already dead? And why had Alderman Trefusis whispered the word 'Dee' when he was dying? And, above all, was I correct in holding the mummers to blame, or was I off hunting yet another mare's nest while the true answer to these Christmas murders still eluded me?

No; I felt certain that after wasting so much time and effort chasing the false hare that Miles Deakin had proved to be, I was now on the right track. Cyprian Marvell had neither denied nor derided my suggestion that his nocturnal visitor had been one of the mummers, or that the link between them and his father had been their service in the French wars. His silence on the subject seemed only to confirm that my guess was the correct one. He had, moreover, admitted to giving the man money; an admission that had to mean some disgraceful episode in Sir George's past; an episode shared, presumably with his contemporary, Alderman Trefusis, who had also been a soldier. And there was a final link with the mummers in that Master Tuffnel, the owner of Sweetwater Manor and the benefactor of Tabitha Warrener and Ned Chorley, was called Cyprian, the baptismal name given to his elder son by the knight. And once again the link was that both men had fought in France. There was a very good chance that they had known one another, that they had been friends.

As for the attacks on myself, one or two of the mummers, if not all of them with the possible exception of Dorcas, had surely been in our house during the wassail of St Thomas Becket's Day when it would have been simplicity itself to slip something into my beaker. They had, of course, been masked, one of them wearing that of the hooked-beak bird; the mask that later, in a little charade, staged, I now felt certain, for my benefit, they pretended had been borrowed and then returned. Had they intended to kill me that time, or had it been merely an attempt to discourage my interest in Robert Trefusis's murder? But why? Because Adela had frightened them when, so uncharacteristically, she had boasted of problems I had solved for King Richard when he was Duke of Gloucester? And when I had shown no sign of abating that interest, they had decided that I, too, must die before I discovered the truth.

It crossed my mind that as they had left the city so early that morning, they might not have realized that they had murdered the wrong man the previous evening. If they thought me dead, it was equally possible that they considered themselves safe at last and would be travelling to their winter quarters in Hampshire at a more leisurely pace. On the other hand, they might have discovered their mistake at the time of the killing, in which case their progress could have become a flight. But either way, it would make no difference. I fully intended to go after them whatever the winter weather held in store. I had liked the mummers. I had thought them my friends. Now I knew them for what they were – a bunch of murderous cut-throats.

I found the knowledge distressing. Adam had liked them, and they had liked him – or seemed to have done. Could I be wrong?

Again? But the longer I thought about things, the stronger the conviction grew that this time I was not mistaken. I suspected that I should now go to Richard Manifold and lay before him my suspicions and my reasons for them. The chase and retribution should now be in the hands of the law, but while the shadow of a doubt lingered I could not bring myself to do so. The sergeant would undoubtedly claim that it was because I wanted all the glory for myself, and who knew but that he might not be right? Had I, over the years, become too set up in my own conceit? Had the general belief that I was an important agent of the king really gone to my head, in spite of all my vigorous denials to the contrary? Certainly, I had been brought to the realization that I had forgotten God, and I recalled Adela's accusation that I encouraged both Adam and Elizabeth in their somewhat heretical view of religion. The trouble was that I could never bring myself to believe in the great God of Wrath and Retribution. He had blessed us with a sense of humour, the ability to laugh at and mock ourselves: therefore, I was unable to feel that he took himself so seriously . . .

I heaved myself away from the chapel wall and found that I was shivering. A man could think too much and never get any satisfactory answers. In the end, I could only be guided by instinct and hope that it was sound; that it was God's way of working through me. Action was what I needed now. Epiphany had come: the Christ Child had been shown to the Magi. It was the Twelfth Day and Christmas was over.

'You're sure about this?' Adela asked anxiously. 'Going as far as Hampshire at this time of the year?'

'Yes,' I said, 'but I'll take my pack. It won't be a wasted journey. People are glad to see pedlars at this time of year when the Christmas festivities are behind them and spring is still a long way off. They're so happy to see a fresh face, they'll part with their money all the more easily.'

Adela sighed. 'We could do with all you can earn,' she admitted. 'This Christmas has emptied our purse. Everything seems to have cost so much more than last year. All the same, you would be able to sell as much if you worked the hamlets and villages hereabouts. If the weather should turn bad, you might find yourself trapped in Hampshire for months.'

She still looked pale and unhappy. I knew why she wanted me to stay; the thought of Dick Hodge's brutal death still lay like a bruise on her spirit, as indeed it did on mine. She needed comforting, but she knew why I had to go: I had explained my reasons to her. She had been shocked and, at first, disbelieving, having looked on the mummers as friends, but I had finally convinced her by my arguments that I must at least go after them and satisfy myself that I was right.

'And what will you do if you are?' she asked.

I admitted that I didn't know and said it depended. 'On what?' she might have asked, but she knew as well as I did that I had no answer. I made her promise to say nothing of the matter to anyone until my return, when I would know more; when I could decide what had to be done.

We celebrated the Feast of the Epiphany that evening at St Giles and said goodbye to Christmas for another year. And in the morning I set out for Hampshire, warmly wrapped up in my new blue cloak against the January weather, and with my pack on my back and my cudgel in my hand.

TWENTY

I t was a fortnight later when I finally discovered the community of Sweetwater, with its moated manor house, tucked away in the countryside between Winchester and Southampton.

The journey had taken me longer than I had expected; though perhaps no longer than I had any right to expect, it now being past the middle of January. The weather had indeed worsened the further the month progressed, with heavy snow showers and driving winds forcing me to seek shelter in friendly monasteries and other religious houses for as much as up to two days at a time. Added to this, of course, I had been peddling my goods around the villages and hamlets through which I had passed, and often been detained by their inhabitants, who were starved of news from the outside world once passing traffic had grown scarce on the frozen roads. Wayfarers were few and far between in the depth of winter, and I was a welcome presence in nearly every dwelling at which I stopped, whether manor, smallholding, cottage or hovel. With Christmas over for another year, and with the days not yet sufficiently longer so as to be noticeable, the inevitable pall of depression was clouding the minds of country folk; and so my advent was hailed with relief and the chance to hear of other people's doings or to discuss such news as had reached them in the summer months rarely passed up.

Of these latter events, most of my customers wanted to know of the happenings in London during June and July, of the new king and, most of all, if the rumours that he had had the deposed young king and his brother murdered in the Tower were true. These rumours now seemed rife throughout the country – the West Country, at least: I couldn't answer for other parts – and I did my best to reassure anyone to whom I spoke that the stories were false. The trouble was that I had no proof to offer as to the young princes' actual fate and found myself resenting the fact. It was high time, I felt, that the king made the whereabouts of his nephews known.

The worst part of the journey was crossing the great plain near Salisbury. I passed the brooding Giants' Dance, the Stone Henge as our Saxon forebears had named it, raised who knew how many hundreds of years before they had set foot in this island. I had encountered a particularly violent, but fortunately brief, snowstorm that afternoon and, for a while, had been forced to shelter among the stones themselves. I can recall even now, after all this lapse of years, how uneasy they made me feel, as if some magic possessed them. I remember how relieved I was when the snow abated and I was finally able to press on.

It was two days later, with a fragile sun riding high in the noonday sky that, thanks to a passing woodsman who knew the surrounding countryside like the back of his own hand, I arrived at Sweetwater Manor. This, as I have already said, was a moated house and the main gate was approached across a wooden bridge, wide enough and strong enough to admit a substantial cart. There was a bell on a rope hanging beside the gate, which I pulled as hard as I could. The sound of its clapper jangled away into the distance and then the silence came creeping back, more profound than before.

The place might have been deserted: there was no sound or sign of any life anywhere. I could see the byres, the pigsties, the sheep pens, but animals were keeping themselves close and not venturing forth in such freezing weather. The outhouses also appeared devoid of life, and I was just beginning to wonder if the whole compound was indeed untenanted when a spiral of smoke went up through a hole in one of the outhouse roofs, followed within a few seconds by the emergence of a young housemaid from a side door of the main building. She skidded across the frozen courtyard in her wooden pattens and disappeared inside the hen coop, presumably to collect the morning's eggs.

I clanged the bell again, louder and more imperatively than before. And again.

At this third summons, the main door of the manor opened and the steward stepped out, a cloak held firmly around him and using his staff of office as a prop to help him walk across the slippery ground. He opened the gate, obviously in a furious temper.

'Where's that fool of a porter?' he demanded.

Not being able to say, I simply shrugged and stepped inside. 'Pedlars round to the kitchen entrance,' the man snapped, having now taken a good look at me.

'I wish to see Master Tuffnel,' I said. 'Master Cyprian Tuffnel.'

For a moment, he was palpably taken aback by my knowledge of his master's name, but he quickly recovered and pointed with his staff to the right-hand side of the building.

'Kitchen,' he said briefly.

I repeated my request, but only succeeded in goading him to a frenzy.

'Kitchen,' he roared again.

'I'm not here to sell anything,' I answered quietly. 'I wish to speak to Master Tuffnel about the mummers to whom he gives shelter every winter.'

'Oh, them!' The steward spoke scornfully. 'Bunch of rogues! I don't know why the master puts up with them.' He flushed slightly, aware of having spoken out of turn, and to an inferior. He drew a deep breath preparatory to ordering me once more round to the kitchens.

He was forestalled by a shout of, 'Oswald!' An elderly gentleman in a furred cloak, and leaning heavily on an ivory-headed cane, was making his precarious way towards us. The steward started forward.

'Master, you shouldn't be out of doors in this weather. You might slip and break a leg. I can deal with this impudent fellow.'

The newcomer paid him no attention, instead looking steadily at me. 'If you're Roger the Chapman,' he said, 'as I presume you are by your pack, I've been expecting you. Give me your arm and we'll go inside. Oswald,' he addressed the steward once again, 'have wine and biscuits sent to the little solar and then see to it that I'm not interrupted.'

So it was that, some ten or so minutes later, I had shed my pack and cloak and was gradually thawing out my grateful body in front of a roaring fire, while my host busied himself with piling yet more logs on the blaze.

'Warmer now?' he asked me. 'You must have had a cold journey.'

I nodded, holding my hands to the flames, but I was not inclined to waste any time on small talk. 'How do you know my name and why have you been expecting me?' I demanded.

'Where are Tabitha Warrener and Ned Chorley? I need to speak to them.'

Master Tuffnel seated himself in a chair opposite mine, on the other side of the hearth. I could see now that, as I had expected, he was an old man, probably in his seventies like Sir George Marvell and Alderman Trefusis.

'One thing at a time, young man,' he said with his pleasant smile. 'I know your name because Tabitha told me about you. She also said that she would be very surprised if you failed to come after her and Ned. And, finally, you cannot speak to them because she, Ned and the others have gone.'

'Gone?' I jerked forward in my chair. 'Where?'

'To France.'

'France?' I stared at him stupidly.

'To France,' he repeated with emphasis.

'When?'

'Over a week ago. In fact, shortly after they arrived here. They set off for Southampton two days later and, as I've heard no more of them, I can only presume that they found a ship's captain willing and able to take them and their gear. There are always a few willing to brave the winter storms in the Channel if, of course, they are offered sufficient money. And I understand that Ned and Tabitha did very well in Bristol.'

'When . . . When will they be back?' I wanted to know.

Master Tuffnel shook his head. 'I fear they won't be coming back. They intend to make their home in France. Both Ned and Tabitha spent so many years in that country that they can speak the language after a fashion. Well enough, at any rate, to make themselves understood. Tobias, Dorcas and her brother, Arthur, will learn it gradually. You need not be afraid for them.'

'Afraid for them!' I was on my feet, shaking with rage. 'Afraid for those murdering ruffians! Do you know that they have brutally killed three men, one of them an entirely innocent young lad, as well as trying three times to murder me? Do you know this? Have they told you?'

At this moment, a serving-man appeared with a tray on which reposed a jug of wine and various plates of small cakes and biscuits. He looked aghast at me towering over his master, my features undoubtedly contorted with the anger I was feeling. I must have looked a menacing figure.

'Are – are you all right, master?' he stammered, setting down the tray. 'Shall I call the other servants?'

Cyprian Tuffnel waved him away with an airy gesture of one hand. 'No, my dear fellow, no! I'm sure I'm perfectly safe with Master Chapman.'

The man went with lagging steps, casting anxious glances over his shoulder. I sat down again in order to reassure him, but once the door had closed, I returned to the attack.

'These people are murderers, sir,' I said, slapping the arms of my chair and breathing hard. 'They deserve no man's goodwill, and certainly not mine.'

'I understand your feelings, believe me,' he said gently, 'and I sympathize with them.' He rose and poured out two glasses of wine, one of which he handed to me before resuming his seat. 'But war, Master Chapman, is a brutal business and those of us who have been soldiers, particularly foot soldiers in the ranks, people like Ned and Tabitha, hold life cheaper than most others.'

'What do you mean?' I asked. 'Ned, yes. But that doesn't apply to Tabitha.'

'Most certainly it does.' He sighed. 'So many people think, mistakenly, that that French girl, the one they burned as a witch at Rouen, was the only woman ever to enlist as a soldier, masquerading in men's clothing. There are dozens of them, I can assure you, in every army of every country throughout Europe. And those that do take up the calling make excellent soldiers. They are far more ruthless than men.'

I was amazed. The idea of women as fighters, braving dangers, brandishing and using weapons, accustoming themselves to the horrors and gory sights and sounds of battle, had never occurred to me.

'And Mistress Warrener was such a woman?' I asked, still struggling to come to terms with the idea. 'A soldier?'

Master Tuffnel smiled gently. 'Tabitha was one of the very best. Not only was she extremely courageous, but she was also a good captain. She cherished the men under her command; looked after them like a mother. She might have them flogged or their ears lopped for disobedience – indeed, I've seen her hang a man herself from the bough of a tree for whatever crime he had committed – but woe betide anyone else who laid a finger on them. And the offence she found the most unforgivable was cowardice, betrayal of one's fellows.'

There was silence for a moment or two, the crackling of the logs on the hearth the only sound in the room, while I marshalled my thoughts and a pattern of events became clearer to me. I remembered Cyprian Marvell's nocturnal visitor and his stubborn refusal to reveal what the man had wanted. He had not denied that it was one of the mummers nor that he had paid him money, but no more. Family honour was at stake. I raised my eyes to Master Tuffnel's.

'Am I to assume that Sir George Marvell stood accused of cowardice and betrayal?' I asked at length. 'And also Robert Trefusis?'

My host shook his head sadly. 'Oh, never to their faces. Never officially. They remained heroes in the eyes of the world. Only those of us who were there knew the truth, and that included Tabitha and Ned Chorley.'

'Who were where?' I asked.

'At the siege of Dieppe.'

'Dieppe?'

'Yes. Why? You sound as though the name means something to you.'

It did. Of course it did. The last piece of the puzzle had fallen into place. Alderman Trefusis had uttered the word 'Dee' as he lay dying. But not the name 'Dee', nor even the first syllable of the name 'Deakin', but the beginning of the word 'Dieppe'. The word carved so savagely into Sir George's chest was not 'DIE', but again the start of that same place name. My theory that the murderers had been interrupted had been correct: the letters 'PPE' should have completed their handiwork.

I looked up to find Master Tuffnel frowning at me in a puzzled fashion. Before he could say anything, however, I leant forward, my elbows on my knees, and said urgently, 'Tell me about the siege of Dieppe.'

Old soldiers love telling tales of past glories, or even, as in this case, past defeats. He settled himself more comfortably in his chair and took a gulp of wine to ease his throat.

'It was forty years ago this August just gone,' he said. 'The year of Our Lord One Thousand, Four Hundred and Forty-three. I know that for a certainty because I had just celebrated my thirty-second birthday. The town had been snatched from us in a daring raid some years before. I forget exactly when. In any case, it doesn't matter. Suffice it to say that in the November prior to my account an English army under the command of the great Talbot of Shrewsbury, including among its officers myself and two of my closest comrades, Robert Trefusis and George Marvell, was at last sent to lay siege to Dieppe and win it back again. This host also counted Tabitha Warrener and Ned Chorley among its ranks. Ned was an archer.

'We weren't in any hurry. Talbot reckoned that King Charles was in no position to come to the relief of the town, and so it proved. A fort was built overlooking Dieppe – an immensely strong affair, like a small town itself – the artillery was hauled into position and we settled down to bombard the walls for as long as it took to force the citizens into surrender.'

Here, Master Tuffnel broke off, staring into the heart of the fire, seeing sights and hearing sounds that I was unable to share.

'And did they?' I prompted him.

He jumped. 'What?'

'Did the citizens of Dieppe surrender?'

'Oh . . . Oh, no. By the following August, against all the odds, they were still holding out, still defying us, but getting near the end of their tether. We knew, because we had intercepted several of the messengers, that the city fathers were imploring King Charles to come to their relief, but none of us, least of all old Talbot, thought that their prayers would be answered. Life was quite pleasant. There was the occasional sortie against the town, but the gunners were doing most of the work. The rest of us diced, played cards, visited the camp whores, caught the usual diseases, slept, quarrelled . . . but in general were quite content to await the inevitable outcome.'

'So what went wrong?' I asked as once again he paused. 'It's obvious that something did.'

Cyprian Tuffnel gave a bark of laughter. 'Oh, something went wrong, yes, indeed. In the middle of August, a few days before the Eve of the Assumption of the Virgin, our scouts brought us

news of the approach of a French army under the command, not
of King Charles, but of the Dauphin, Louis. That's the King
Louis who died this past year. I don't know if you ever saw him
or know anything about him?'

'As a matter of fact, I do,' I replied. 'I saw him at a distance
eight years ago on the bridge at Picquigny, but I was also once
acquainted with a young woman whose father had served in
Louis's Scots Guard. She admired him greatly and thought him
one of the cleverest, most shrewd men she had ever known,
whose natural cunning made up for the fact that he was no
soldier.'

My host nodded. 'Your friend was right, but at the time I speak
of no one, at least on the English side, was aware of his brilliant
mind. All we knew was that he had a poor reputation in battle,
that he dressed and looked more like a mountebank than a prince
and was generally considered hopeless as a fighter. So when we
stopped laughing, we just widened the ditches around the fort a
little, altered the position of a few guns and calmly awaited his
arrival. What our scouts hadn't told us, because their information
was faulty, was that Louis had with him Dunois, the Bastard of
Orleans and the Count of Dammartin, a brilliant captain of the
Ecorcheurs. He also had artillery.

'The upshot was that we were taken entirely by surprise by
the scale and ferocity of the attack, which was of sufficient
strength to breach the walls of the fort and to enable a vast
number of the French to get inside. By the time darkness fell we
had just about managed to drive them out, but inside the fort it
was a shambles. No quarter had been asked and no quarter had
been given. The place was a charnel house and the atrocities
committed on both sides had been vicious. Neverthless, we
thought that was that: the French must surely have had enough
– their casualties had been as great as ours – and they wouldn't
attack again.' He took a deep breath before continuing, 'That
statement, however, is not quite true. I should have said that most
of us thought that the French would not attack again. But there
were a few so appalled by the day's carnage that they decided
not to wait and find out. Some time during the night they slipped
out of the back entrance to the fort and disappeared into the
darkness . . .'

I interrupted. 'Don't tell me,' I said. 'Let me guess. George Marvell and Robert Trefusis were two of those who deserted.'

Master Tuffnel curled his lip. 'It didn't need much guesswork, did it? But you're right, of course. My two best friends' – he spat into the fire where the spittle boiled and sizzled – 'had run away. Later, they declared that they had gone for help, and because of their good name they were given the benefit of the doubt. But no one who was left in that fort believed them.'

'And did the French attack again next day?'

My host's face grew grim. 'They did, and they took the fort within three hours. The atrocities that followed were horrific. Louis and Dunois and Dammartin did what they could to control their men, but they were really able to do very little. The citizens of Dieppe all flocked out to join in the slaughter and avenge their sufferings.' He gave a wry smile. 'I suppose one can hardly blame them. Ned Chorley was captured and his captors had just started to get to work on him – they had chopped off his bowstring fingers and were trying to gouge out his eyes – when Tabitha and some others managed to rescue him, killing quite a few of the enemy in the process. After that, it was every man for himself. Some of us managed to get away and lose ourselves in the surrounding countryside before somehow or other getting back to Calais, but the men who had deserted during the night were never forgiven by the rest of us, and never will be. I understand that George Marvell had the gall to name his son after me. Well, I never had a son.' His voice grew bitter. 'But if I had I'd have strangled the child at birth rather than call him George.'

There was another, even longer silence when he had finished speaking while we both sat quietly, thinking our own thoughts.

I could only guess at what Master Tuffnel's were. The terrible sights and sounds of that long-ago battle, imprinted forever on his memory, must have been rolling around in his head, his feelings toward the men who had betrayed them as simple and uncomplicated as they had always been. Mine were far more confused.

To begin with, I suppose my sympathy was with the two mummers. They had seen their fellow soldiers butchered in the most horrible ways, and although no doubt the outcome of the French attack would have been the same even if the deserters had stayed, no one relishes the thought of betrayal. If Tabitha Warrener and Ned Chorley had confined their murderous activities to Sir George and Alderman Trefusis, I might have been inclined to pardon them. But they had come after me and, in doing so, killed Dick Hodge in the process. For that I could never forgive them.

'Did they tell you,' I asked Master Tuffnel, 'that they tried their best to murder me? That an innocent young man mistakenly had his throat cut instead because he was wearing an old cloak of mine which I had given him? Did your precious friends, the mummers, tell you that? Or hadn't they realized their error?'

My host gave an involuntary shiver. 'Oh, yes, they'd realized it and were distraught. They guessed that you would come after them and thought that you would bring the law with you. That is why they travelled as fast as they could to get here, and why they decided they must go to France, if they could find a ship, and settle there, in spite of Dorcas's condition. Tabitha said that if they were unable to find a ship's captain who would risk crossing the Narrow Sea in midwinter, then they would lie low until the spring. But whatever happened, they would not return here.'

'I should have brought the law,' I said bitterly, 'but I wasn't absolutely certain that I was right. Almost, but not completely, and I wanted to hear what they had to say first.' A red mist of rage swam before my eyes and I cursed my own folly. 'But they would have escaped anyway, wouldn't they?' I consoled myself. 'You wouldn't have helped to detain them, would you, Master Tuffnel? Not your precious friends whom you've known nearly all their lives? You're as bad as they are.'

I was suddenly conscious that I was shouting at the top of my voice and, before I could stop myself, I shot out a hand and sent the wine jug and beakers and plates of sweetmeats flying, spilling all over the floor and rolling on to the hearth. I don't know what I looked like, but my host shrank back in his chair and raised his arms as though to defend himself.

Two of the servants came bursting in, obviously disturbed by my raised voice. One was holding a club between his hands and, having taken a glance at the scattered things on the floor, they advanced ominously.

Master Tuffnel, recovering from his initial fear, waved them away.

'An accident,' he said quietly. 'Master Chapman was explaining something to me and hit the jug off the tray. Just pick up the plates and beakers and bring more wine. That will be all.'

The servants obeyed reluctantly and then withdrew, keeping a wary eye on me throughout. They plainly didn't think it an accident. Feeling somewhat ashamed of myself, I sat down again.

'I'm sorry,' I apologized roughly. 'I shouldn't have behaved like that. But I was very fond of Dick Hodge, the boy who was murdered.'

Master Tuffnel nodded. 'I understand that. And I really have nothing to offer in Tabitha and Ned's defence, except that evil begets evil. And in spite of having been a soldier, I have always thought that war is an evil. It is not a popular point of view, I know, but one to which I strongly adhere. It brutalizes men – and women – and I have often regretted helping Ned and particularly Tabitha to lead that life. But I love them both and couldn't have held them here with the prospect of seeing them end on the gallows. Although I have reason to believe that it was Dorcas's brother, Arthur Monkton, who actually made both the attempts on your life and killed your young friend, I can't pretend that the others, with the exception of Dorcas, were ignorant of his intentions. In fact, I know they weren't. And I beg you not to think that I approve of what they did. I am a Justice of the Peace and do not believe in people taking the law into their own hands. But I also understand how their sudden encounter with George Marvell and Robert Trefusis affected them, even after forty years. Ned and Tabitha had spent a lifetime hating them, and that hatred boiled over when they clapped eyes on them again.'

And with that I had perforce to be content. Besides, I could not rid myself of the uneasy feeling that if I had not meddled, if I had left the law to take its course, Dick Hodge would still be alive. In any case, there was nothing I was able to do now. The mummers had gone beyond my reach, and the reach of justice. I should just have to accept the fact.

Master Tuffnel begged me to stay the night beneath his roof, but although I was very tired and would have welcomed a decent bed, I refused the offer. He was too closely associated with the mummers, obviously finding it difficult to blame them for what they had done, for me to feel comfortable in his company. So I refused, and he directed me to the nearest decent inn, where he assured me I would be well fed and housed without being robbed.

And the next day, I started on my homeward journey.

What else was there to do?

With luck, I should be home in time for Candlemas, and soon a new year would be beginning.